Tomorrow's Promise

What Reviewers Say About Bold Strokes' Authors

Kim Baldwin

"Her…crisply written action scenes, juxtaposition of plotlines, and smart dialogue make this a story the reader will absolutely enjoy and long remember." – **Arlene Germain**, book reviewer for the *Lambda Book Report* and the *Midwest Book Review*

Rose Beecham

"…a mystery writer with a delightful sense of humor, as well as an eye for an interesting array of characters…" *MegaScene*

"…her characters seem fully capable of walking away from the particulars of whodunit and engaging the reader in other aspects of their lives." – *Lambda Book Report*

"…creates believable characters in compelling situations, with enough humor to provide effective counterpoint to the work of detecting." – *Bay Area Reporter*

Jane Fletcher

"…a natural gift for rich storytelling and world-building…one of the best fantasy writers at work today." – **Jean Stewart**, author of the *Isis* series

Radclyffe

"Powerful characters, engrossing plot, and intelligent writing…" – **Cameron Abbott,** author of *To the Edge* and *An Inexpressible State of Grace*

"…well-honed storytelling skills…solid prose and sure-handedness of the narrative…" – **Elizabeth Flynn**, *Lambda Book Report*

"…well-plotted…lovely romance...I couldn't turn the pages fast enough!" – **Ann Bannon**, author of *The Beebo Brinker Chronicles.*

"…a consummate artist in crafting classic romance fiction…her numerous best selling works exemplify the splendor and power of Sapphic passion…" – **Yvette Murray, PhD**, *Reader's Raves*

Tomorrow's Promise

by

RADCLYfFE

2005

TOMORROW'S PROMISE

ISBN 1-933110-12-0

This Trade Paperback Original Is Published By
Bold Strokes Books, Inc.,
Philadelphia, Pa, USA

First Edition: July, 2003
Second Printing: October, 2004 Bold Strokes Books, Inc.
Third Printing: June, 2005 Bold Strokes Books, Inc.

Credits
Executive Editor: Stacia Seaman
Editor: Laney Roberts
Production Design: J. Barre Greystone
Cover Photo: Radclyfe
Cover Design By Sheri (GRAPHICARTIST2020@HOTMAIL.COM)

By the Author

Romances

Safe Harbor
Beyond the Breakwater
Innocent Hearts
Love's Melody Lost
Love's Tender Warriors
Tomorrow's Promise
Passion's Bright Fury
Love's Masquerade
shadowland
Fated Love
Distant Shores, Silent Thunder

Honor Series

Above All, Honor
Honor Bound
Love & Honor
Honor Guards

Justice Series

A Matter of Trust (prequel)
Shield of Justice
In Pursuit of Justice
Justice in the Shadows
Justice Served

Change Of Pace: *Erotic Interludes*
(A Short Story Collection)

Acknowledgments

This book, like many, has a checkered past. It was once, long ago, accepted for publication, but only under the condition that I change things that, to my mind, were essential to the heart of the work. I declined the offer, and the manuscript remained tucked away for quite some time. After I posted an early version on the web in 2000, many readers wrote to tell me how much this work meant to them, and I was inspired to resurrect it. I have since revised the text, but not the story, for the story is, after all, the soul of any book. Here at last, in this form, *Promise* has come to rest.

Laney Roberts and Stacia Seaman are excellent editors, and I am ever thankful for their skill, professionalism, and willingness to deal with my eccentricities. My friends and beta readers, Athos, Diane, Jane, JB, and Tomboy, helped enormously with each review of the manuscript.

Many thanks to HS for her gracious efforts in keeping the Radlist running smoothly and to all the group members for their enthusiastic support and patronage.

I took the cover photograph of the jetty at Long Point in Provincetown in the summer of 2001. It is a beautiful place that Sheri has rendered even lovelier with yet another superb cover.

Each day, Lee comes home and asks, "Did you write me a story today?" Her love and support have made it possible for me to tell these stories. There are no words to describe what that gift means to me. *Amo te.*

Radcly*f*fe 2005

Dedication

For Lee,
For Every Tomorrow

PROLOGUE

"Come on in, the party's just getting started," the blond exclaimed. She kissed the dark-haired youth in the low-riding ragged jeans and scuffed leather jacket on the lips for perhaps a moment longer than was customary for a casual greeting. "Hey, I heard that you were long gone, but I didn't believe it."

"Still here." The newcomer shrugged nonchalantly while casting an appraising eye over the women and men already gathered in the shabby-chic living room of one of the mixed-gender college houses. "Did I miss anything?"

"You mean did you miss *anyone*, don't you?" Charlene Belvedere coyly rested her fingers on the boyish young woman's hip, stroking her blatantly as they stepped out of the path of other arriving guests.

"Is she here?" Tanner Whitley ignored the caress. She'd been pointedly avoiding Charlene's hints all fall, but it hadn't seemed to put a damper on the blond's interest.

"Uh-uh. Word has it she left the minute the two of you were released. I knew it would take more than a night in jail to run *you* out of town, though."

Tanner's stomach clenched at the not-so-subtle reminder of her most recent brush with notoriety, but her face revealed nothing. There wasn't any point in explaining that she had only been detained, not actually arrested. The rumors had already become legend. "Well, it's almost mid-semester break anyhow. I guess she decided to go home early."

"Her parents showed up yesterday morning and practically packed her belongings themselves, then hustled her into the car. All rush-rush," Charlene continued, unperturbed by the sudden stiffening of the muscled leg under her fingertips or the blaze of anger that leapt to Tanner's dark eyes. "I don't think Grace will be coming back to

Bennington in January." She laughed a little maliciously. "God, if they ever figure out that she was actually *screwing* you, they'll probably send her to a convent."

"Did Grace say we were sleeping together?" Tanner asked, feigning confusion. She knew Charlene was just trolling for information. Grace would never have mentioned what had transpired between them—not because she was ashamed, but because she was private about her personal life. Tanner liked that about Grace Weston. She didn't pry, and she respected the same desire for privacy in others. Charlene, for all her good looks and brains, was incredibly insecure about both and loved nothing better than reveling in other people's misfortune.

"Well, I just assumed..." Charlene whispered knowingly, leaning close enough that her breasts brushed Tanner's arm. A steady stream of students arriving for the party had forced them back against the wall in the small entrance alcove, but she wasn't complaining about the contact. Tanner Whitley was hot, rich, and wild. She'd been trying to get a date with her for weeks, but she never seemed able to catch the always-in-demand Tanner between women. Someone had actually said Tanner had been dating an English prof, but no one could say who it was for sure. "What woman would pass up the chance at you, and it's not like you're tied down to anyone. So, when I heard the two of you were going out..."

"Grace never gave me a second look," Tanner lied. If Grace was in trouble because of her, she wasn't going to add fuel to the fire. Let them all wonder. "I was still working on getting her attention."

"Oh, so that's the reason you took her to that *très* elegant place in the Berkshires for the weekend. You were trying to get her attention?" Charlene's tone suggested that she didn't believe Tanner for a second. She took Tanner's hand and led her into the living room. "Tell me another one."

Tanner shrugged. She had no intention of discussing her love life with anyone, least of all someone who was likely to repeat every word she said before morning to anyone who would listen. "You have to start somewhere."

"Well," Charlene pronounced with finality, "she's yesterday's news now. Almost, anyhow. I suppose walking away from a totaled Mercedes and getting busted for public intoxication will be topics for discussion for another week or so. But at least she wasn't driving."

"Yeah," Tanner remarked vaguely as she attempted to follow a group of jostling partygoers toward the rear of the house. The bar must be back that way, because it was definitely the area with the most activity. *"At least she wasn't driving." So that's what everyone thinks. Good, let them. Grace doesn't need that kind of baggage following her around for the rest of her life.*

"What about you?" Charlene clung persistently to Tanner's arm in the crowd. "Are you in any trouble?"

"Me?" Tanner asked in mock surprise, flashing a grin that didn't quite reach her eyes. With her smoky dark gaze, thick black hair that slashed across her forehead, and devil-may-care good looks, she resembled James Dean at his finest. "No. It's not a problem."

Not much *was* with a cadre of lawyers at her disposal. As much as she resented the corporate superstructure that loomed in her background like a black hole waiting to suck her into high-powered institutional obscurity, she'd been glad of its presence when she'd found herself behind bars facing a slew of felony charges, including DUI, reckless endangerment, and resisting arrest.

Still, better her than Grace, who'd been too drunk to remember any of the details of the car wreck and couldn't contradict Tanner's explanation of just how they had ended up off the road halfway down a mountainside in Vermont. Grace had been accepted to Yale Law School and couldn't afford this kind of fuck-up on her record.

Tanner figured it was the least she could do to take the rap for her, considering that she had been the one to buy the last bottle of champagne, at which point neither of them had been exactly sober. Besides, *she* didn't have any grand designs on the future, so what did it matter? She'd always known what the shape of her life would be—at least she had once she'd passed beyond the blissful ignorance of childhood.

She was a Whitley. In fact, she was the last Whitley, and it was her destiny to continue the tradition as head of the Whitley family empire. The fact that business dealings and venture capitalism left her absolutely cold was never an issue. Her only goal at the moment, however, was to avoid being swallowed by the giant gaping mouth of the Whitley company monster. So far, she had succeeded, but she knew her days were numbered.

"Uh...scotch, I guess, double up," she said to the guy pouring drinks with both hands behind a makeshift counter in the kitchen. She didn't want to think about what awaited her after college, or to remember why she would be assuming the mantle of leadership many years too soon. Somehow, though, she had a feeling it was going to take more than the scotch to make her forget it. She needed something to engage all her restless energy, not just dim her memories. Glancing at the woman still glued to her side, she asked, "Want something?"

"You know I do." Charlene softly parted her lips in a seductive smile. "Just say when."

"Go, Tanner," the bartender muttered, and both women laughed.

"As in *to drink?"* Tanner repeated, but her hand was on Charlene's waist now. What the hell. The lithe blond was gorgeous and willing, and the night would be long and cold if she had to sleep alone. So, why not? Tanner slugged the scotch and waited.

"Wine now," Charlene whispered. "You later."

Why not?

CHAPTER ONE

Four Years Later

Hello? Anybody here?" Adrienne Pierce called into the open bay of the small roadside gas station. She glanced at her watch. Seven p.m. already. Damn. "Excuse me—hello?"

"Ayuh," a voice answered from somewhere inside the repair area. A thin, friendly looking man in his late fifties dressed in stained coveralls came out of the building. He wiped his hands casually on a grease-spattered rag and smiled at Adrienne expectantly. "Help you?"

"I hope so," Adrienne replied. "I'm looking for the turnoff to Whitley Point. My directions said it should be near here, but I can't seem to find it."

"Traveling long?" he inquired conversationally, his broad New England accent contrasting sharply with Adrienne's clipped, precise cadence. Busying himself with cleaning the road grit from the windshield of her blue mid-sized rental, he studied her from the corner of his eye. He knew the type—seen them enough on their way to the island—another wealthy summer visitor, most likely. Golden-blond hair just beyond short, subtly layered and carelessly pushed back from her face. Tall, trim—very elegant even in casual chinos and a pressed cotton shirt. Yep, stylish, the way Hepburn and Stanwyck were—cool beauty and a core of iron. "Not from around here then, are you?"

"I guess that's pretty obvious." Adrienne smiled, a smile tinged with sadness. "I'm from the West Coast, but I just drove up from Philadelphia today." Had it really only been twelve hours since she had awakened in her childhood bedroom, a room she hadn't slept in for twenty years until a week ago? The landscape of her life was changing so quickly she barely knew where she was any longer.

"Why do you want to spend the summer by yourself?" her mother asked, unable to hide her hurt. "You know we want you here—especially now."

"It's been good to be here, it has," Adrienne said as calmly as she could manage. She didn't want to add to the hurt by explaining that she was suffocating under her mother's well-meant attentions and her father's awkward silences. "I need to make some decisions. Sort some things out."

"Why?" her mother repeated anxiously. "Why now? You said everything was all right."

"Yes, it is," Adrienne assured her quickly, ignoring the small kernel of fear that never quite left her mind. Fear, her new companion.

"Then why?"

"I'm sorry. I need to go. I'll call you."

"You're pretty far from home, I'll say that," he said, reaching into his pocket for a cigarette.

You have no idea how far.

"Got friends on the Point?" He seemed not to mind that she hadn't answered. He leaned against the bumper, rolling the cigarette idly between his fingers, appearing for all the world to be settling in for a long chat.

Adrienne looked at him, struggling between annoyance and amusement. Obviously, he wasn't in any hurry, and, since she *had* come all this way to relax and leave the turmoil of the last few months behind, she might as well get used to it. Striving to put a conversational tone in her voice, she replied, "I don't know a soul at Whitley Point. I'm leasing a house there for the next three months, and I'd really like to find it before dark."

"I'm trying to quit, so I only smoke them halfway down," he offered as if he needed to explain. He gave a last swipe at the spotted windshield and stubbed his half-smoked cigarette out with the toe of his reinforced boot. "It's a real pretty place, Whitley Point. I used to work out there when I was a boy, back when Charles Whitley, Sr. was still alive. Only the family summered there then, before the island was developed."

"I thought the island was privately owned by the Whitleys." She'd read some of this while researching the place. A realtor's ad she had come across by chance in a magazine had described houses for rent on the island, and it had seemed the perfect solution to her current anchorless state.

"Still is," he continued. "The whole north half of the island is the Whitley family estate, but there are a handful of private homes, too, on the southern end."

"Isn't the younger Whitley dead now, too?" Adrienne was interested in spite of her urgency to get back on the road. The idea of a family dynasty as powerful as the Whitleys' intrigued her. It was far different than her own experience growing up in a comfortable, though hardly affluent, middle-class family, and it was partly that fascination that had prompted her to rent the house on Whitley Point. At the time, the idea of a remote island off the coast of Maine had seemed romantic in a *Wuthering Heights* kind of way, and about as far away from her memories as she could get.

"Yep, Whitley Jr.'s gone, too," her companion informed her. "Died almost ten years ago in a freak storm out at sea. They found his body way down the coast days later. Never could understand how he let himself get caught so far out to sea in gale weather. Any native knows how fast those storms blow in—and Whitley was a mighty fine sailor. Maybe it was fate. Anyhow, now his daughter manages things on the island, although I hear she leaves most of the business matters to the corporation." He squinted up at the quickly setting sun. "Well, I guess you'll want to be gettin' on."

"Yes." Adrienne suppressed a smile and nodded solemnly. "Perhaps I should."

"So," her new acquaintance advised, pointing the way, "the sign for Whitley Point is about two miles further down the road. You can't miss it. Once you make the turn off the mainland and cross over the causeway, you ought to reach the southern end of the Point in less than half an hour."

"Thank you." Adrienne said goodbye with some reluctance. She couldn't remember the last time she had held a conversation that hadn't been filled with embarrassed pauses or uncomfortable silences. It was good to be treated like an ordinary person again. She waved as she pulled out of the parking lot, suddenly eager to reach a safe haven.

Safe haven. Is there really such a place for me?

She had come three thousand miles in search of one.

After crossing the causeway, a narrow two-lane road surrounded by water that connected the island to the mainland, she followed the coastal road that wound north on the ocean side, marveling as she drove at how untouched by the modern world the surrounding shore appeared. Only her headlights broke the descending darkness as she carefully followed the twisting road. Occasionally, she caught glimpses of lights through the trees, but she couldn't make out any structures from the moving car. The sea breeze gusted in through her open windows, bringing with it a sudden pang of nostalgia. How she missed the ocean! Despite her melancholy, being near the water soothed her, and even after many hours on the road, she felt strangely rested.

Her mind drifted, lulled by the sounds of the sea, and she almost passed the small painted sign that announced the turnoff to Eagle Lane. Braking quickly, she negotiated the turn faster than she had intended, feeling the chassis shake. Heart racing, she pulled the car out of a near-spin on the unpaved, rutted road.

I'd better stay awake if I'm going to get there in one piece. After all this, it would be rotten luck to die in a car crash.

She drove with all her attention on the road until she found the house, looming up in the darkness against a moonlit sky, all angles and edges. Then she sat in her car for a few moments, staring. It was huge. She could make out a wide porch bordered by pines and what looked to be a top-floor deck winding around one side toward the rear. The ground level was comprised of a garage and a semi-enclosed storage area with the main living space actually on the floor above—a precaution against tidal floods, she imagined.

Finally, she gathered her suitcases, maneuvered them up the front steps, and dropped them inside the front door. Despite her fatigue, she was anxious to explore her new home.

The spacious master bedroom, she discovered to her delight, was in the rear and opened onto the deck she had seen from the driveway. She immediately opened the sliding glass doors to admit a breeze and stood in the doorway, looking past the shore a hundred yards below to the endless expanse of sea, black beneath the purple sky. It was a beautiful setting, and for a fleeting instant, she wished she had someone with whom to share it. She quickly banished that thought, as she had done so many times in the last months. That, too, was part of her past.

Suddenly weary, she kicked off her shoes and stretched out on the bed, fully clothed. Within seconds, she was asleep, and mercifully, she did not dream.

❖

Five miles up the road, Tanner slammed the door of her seaside bungalow and sprinted toward her Jaguar. Gunning the powerful engine, she roared from the drive amidst a shower of gravel, tearing down the coast road, her headlights slashing through the night. Had she left ten minutes earlier, she would have passed the summer visitor's car on the road. As it was, she saw no one as she hurtled toward her destination. Despite the chill night air, she had the top down on the sleek convertible and the radio turned up, all six speakers blasting. Drumming her fingers impatiently against the steering wheel, humming snatches of the melody, she maneuvered the twisting turns from memory, having driven the road thousands of times.

When she pulled into a hidden driveway near the south end of the island, careening to a stop behind a long line of sports cars and roadsters, the party was already in full swing. All of the second-floor windows of the large cedar and glass house were open, loud music mixing with the din of voices pulsating into the night.

Tanner sauntered through the crowd of people gathered on the wide front stairs and made her way inside, nodding to friends who called a greeting as she passed. She edged between jostling bodies toward the bar that was set into an alcove on one side of the spacious living area.

"Tanner!" a young flaxen-haired man shouted as he came up beside her, trying to be heard over the pounding music and roar of animated conversations. "Heard you were home. Glad you could make it. What are you drinking?"

"Scotch." She accepted the drink from him a moment later, and they both turned to survey the other guests.

"Great, huh?" he enthused. "Everybody's here."

"Yeah. Great."

It was a familiar sight. Most of the island's younger set was present, all of them eager to initiate the summer season with abandon. For three months, there would be an endless stream of house parties, dances, and barbeques as the wealthy gathered to escape the heat of the cities and the demands of their professions, just as had been the custom for a hundred years. Most of the faces she recognized—they were the women and men she had known since childhood, some home for the summer from exclusive universities, others simply idling away time.

Other than the fact that she was a year-round resident of the island and not just a summer visitor, Tanner was no different. She had just returned from a six-week tour of Europe that she had found repetitive and boring, but it had been better than the alternative—being locked in a boardroom with humorless representatives of the Whitley Corporation.

"So, what are your plans?" the handsome blond asked when they had finally found a quiet corner where they could hear each other.

"Plans?" She shrugged, then sipped her drink, not really tasting it. She simply waited for the burning to dissolve into a few hours of numbness. After Bennington, she had dutifully moved into a corner office right on schedule. She was born to it as much as she was born to the island and tied to it in some deep way that defied rationale. Fortunately, her presence mattered more than her participation, and she came and went as she pleased. Unfortunately, keeping apathy at bay was a losing proposition. "No plans."

"Still waiting for Princess Charming?" Todd Barrow prodded good-naturedly. He had known Tanner since they were children, and they'd even dated semi-seriously during high school. Both their families had assumed that they would someday marry. It seemed like a natural match. Even after Tanner had told him she wasn't interested in anything other than friendship, and why, they had remained friends. Todd regarded her now with a mixture of bewilderment and fondness.

"Afraid not." She laughed bitterly. "I've outgrown fairy tales." *About ten years ago.*

"Really? I thought the young and the innocent were your favorite types," he responded flippantly.

"Innocence is the last thing I want." Her voice was strangely hollow. *Let them find out from someone else that tomorrow is just a myth and that dreams don't come true.*

"Are you getting cynical in your old age?" His tone was still light but his eyes serious. It was a rare thing for Tanner to admit she had doubts or reservations about anything. Despite their long friendship, they hadn't talked intimately in years. Tanner had always been an intensely private person, and perhaps the reason they had remained friends for so long was that he never pried. If she wanted people to believe that she was no more than the rich playgirl she appeared to be, Todd saw no reason to challenge that image. But he remembered the nights lying beside her out on the beach, watching the stars, sharing their hopes and their fears. Once upon a time, she had dreamed.

"I don't know what you'd call it," Tanner admitted, turning from him to face the open window at her shoulder, seeking comfort in the night. The feeling of emptiness had been a part of her for so long she didn't even think about it any longer and certainly didn't try to explain it. It was easier just to ignore it, or obliterate it. "I just don't find the chase quite as much fun anymore."

"Too easy?" He knew from his own experience that it was often his money and status that attracted others, not him personally. He'd seen the same thing with Tanner—girls wanted her because of who she was. Of course, it was more than that, too. Tanner, good-looking to a fault in her faded jeans, boots, and signature white shirt, was the epitome of indifference, which made her nearly irresistible to a lot of girls. *She* never seemed to believe it was anything but her name that attracted attention, though. "No challenge any longer?" he teased.

"Not that so much," she continued with unaccustomed reflection. "I just don't enjoy winning anymore." Impatiently, she laughed at herself, shaking her thick, unruly dark hair out of her eyes. "Come on—let's go find some other kind of action. This is a party, right?" She didn't feel like being serious tonight, and she most definitely didn't feel like thinking about the women that she had left in tears or the broken hearts she had never wanted in the first place.

"I know just what you need," Todd said with a grin, slipping his arm around her waist. "Come on."

She followed him to another room filled with women and men, some of whom passed a joint while others sat around a low table where lines of white powder were carefully arranged. Conversation flowed as people casually sampled the various substances available.

"What's your pleasure?" Todd asked.

"I'll stick with this," Tanner replied, raising her glass as she sat down with several friends and returned their greetings.

She stayed a while and then followed the exodus of people outside onto the expansive deck. She picked up another scotch on the way and settled comfortably into a lounge chair, feeling the soothing effects of the alcohol and wondering why she had been so bothered earlier. Nothing ever really changed, and she was a fool to expect anything different.

Eyes half-closed, she sought solace from the sea. Starlight illuminated the sky, and moonlight glinted off cresting waves like splinters of glass, lethally beautiful. Surf thundered distantly against pristine shorelines, the ocean's power tamed and finally captured. Even though she had seen it thousands of times, it stirred her still, and for one brief moment, she longed to escape onto the water. She could be at the marina in ten minutes.

A young redhead she had never seen before leaned over her and offered a joint. Tanner accepted automatically, then passed it back.

"Great party, isn't it?" The girl exhaled the smoke in a long thin stream.

"Sure," Tanner replied, her starkly handsome features flickering with dark amusement. "First time out here?" The shapely youth looked to be eighteen—maybe.

"How did you know?" the redhead asked in surprise. Sliding onto the chaise, she rested her hand casually on Tanner's bare forearm below her rolled-up cuff, stroking very lightly.

Tanner shifted to make room, eying the trim figure and pretty features appreciatively. Grinning, she replied, "Because I know everyone on this island, and I've never seen you before. I'm sure I'd remember if I had."

"Well, I know who *you* are," her companion responded coyly, turning so that she was very nearly reclining against Tanner's side. Her nipples, tight beneath the thin silk of her scoop top, brushed against Tanner's arm. "I saw you at the Davises' beach party last year. Except then you weren't alone."

"Really?" Tanner played the game that was second nature to her. "Well, I am tonight. What's your name?"

"Jeanette."

The girl's hand fell in a practiced move to Tanner's thigh, and the caress of her fingers along the inside of her leg made Tanner's breath quicken. Noting the eager look in the redhead's eyes, she allowed herself to imagine how it would feel to have her naked. How easy it would be...and how pointless. She shook her head, ignoring the pulse of arousal beating between her thighs, not wanting to pursue that thought.

Her body was eager, but the conquest didn't interest her, even with such an attractive partner. And that was new.

"You should be careful, Jeanette." Tanner gently pushed the hand from her leg. "Sometimes you get more than you bargained for at these parties."

"I know what *I'm* bargaining for," Jeanette whispered, her lips very close to Tanner's neck. "Do you?"

"Nothing, tonight."

"Look me up later—if you change your mind," Jeanette urged as she finally moved from the lounge chair. By the time she slipped away into the crowd, she was already looking for the next interesting face.

Tanner closed her eyes, imagined the sway of the boat under her feet and the sound of the wind whipping the sails. The water surrounded her—so beautiful, so peaceful...so deadly.

"Find what you were looking for in Europe?" A low sultry voice very near her ear stirred Tanner from her reverie.

Her eyes still cloudy with memory, she looked up at an older brunette in a very revealing black sheath. In a tone languid and rich, she asked, "What makes you think I was looking for anything at all?"

"Because you've been looking for something for years. I'm just glad you didn't try to find it with that cute little piece of jailbait." The woman laughed, settling herself on the chaise and placing her hand deliberately on Tanner's leg in very nearly the same spot that Jeanette's had just vacated. "But that's why you never stay in one place for long. And why you never stay with one person either."

"You make me sound very mysterious." Tanner drained her scotch and traced a finger along the older woman's hand.

"Just hard to please."

"I never noticed you had much trouble in that department," Tanner responded playfully. The woman was so close her breath warmed the skin on Tanner's neck. Here was a heart she didn't need to worry about breaking.

"I didn't think you remembered." Slowly, she edged her hand higher.

"I haven't forgotten, but my memory could use a little refreshing." Tanner shifted so that her companion's hand rested against her crotch. Already aroused, she found the teasing strokes enticing and pleasant but not nearly enough to satisfy.

The woman searched for a sign of welcome in Tanner's dark eyes but found them as unreadable as the ocean's depths. She didn't have any trouble reading her body though—the subtle rise of Tanner's hips beneath her fingers told her all she needed to know. She stood, tugging on a willing hand. "Let's go for a ride. Maybe I can improve your recollections."

CHAPTER TWO

Whitley Point looked different to Adrienne by daylight. She had awakened to early morning sun streaming through the open windows onto her bed. She showered, luxuriating in the cool stream of water that seemed to wash away more than the aftereffects of a twelve-hour drive, and began to relax for the first time in weeks.

The ocean beckoned to her, and she looked forward to a walk on the beach. The May morning was cool, so she pulled a sweater on over a T-shirt and jeans. She frowned at the loose fit of her clothes. She *had* lost weight, and at five-eight, she had never had much to spare even when at her healthiest. *That's behind you now,* she reminded herself, wishing she could believe it.

Following a well-worn path that wound between rippling dunes, she made her way through the scrub brush and small pines that separated the beach from the inner island. As she walked, she noticed a few houses, which hadn't been apparent the night before, secluded behind clusters of trees. Even now, they blended unobtrusively with the landscape, and she noted appreciatively how the construction and clean, simple design of the buildings preserved the natural beauty of the environment. It was obvious that someone had gone to considerable effort to protect the wild character of the island.

The sound of the surf led her north, and when she rounded the last dune, she halted abruptly. Stretched before her was one of the most beautiful coastlines she had ever seen. In either direction, the beach undulated between the ocean and the rising sands as far as she could see. On the seaward side of the island, the waves came in at full strength, cresting and breaking off shore. The East Coast was very different from Southern California, where she had lived for most of the last fifteen years. The shoreline was lower, less threatening, the ocean somehow more mellow. The ever-present power of the raging Pacific was absent here, but the sea nevertheless remained fathomless, full of secrets.

She stood still for some time, listening to the rhythm of the sea, missing home. Finally, she headed toward the far end of the island, skirting the water at the edge of the irregular shoreline. The tide was on its way out, and hundreds of tiny sand crabs scuttled along the wet beach, disappearing into holes in the sand as she drew near. They were private creatures. She used to make a game of trying to sneak up on them, but she had never gotten close. Now she didn't impinge on their desire for solitude. She understood it. In fact, lately she felt somewhat like the shy creatures, withdrawing into herself as instinctively as the little animals did into their sanctuaries in the sand...

"Adrienne, please! Why are you leaving? Nothing has changed!"

"Are you crazy? Everything *has changed! Have you seen the way people treat me?"*

"It's only because they care about you."

"Is that why no one can look me in the eye? Is that why you *can't?"*

"That's not fair!"

"I know. I'm sorry. It's not your fault. It's not anyone's fault."

"Adrienne, you're so far away. You won't talk to me; you won't talk to anyone. Can't you see how much you've cut yourself off from everyone?"

"That's why I'm going."

"Adrienne. You're already gone."

She stopped walking and concentrated on the wind from the water, letting the cold salt air blow the memories away. Unexpectedly invigorated, she wished she had worn running shoes. That thought produced a smile as she reminded herself that she hadn't run in months. It had once been a daily ritual—to rise early and run on the beach. Exercise first thing in the morning had helped her to face the hours of meetings and indoor obligations with equanimity. It had taken being near the water again for her to realize how much she missed it.

Tomorrow. Tomorrow I'll run.

As she came upon a secluded section of beach more than a mile from where she had started, a large, dark, shaggy shape rose up out of the sand not twenty feet in front of her. She stopped suddenly, stifling a cry of surprise, and stared at the apparition. After a moment, she laughed quietly to herself, recognizing the square head and massive body of a Newfoundland. The dog stood motionless, surveying her with a calm but curious expression.

"Hi there, pooch," Adrienne called softly, advancing slowly. "What are you doing out here so early, huh?"

The dog didn't seem at all disturbed by her presence, but Adrienne was wary. She didn't relish the thought of an early-morning sprint down the beach with an angry dog nipping at her heels. *Of course, I did want to go running.* She laughed out loud again at the thought, but the laughter turned to a gasp of shock when she drew close enough to see a body crumpled in the sand on the far side of the vigilant animal.

Images from too many moody mysteries where the faithful companion was found guarding its master's dead body flashed through her head. Steeling herself for the horrible sight she was sure would materialize, she moved cautiously nearer, continuing to murmur to the dog in what she hoped was a reassuring voice.

"Oh, Christ," she muttered when she was close enough to see that the figure, half-turned away from her, was that of a woman. The curve of hip and partly bared shoulder left little room for doubt. Instinctively, she looked over her shoulder, wondering if some psychopath still lurked behind the dunes. The beach appeared deserted except for the dog and the still figure in the sand.

The dog's tail was wagging, and Adrienne decided she could risk a closer look. Taking a deep breath, she leaned down, grasped an arm and rolled the body over. The pale face was framed with tousled black hair, scattered throughout with bits of twigs and sand. Her features were boldly sculpted, with a strong nose and square chin framing full, rich lips.

Just as Adrienne reached out tentatively to touch the woman's face, nearly translucent eyelids fluttered open to reveal dark, unfocused eyes. Adrienne stood transfixed, staring down, captured by those eyes. For an instant, there was a hint of innocence and something terribly lost swirling in their depths. It wasn't until the searching gaze settled questioningly on Adrienne's face that she found her voice.

"My God, you frightened me. Are you hurt?"

"Eternally," a husky voice replied.

As a powerful wave of alcoholic fumes exuded from the prone

figure, Adrienne rocked back on her heels.

"Bull," Adrienne uttered in exasperation, annoyed now at her earlier fears. "You're not hurt, you're just drunk."

The dark-haired stranger made an attempt to sit up and fell back into the sand. "Right now that amounts to the same thing." She groaned. "Why is the sun so bright?"

The whole scene was so ridiculous Adrienne had to laugh. Regarding the moaning woman, she asked, "How long have you been here?"

"That depends," came the weak reply. "If today is still Saturday—a few hours. If it's not, then you'll have to tell me."

"Must have been some party," Adrienne muttered, straightening up as she watched the young woman finally manage to attain a sitting position. Her light cotton shirt was half-unbuttoned, and Adrienne hastily averted her eyes from the full curve of barely covered breasts beneath. The arms supporting the woman's bowed head were firmly but sleekly muscled, as were the denim-clad legs. She looked to be in her mid-twenties, a good ten years Adrienne's junior. Adrienne was caught staring as deep charcoal eyes, now clear, suddenly fixed her with piercing intensity, and the pale face lit up with a brilliant smile.

"Hello, by the way. I'm Tanner."

"Adrienne Pierce," Adrienne answered somewhat stiffly, irritated that she had been caught up in such an absurd melodrama. All she had wanted was a quiet walk on the beach. What she did not want was a conversation with a barely sober girl.

Tanner leaned her cheek on her knee and studied the woman standing ramrod straight before her. Blue eyes like chips of flint met hers coolly. The face seemed flawless except for the signs of strain that showed in the fine lines around her mouth and eyes. Tanner wondered briefly what was bothering her so much, but the thought passed quickly as a pounding headache penetrated her slowly awakening mind.

"Ugh!" She grimaced. "If I look half as bad as I feel, I'm surprised you didn't run immediately for a body bag."

Adrienne thought Tanner looked remarkably attractive for someone who had just spent the night in a drunken stupor on the beach, but she certainly wasn't about to say so. "Well, I can't say much for your choice of sleeping places," she commented dryly. "Besides, your dog may be good company, but she isn't big on protection. She let me walk right up to you."

Tanner managed a slightly flirtatious grin despite her splitting headache. She wanted to crack that ice-cold façade. She wasn't sure why it should matter, but it did. "Sam probably knew I would be safe with you."

Adrienne remained impassive. Tanner was lovely, to be sure, with her devilish grin and confident charm, but she also was obviously trouble. "Now that you're awake and reasonably oriented in time and space, I'll leave you to find your way home when you're up to it." She turned to go but was restrained by a surprisingly firm grip on her arm. Tanner had risen quickly and stood unsteadily beside her.

"Wait a minute, please," Tanner said anxiously. "I don't even know where you live. I'd like to talk to you sometime when I can make a more civilized impression."

Adrienne laughed softly. "I have a feeling you're never entirely civilized. Besides, I doubt that we'd have much in common. I'm here on R and R—that's short for *reading and resting* at this particular point in time. A sabbatical of sorts from the real world. I'm sure you'd find that dull."

"You're mistaken." Tanner regarded her intently, the expression on her face impossible to decipher. "Actually, Adrienne, all of us on Whitley Point are attempting to escape life in one way or another. It seems that you've come to the right place if it's the real world you want to avoid."

Adrienne was surprised by the thinly veiled bitterness in Tanner's voice, but she didn't care to probe for its source. She didn't have the energy for someone else's problems. She could barely manage her own.

"I didn't mean it quite the way it sounded," she amended lightly. "I'm just not very interested in socializing these days. Perhaps we'll run into each other some time. Take care of yourself," Adrienne finished lamely as she resolutely turned to leave.

For a few seconds, Tanner watched the tall, thin figure striding purposefully away before calling to her retreating back, "Goodbye, and thanks for rescuing me!"

She thought she heard faint laughter, but the blond did not alter her step. Tanner continued to stare after her until she rounded the curve of the shoreline and disappeared from view. She then ran both hands through her disheveled hair and straightened her shirt. Moving slowly in an attempt to reduce the force of the cannon barrage in the back of her head, she made her way over the dunes toward the main house. When she entered the kitchen, the housekeeper fixed her with a stern glance.

"And where have you been? You look like a vagabond." May's annoyance was clearly displayed in the flash of her dark eyes.

Tanner held up one hand and gave May a pleading look. "Coffee, please, and don't go on at me right now. I'm suffering enough, I promise you."

"Hmph," the older woman snorted. She poured the steaming liquid into a mug and set it in front of Tanner, who had slumped into a chair at the table.

"Thanks," Tanner mumbled.

May had been the housekeeper for the Whitley family long before Tanner was born, and she had always considered it well within her province to bring Tanner to task for her behavior. In truth, when Tanner had been a teenager, May had often been the person who managed to prevent her escapades from coming to the attention of her mother. Tanner knew it, and she was grateful.

"Your friend was up here looking for you earlier," May commented reproachfully. "I had Richard give her a ride back to the mainland."

"My friend?" Tanner looked puzzled for a moment, until she suddenly recalled the events of the previous evening. "Oh, right. Thanks."

She sighed heavily, wishing she could push the coffee into her veins. Now she remembered how she had ended up on the beach. At first, there were only fragmented images, more impressions than actual memories—wild urgent need and an aching, desperate desire shot through with a loneliness so pervasive she almost bled. They had made love furiously, frantically, until dawn, when Lois had finally fallen into an exhausted slumber. Ironically, Tanner hadn't been able to sleep with Lois in her bed, so she had risen quietly and pulled on clothes from the pile they had left on the floor in their eagerness to undress. Lois had not awakened as she left. Funny, she could remember what had happened, but her body still seemed empty, as if she had never been touched.

"Where's Mother?" Tanner asked suddenly.

"On the terrace. And you had better not go out there looking like that. Go shower and change your clothes." May looked at Tanner with a mixture of fondness and concern. "Are you all right?"

Tanner smiled wanly and rose to her feet. "Sure," she said, giving May a quick hug as she left.

An hour later, refreshed from her shower and dressed in a casual white linen shirt and loose drawstring pants, she climbed the winding outside stairs to the terrace. Her mother looked up from her reading as Tanner approached and smiled.

"Hello, darling."

"Hello, Mother," Tanner said softly, stooping to kiss her lightly on the cheek. She was often moved to tenderness at the sight of her mother's calm, gentle face. Just her presence, somehow, seemed soothing. Even though they rarely spoke directly of personal things, they were deeply bonded to one another. Tanner stretched out in an adjoining chaise and leaned her head back with a sigh.

"Are you here for the summer?" Constance looked fondly at her daughter.

"Hmm?" Tanner asked lazily, growing sleepy as the late spring sun suffused her with warmth. "Probably. The boat is here."

"Of course, you'll want to sail," her mother said quietly. *The water, always the water. So much like him.* "It's so nice to have you home."

Constance rested her hand affectionately on Tanner's suntanned arm. When there was no reply, she realized her daughter was asleep. Studying Tanner in repose, Constance thought how young she seemed when the shadows that often flickered across her features and haunted her deep-set eyes were gone. It was the only time she seemed at peace.

Unhappily, Tanner's seething unrest was far too familiar to Constance—it was the same barely contained energy, that same wild spirit, which had driven her husband for most of his life. It was the essence she had loved—and feared—most about him. That kind of passion could produce great achievement, but without purpose, it could end in self-destruction. Tanner was so like her father; Constance fervently hoped her daughter would not become a victim of her undisciplined desires, as he had.

CHAPTER THREE

Adrienne arrived back at the large empty house feeling strangely unsettled. She couldn't seem to get the encounter with the girl on the beach out of her mind. Something about the mixture of amusement and self-deprecation in the younger woman's manner had captivated her. *Probably because she's the first person you've met in months who's in worse shape than you,* she chided herself, trying hard to forget the dazzling smile and flirtatious charm. Tanner reminded her of so many of the young Californians, wild and reckless, who flocked to the bars and beaches ready to try anything, or anyone, that happened along. If she had ever been that young, or that vital, she could no longer remember it.

She let herself in through the sliding glass doors to the sun-filled bedroom, shaking her head impatiently. With a determined glance at the suitcases piled next to the door, she put herself to the task of unpacking. She hung her clothes neatly on hangers in the spacious closet, smoothing out her service dress uniforms and pushing them to the rear along with the rest of her regulation clothing, wondering absently why she had brought them along. Old habits. Immutable patterns of a lifetime.

The afternoon passed quickly as she attempted to bring order to her new surroundings, stowing her few supplies in the vastly oversized kitchen and unpacking the books and personal items she had shipped cross-country. There were only two cartons; she had just walked away from everything else.

Late in the day, she discovered to her delight an amply stocked bar in a small recessed area off the living room, courtesy of the absent owners. She poured herself a brandy, wandered barefoot outside with a copy of the *Whitley News*—a small weekly periodical listing local events that the realtor had left with the keys—and settled into a canvas deck chair. She looked to the water, reminded of the many evenings she had spent this way at home, just relaxing after a long day at the base. The only difference now was that she was alone. She had never felt so alone, in fact, so unable to confide in anyone, and the loneliness had slowly become a familiar companion.

She wondered if she hadn't made a mistake coming here instead of returning to the West Coast and resuming the life she knew. Then she reminded herself again of all the reasons she had decided not to do that. But what could she hope to find on the lonely expanse of this foreign shore? Time was what she needed most—time to adjust to the new circumstances of her life, time to chart a quiet course to order her days, time to seek a calmness of spirit in order to face her uncertain future without fear. Perhaps here, on this isolated island where time itself seemed suspended, she would find peace, if nothing else.

❖

"South Point Sports," she read from the single page devoted to nearby business establishments. After six days of rising early to walk on the beach, followed by leisurely hours spent reading in the sun, she felt better than she had in months. *Time to start some serious exercise again.*

An hour later, she was leaning on a chipped Formica counter in a one-room storefront gym. No one would ever consider calling this place a health club. From what she could see beyond the counter, there were two tiny bathroom/changing rooms in opposite corners of a garage-like space lit with overhead fluorescents, stacks of free weights, benches with taped-over tears, and a crowded collection of cast-off exercise equipment that had seen better days. It smelled like a locker room—sweat and machine oil and vinyl. It smelled like life.

"Help you?"

"Yes," Adrienne said, turning to face the woman behind the counter. She was suntanned, wind-blown and a hundred thirty pounds of muscle and bone. On a ship she would have been a machinist mate. "Uh, do you have a membership plan or a daily fee?"

"We're flexible," the woman replied, trying to place the tall, blue-eyed blond. She wasn't a native, and she didn't look like one of the soft, pampered summer crowd. Too early for that bunch anyhow, and they usually preferred the swankier places on the mainland. "Five dollars a day, thirty for the week, ninety for one month or one seventy-five for three."

Adrienne hesitated, then pulled her wallet from the back pocket of her jeans. *Time to commit.* "Let's do three."

"Staying on the island?" the woman asked as she ran the card.

"Yes."

"I'm Finch. Towels are inside, bring your own lock. If you need anything, give me a yell."

"Thanks. Adrienne Pierce," she said, extending one hand as she took her credit card in the other.

Finch smiled and held her hand a beat. "Pleasure."

Grinning, Adrienne threaded her way between the equipment to the closet-sized locker room. If that was a pass, it had to have been the first one in years. Well, maybe only the first she'd noticed. Silly to care, but nice just the same.

Thirty minutes later, the farthest thing from her mind was whether anyone found her attractive. Every muscle screamed, she couldn't get a deep breath, and the sweat that dripped into her eyes in the decidedly non-air-conditioned gym had to be mixed with blood. The months of inactivity had taken their toll.

Three more reps. Come on, you used to do fifteen like it was nothing.

"Need a spot?"

Adrienne looked up between her braced arms, past the horizontal bar of the barbell, into smoky dark eyes. She kept pushing the bar up, but her arms were shaking. "Yes, thanks," she gasped.

Tanner spread her legs on either side of the weight bench and bent her knees, then extended her hands under the barbell, fingers just lightly touching it, ready to grab it if it started to fall. "You're taking more of the weight on your left arm," she commented. "The right okay?"

"Old...injury," Adrienne said through gritted teeth, lowering the bar toward her body. Her entire chest and right shoulder were on fire. Tears leaked from the corners of her eyes. She hoped it looked like sweat. "One more."

"Go, all the way up to the count of five. One...two..." Tanner leaned a little closer until she straddled the top of the bench just above Adrienne's head. She looked down and lost the count. Adrienne's face was a vista of stark, unmitigated beauty. Her eyes were the blue of the bay at sunrise, and for an instant, Tanner went under, soothed as she imagined she would be as she drowned. Distantly, she heard a strangled groan of pain. Heart pounding, she asked quickly, "Stop?"

"No," Adrienne rasped stubbornly. The right side of the bar dipped precipitously. "Oh God!"

The bar dropped.

Tanner flexed her legs, tensed her shoulders, and caught the weight before it hit Adrienne's chest. "Stay still," she grunted, hefting the barbell back up to the support cleats.

"Sorry," Adrienne whispered, closing her eyes against the agony in her chest. "I—"

"It's okay." Tanner knelt by the bench, a fist of anxiety knotted in her throat. "Are you hurt? Did you tear something?"

"No," Adrienne answered weakly. "Just...a spasm."

"I can get some ice."

"No, please." Carefully, Adrienne sat up, massaging her shoulder with her left hand. Tanner was very close to her, her face creased with worry. Embarrassed, Adrienne blushed. "You saved me from a nasty crush. Thanks."

"Don't mention it," Tanner said, finally breathing easier. The pain was beginning to clear from Adrienne's face. "We're even now."

"What?"

"You rescued me, remember?"

"Hardly." Adrienne laughed despite the ache that pulsed with each heartbeat. "Sunburns are rarely fatal."

"Depends on where you get burned." Tanner's voice was low and suggestive. Now that the other woman's color was better and the tight mask of pain was gone from her face, Tanner relaxed. And appreciated again how attractive the new visitor was. Even in a baggy T-shirt and loose sweats, there was no denying it. "How about lunch?"

"Thanks, no." Adrienne stood abruptly. "I need to get home and take a shower. Thanks for the spot."

"Some other time, then?"

"Perhaps."

Tanner watched her walk away, feeling dismissed and, strangely, defeated. *That was a pretty clear no. It's not the first time you've heard it.*

It was just the first time in a long time that it mattered though, and she wondered why.

❖

Adrienne stood under the steaming spray, letting the water beat gently against her chest, eyes closed against the lingering pain. *It doesn't mean anything. Just a little too much a little too fast. You'll get it all back.* She lathered her skin, massaged her sore muscles, her body like a stranger to her. *Will I? Will anything ever be the same?*

Impatiently, she reached for the shampoo, working the soap into her hair. *Questions with no answers. Ridiculous to dwell on it.* She thought of the young woman who had asked her to lunch. *Tanner.* Sleek and strong and confident in a sleeveless T shirt that revealed so much more than muscle. A young animal—arrogant, prowling with energy, so sure of herself. She envied her that certainty.

CHAPTER FOUR

Over the next few days, Adrienne's life quietly settled into a routine. She explored the island enough to acquaint herself with the general store where she bought the few supplies she needed. Walking the aisles, she nodded politely to the pleasant hellos of several of the island's long-time inhabitants but didn't attempt conversation. One afternoon, she wrote notes to a few friends and made an obligatory call to her family, but other than that, she had no contact with anyone.

If she was lonely, she did not recognize it as such. When she grew restless, she had only to return to the sea to find the comfort her soul craved. The sea was her constant companion. In the morning she ran and at sundown she walked the beach, surrounded by such beauty she couldn't think of anything else.

Four days later, she visited the gym again. Halfway through her workout, Tanner appeared. With a brash grin and a bit of a swagger, she walked over to the leg extension machine where Adrienne was silently counting reps.

"Need a partner?" Tanner settled her hands on her hips, well-muscled legs slightly spread.

"Thanks, no," Adrienne replied. "I'm taking it easy for a while."

"The offer for lunch is still open."

"We've had this conversation before." But she couldn't help but smile fleetingly. As annoying as the girl was, she had her charms.

"I know, but things change," Tanner responded, watching Adrienne's face closely for a sign as to what she was thinking. The blond's cool façade was nearly impenetrable, which only made Tanner want to try harder. She wanted her to smile again, because when she did, it was like sunshine, hot on her skin.

"This won't," Adrienne said softly, deliberately meeting the girl's smoldering gaze. "This time no is really no."

"I understand," Tanner said quietly. "Sorry to bother you. I'll let you get back to your workout."

Adrienne did not see her again that day or the next, and she was glad. There had been something beneath the cocky banter that had sounded like pain. Hearing it, she had wondered what it was, all the while knowing that she could not afford to ask.

❖

While unpacking groceries from her car one morning, Adrienne was startled by the sound of a ringing phone. It was such a rare occurrence, it took her a moment to realize what it was. *Surely a wrong number*, she thought, as she dashed indoors to snatch up the receiver.

"Yes?"

"Ms. Pierce?" a well-modulated voice inquired.

"Speaking," Adrienne replied, puzzled. She did not recognize the voice.

"This is Constance Whitley, your neighbor to the north. You've settled in comfortably, I hope?"

Nonplussed, Adrienne hesitated, wondering how the Whitleys knew of her presence. *Of course, in all likelihood, little escapes the attention of the Whitleys on Whitley Point.*

"Yes, I have. Thank you," she replied after a second.

"I'm delighted to hear that. I'm calling to invite you to our open house on Saturday evening. It's rather a tradition on Whitley Point. Everyone on the island celebrates the beginning of the summer season at a barbecue dinner-dance at our home. I do hope you can attend."

"Well, I..." Adrienne began, desperately seeking a polite way to refuse an invitation from the island's most prestigious family. When she could think of none, she replied, "I would be happy to. Thank you so much for thinking of me."

"Not at all, my dear. Dress is informal. We'll expect you around seven." Constance Whitley rang off with a polite goodbye.

Adrienne was left staring at the phone. "Damn," she muttered under her breath. "Just what I do *not* want to do. But I guess I can't refuse the first family."

As Saturday approached, Adrienne found her hard-won peace of mind slipping away. She was nervous about the evening's festivities because she hadn't attended a public function in months and wasn't at all sure she was up to the social niceties. Throughout the day, she was plagued by a vague ache in her right arm and shoulder, the first time she'd been bothered by it in over a week. Annoyed with herself, she tried to read, but she found she couldn't concentrate. When she realized that she had read the same paragraph three times and still didn't know what it said, she tossed the book aside in disgust. She found herself craving a cigarette after six months without one. *Oh, what the hell.*

She grabbed her keys and stomped down the steps to her car. On a mission, she wheeled the vehicle around the cul-de-sac and headed toward the intersection with the shore road. Just as she pulled out, a silver Jaguar hurtled around the curve and barreled down on her. A horn blasted, she swerved, and only her quick reflexes saved her from being broadsided.

As her car skidded, Adrienne yanked the wheel hard to the right, slamming to a stop just on the edge of a ditch that ran along the shoulder of the road. The sports car roared away. She caught only a glimpse of the rear of the convertible as it disappeared around a corner. She couldn't see the driver, but the letters *THW* stood out clearly on the license plate.

"Damn!" Adrienne cursed aloud, trembling slightly. She waited for her breathing to quiet before backing the car carefully onto the road and driving at a sedate pace to the store.

"Good morning, Mr. Simms," she said to the familiar face behind the counter. "Could I have a pack of Dunhills, please?"

"Sure thing. Beautiful sailing weather, isn't it?" he responded with a smile.

Still shaken by the near-accident, Adrienne bit back a sarcastic comment and turned to look out a window to the marina below. After all, he was just being friendly. An impossibly blue sky, decorated with picture-postcard clouds, joined a brilliant expanse of ocean as far as she could see. "You're right, the sea is perfect."

"Do you do much sailing, Ms. Pierce?" he asked as he rang up the sale.

"I have. Not this summer, though."

"Well, there are some nice little boats here you can rent if you ever get the urge."

"Thank you. I'll remember that," Adrienne replied calmly as she accepted her change.

She drove home along the beach road remembering the feel of the sails in her hands, the exhilaration and the freedom. The cigarettes remained unopened on the seat beside her. *Why not? I'm strong enough now.*

Some small part of her soul, long dormant, flickered to life.

❖

It wasn't difficult to find Whitley Manor since it occupied the entire north end of the island and the main road stopped at its massive iron front gate. Adrienne followed a line of cars up the curving drive and parked her modest rental car beside a row of Mercedes, Jaguars, and BMWs. She caught her breath when she saw the house.

It was hidden from the beach by a copse of trees, and though she had glimpsed it from the shore, she had never realized how impressive it was. Three stories and one of the few stone edifices on the island, it had been carefully designed not to detract from the landscape surrounding it. Sunken pools accented by recessed lights bordered a meandering flagstone walkway through terraced gardens to a wide front staircase. A spacious porch led from the main level around the side of the house, with a second open deck one floor above. The verandah was already crowded with guests.

I'm here now; I might as well go up.

She handed her keys to the handsome young man who was parking cars and took a deep breath, trying to steady her nerves as she climbed the stairs. She wasn't looking forward to greeting a crowd of strangers, especially alone. She had chosen a pale blue silk suit, comfortably simple yet elegant enough for the occasion. As she glanced over to the portico off the right of the drive, she noticed a silver Jaguar XKE with a familiar license plate parked halfway up on the lawn. The vehicle that had nearly hit her earlier in the day.

Well, at least THW made it here in one piece.

Suddenly, her nervous self-consciousness was replaced with anger. She still remembered her panic, and the last thing she needed was a further reminder of life's fragility. Struggling to put it from her mind, she joined the flow of people making their way to the rear reception area. A passing waiter offered her a glass of champagne, which she gratefully accepted.

The patio in the rear of the house overlooked an impeccably groomed garden. She leaned against a pillar and attempted to get her bearings while watching with interest the people around her. The men and women all looked sleek, healthy, and supremely confident. They all seemed to know their place in the world, and it was obvious that it suited them. A gentle hand on her arm interrupted her quiet surveillance.

"Ms. Pierce?"

Adrienne turned to find a woman in her mid-forties standing by her side. Dressed in an exquisite pearl-gray dress set off by a simple emerald necklace, the woman was the epitome of aristocratic elegance. Adrienne stared at her for a moment, uncertain, then found her voice.

"Yes?"

The woman smiled kindly at her obvious consternation. "I'm Constance Whitley. I'm so glad you could come."

Her voice was soft, like her eyes, and Adrienne found herself holding her breath, half expecting this gentle apparition to disappear. Aware of the slightly puzzled look on her hostess's face, she quickly extended her hand in greeting. "Thank you for inviting me. Please forgive me for staring. It seemed for a moment that I had met you before."

"Well, perhaps it's my rather ordinary face." Constance laughed quietly, her eyes suddenly lively.

Adrienne blushed, feeling foolish. "It is hardly ordinary, Mrs. Whitley."

"Please call me Constance," she said as she hooked her arm through Adrienne's. "Come, let me introduce you to a few of your neighbors."

Adrienne allowed herself to be taken in tow by this charming woman, nodding hello as she was introduced to one smiling face after another. She was certain that she wouldn't remember a single name. They were making their way through the crowd when a familiar voice boomed out.

"Commander Pierce! Is that you?"

Startled, Adrienne jumped, blushing as she saw heads turn in her direction. A large man in summer whites bore down upon them, and she couldn't help but smile despite her acute embarrassment and considerable surprise. "Admiral Evans—how nice to see you, sir."

"An unexpected pleasure, out here of all places. Small world, indeed. How are you, Adrienne?" he asked kindly. They walked over to the rail, out of the way of the throng of people milling about.

"I'm fine, sir, really. I'm on leave still."

"Hmph," he muttered. "Of course, I knew that. Damn shame what happened."

Adrienne looked away uncomfortably. Until his recent relocation, she and the admiral had been stationed in the same area, and she supposed at some point paperwork concerning her had crossed his desk. "Yes, sir. Thank you, sir. Well, the sea air has always agreed with me."

"Quite right, quite right." He looked chagrined and hastily changed the subject. "How are you enjoying Whitley Point?"

"It's charming," she replied honestly. "Do you have a house here?" Despite the memories the admiral stirred, she was quite happy to see a familiar face among the crowd of strangers.

"Here? Oh, no. Just visiting. I've known Constance Hughes—well, Whitley now, of course—since she was a child. Now that I'm stationed fairly close—just down the coast—I come here as often as I can find an excuse. She's a wonderful woman."

"She certainly seems to be."

"It's a wonder, really, her being widowed so young—with a daughter to raise as well as the entire Whitley fortune to manage. She's done remarkably well."

"I can see that," Adrienne commented blandly. She was truly fond of the admiral, but she wasn't in the mood for light gossip at the moment. Suddenly she felt very tired, and she didn't think it was entirely physical. Watching couples stroll together, hearing the sounds of so many happy people enjoying themselves, she was acutely aware of how solitary she had become.

"Would you excuse me, sir? I'd like to wander around for a bit."

"Of course, Commander. I'll look for you later."

Retreating quickly down into the garden, Adrienne soon found a seat on a secluded bench that was separated from the stone walkway by a hedgerow. She sipped her champagne and tried to collect her thoughts. Seeing Admiral Evans had reminded her all too clearly of how far she had strayed from her previous way of life. It was more than unsettling; it was literally disorienting. *Truly at sea*, she thought bitterly, lowering her head into her hands and closing her eyes.

"A bit much, isn't it? The party," a cool voice said at her elbow.

Adrienne raised her head quickly to discover Tanner, resplendent in a nearly sheer white silk shirt and black tuxedo trousers, standing casually beside her, a champagne flute dangling from one hand and a nearly full bottle in the other. Her athletic figure was well displayed in the finely tailored clothing, and for a moment, Adrienne simply stared. Finally she said, "You keep turning up. I'm beginning to think it's planned."

"Maybe it's fate," Tanner remarked, her voice oddly serious.

"More like a very small geographic area."

"So, it's Commander, is it?" Tanner took a seat beside Adrienne on the stone bench and deposited the champagne bottle nearby.

"Were you eavesdropping?"

"Guilty, ma'am." With a disarming grin, she tossed a fairly good salute to emphasize her words.

"Oh stop!" Adrienne laughed despite herself. "And no, it is *not* Commander—not here at any rate."

"Stationed near here like the admiral?"

"No," Adrienne replied reluctantly. "I'm on extended leave...and that may become permanent."

"Really?" Tanner continued flirtatiously. "I would think you have many good years of service left."

Adrienne paled slightly and turned away, searching in her handbag for the cigarettes she had tossed in at the last minute before leaving her house. She was annoyed to find that her hands were trembling.

"I'm sorry." Tanner touched her arm, recognizing her discomfort. "I always seem to say something stupid when I'm around you." She reached quickly for the matches in Adrienne's hand and lit the cigarette for her.

"Thank you." Adrienne exhaled the smoke slowly and smiled, her eyes on Tanner's worried face. "It's all right. It's just a very long story, and not one I'm fond of telling."

Tanner held up a hand and shook her head. "I understand. It's none of my business, really. There are things I'd rather not talk about, too. But I am very glad to see you again." She took the cigarette that Adrienne offered and sat silently, wondering what Adrienne had been trying to escape from, down here away from the crowds. They seemed strangely alone, isolated by the dense shrubbery, despite the people passing by just yards away.

"Better?" Tanner inquired finally.

Adrienne smiled, stubbing out the cigarette she discovered she didn't really want. "Yes, I'm sorry. I seem to have lost my sense of humor somewhere this past year."

Tanner gazed intently up at the people gathered on the verandah above them. "Perhaps you'll regain it here on our peaceful island," she said darkly.

It was Adrienne's turn to stare, taken aback by her companion's bitter tone and the hint of pain in her eyes. "Don't you find it peaceful here?"

"Hardly." Tanner laughed without humor. She lifted the champagne bottle resting by her side and filled Adrienne's glass. "But then that's my story, isn't it?" she responded abruptly.

"Let's just say we both have our stories, and let it go at that," Adrienne said quietly, finding that she wasn't offended by the curt reply. She knew how important her privacy had become to her, and she could more easily accept it in others. Besides, she hadn't the energy to probe another's anguish, nor the strength to offer solace. Searching for neutral ground, she asked, "Do you live near here? You never said."

Tanner nodded. "I'm a native. Can't seem to escape. I've tried New York and Boston, but I always seem to return to the Point. I never feel really whole unless I'm near the sea."

"I know what you mean. I love it, too."

"So you chose the Navy?"

"Yes. Sixteen years. I don't know what attracted me the most at first—the uniform or the sea," Adrienne acknowledged with a laugh. "After a while, though, it was definitely the sea."

"I'll bet you look absolutely smashing in a uniform." Tanner couldn't help a grin.

"You watch too many movies," Adrienne accused, suddenly uncomfortable. There was something a little too appealing in Tanner's persistent flirtations.

"Nope. I read too many books."

"Oh, all right, you win." She couldn't help but admit it. "I *did* like the uniform."

Then they both laughed and, sipping champagne, watched in silence as the sky darkened, a spectacular sunset giving way to the soft glow of the moon and stars. The scene was achingly beautiful, and Adrienne was acutely aware of the woman beside her. She glanced at the chiseled profile, wondering if Tanner felt it, too. *Don't,* she chided herself, *don't even wonder.*

"Hungry?" Tanner inquired.

"Famished," Adrienne replied, realizing it was true. "I take it there's food nearby?"

"Scads. Come on—I'll lead the way."

They were helping themselves to the ample buffet when Constance Whitley approached them with an engaging smile.

"I see that you've met my daughter, Ms. Pierce."

Adrienne looked quickly from Tanner to Constance, momentarily taken aback. Then she realized why Constance had seemed familiar. "Of course. I don't know why I didn't see it sooner. The resemblance is striking."

"You compliment me, Ms. Pierce." Constance smiled fondly at Tanner, reaching out to stroke her cheek gently before moving away.

Tanner stood quietly in the uncomfortable silence, waiting for Adrienne to react. She was used to the response her status evoked, especially from women. Inevitably, they either became exceedingly cold or insufferably solicitous. She was totally unprepared for Adrienne's response.

"It was you!" Adrienne exploded angrily, finally putting all the pieces together. "THW—that's Tanner Hughes Whitley, isn't it?"

"Yes, but..." Tanner began, clearly confused. *Now what have I done?*

"You damn idiot." Adrienne was seething. "You nearly killed me today. Haven't you ever heard of speed limits?"

Tanner stared at her, dumbfounded. "What are you talking about?"

"On the shore highway this afternoon. You nearly ran me off the road." Adrienne struggled to keep her voice down as her temper threatened to detonate. Just thinking about it made her heart pound with the memory of the fear.

"Today?" Tanner searched her memory and drew a blank. "I'm sorry. I don't remember. I was...uh, a little...out of touch this afternoon."

She was embarrassed, recalling the afternoon's entertainment that she had shared with some friends on the beach. She didn't clearly remember even driving into town.

"Well, perhaps the next time you're drunk, or stoned, or whatever it is that you do, you'll do the rest of the world a favor and stay off the roads." Adrienne turned abruptly and pushed her way through the crowd of people gathered behind them trying to get to the buffet. She didn't know what incensed her more—the fact that Tanner had nearly killed her, or the fact that Tanner might have killed herself. And it infuriated her that she even cared.

Tanner was left staring after her. "Fuck," she cursed vehemently. "I can't seem to do anything right when it comes to that woman."

Stung by the rebuke and angry with herself for inciting it, she went off to find another glass of champagne. This evening was turning out to be as bad as she had expected it to be. The only pleasure had been in those few brief moments that she had been able to share with Adrienne, but that was over now.

Chapter Five

It was late when Adrienne finally escaped. Admiral Evans had monopolized her attentions for the remainder of the evening, insisting that she meet half the population of Whitley Point. While her anger burned dangerously close to the surface, she had attempted to make polite conversation with people she had no intention of ever seeing again. All she could think was what a monumental mistake on her part it had been to come to the party. She had been so much happier by herself and couldn't wait to be alone again.

Tanner had seemed about to approach her several times, a conciliatory look on her handsome face, but Adrienne had managed to avoid her. The last thing she had wanted was another confrontation with someone who seemed to rouse her own worst traits. Pointless anger would do neither of them any good. She had enough conflict in her life already. The last time she had seen her, Tanner was being led away by an attractive blond in a low-cut evening gown. For some reason, that sight incensed Adrienne even further.

Home finally, she went directly upstairs, irritably stripped off her clothes and, uncharacteristically, tossed them aside without a second thought. She kept seeing Tanner, an arm around the woman's waist, a bottle of champagne in her free hand, heading off into the dark. She was irate that the memory angered her.

So what if she made a spectacle of herself, letting that woman hang all over her. She'd had enough champagne—she probably needed the help. Oh, what do I care? She's obviously capable of taking care of her own needs. Or finding someone who will. God—what difference does it make to me what she does to herself or who she does it with?

She wasn't at all sure why a woman she hardly knew could have such a disquieting effect on her. Tanner *did* seem to be adrift, more than likely a result of never wanting for the things ordinary people struggled a lifetime to attain. She had money and privilege, but neither seemed to have brought her happiness. Still, there had been something more than that in Tanner's eyes, something that Adrienne recognized—despair or some deep anguish—that seemed to echo her own desperation. She felt it, and she had wanted to reach out to her.

Don't be ridiculous. You can barely look after yourself. She's probably just bored.

Her own situation, she admitted, was probably far more incapacitating. She didn't trust herself. She didn't trust her future. Without a clear idea of where her life was headed, she seemed, in fact, to have nowhere to go. Now she was lost, uncertain of her next move—unsure of what the next day might bring. She struggled to accept a life without dreams, without passion. She had thought she was succeeding until this dark-haired youth with eyes deep as the fathoms had walked into her life. Now, she felt a great deal more than she wanted.

Let it go. You can't help her. You have no right to even think of it.

She collected her scattered garments and hung them carefully in the closet, then pulled on a faded pair of cut-off chinos and a loose cotton shirt. Wide awake, she wandered out onto the deck. Overhead, the sky was velvet black, punctuated by bright points of flickering starlight.

Reclining in the chaise with a sigh, she stretched her long legs out in front of her and tried to relax. The sounds of the distant surf failed to have their usual calming effect. She was agitated and restless, and her thoughts kept returning to issues she wasn't prepared to face.

Months ago, she had given up trying to understand why her life had taken such an unexpected turn. Circumstances had led her on a journey that had culminated in her arrival at Whitley Point, and now she was here, far from the settled, predictable world she had grown used to. If there was some logic to it, some hidden reason to the events that had completely changed her life, she couldn't identify it. At the moment, she didn't want to try. All she wanted was to learn to deal with what had befallen her. She had thought she was succeeding, until she met Tanner. Now her hard-won peace of mind was threatened by the reflection of her own loss mirrored in Tanner's dark eyes. She rubbed her aching shoulder and pushed herself up.

If I can't sleep, I might as well walk. Anything to stop this pointless train of thought.

She climbed down the stairs toward the beach and followed the path through the shadow of the dunes by memory. As she walked, night sounds surrounded her—the wind bent blades of grass; the waves rushed to destruction in the shoals; the small living creatures fled her approach on scurrying legs.

Her thoughts were of Tanner; she couldn't seem to put her mind on anything else. Tanner's eyes, her voice, the brazen curve of her smile—everything about her was alive and so vibrant. It was incomprehensible how someone with so much to live for could be so heedless of her own well-being. If there was one thing Adrienne had learned to appreciate in her journey, it was the vagary of life.

It seemed to her now, reflecting on her own situation, that life was dangerously unpredictable, ready to spin away, out of one's grasp, at any moment. She would give anything to feel in control of her own fate again. Tanner's face flickered into her mind once more, something bitter and hard glinting in her beautiful eyes. Something dangerous and lost in them, too.

She doesn't care. God, what a waste. Surely, if there is sin, it must be that—to throw life away as if it were nothing. What I wouldn't give... She shook her head angrily. *Stop it! You should be used to times like this by now. You know damn well there are no reasons, no explanations, no answers. No going back.*

She continued to walk, unmindful of destination, forcing the dark memories from her mind. The beach was still—even the waves seemed to realize it was nighttime, breaking softly and rolling gently onto the shore. The half-moon cast soft shadows over the sand. Finally comforted, she fell into step with the rhythm of the sea, walking steadily along the edge of the tide pools. She half expected to come upon some weary castaway in this unreal world of sound and shadow, so she was only slightly startled when her solitude was shattered by a husky voice calling out to her from the darkness.

"Are you lost, Commander?"

Adrienne squinted into the shadows, finally making out a still form hunched over in the protection of a gently rising swell of sand. She approached silently and sat down on the moist ground. "Where's your friend?"

"Asleep in my bungalow."

"What are you doing out here?" Adrienne studied Tanner's set features. The effects of the alcohol appeared to have worn off. She looked tired but composed. "It's much too cool to spend the night on the beach again."

"Couldn't sleep," Tanner answered lightly. She never could figure out why the presence of another person in her bed disturbed her, but she was always wide awake after sex, unaccountably restless. "How about you? Pretty late for a walk, isn't it?"

"The ocean relaxes me." Taking a deep breath, Adrienne continued, "Listen, I'm sorry I went off at you back there at the party. It's just that—"

"No need," Tanner interrupted with a shake of her head. "You were right. If I'm going to screw myself up, the least I can do is have the decency not to involve other people. I'm sorry I frightened you. I never meant that."

Adrienne stared at her, shocked by the hollow note in her voice. This was not the cocky, confident woman she had verbally jousted with only hours earlier. Tanner seemed to have surrendered to whatever demons had been plaguing her, and, to her surprise, Adrienne found that she much preferred the young woman's maddening arrogance to this.

"That's not what I was trying to say to you. I was worried about you—and angry at you, too. You could have really hurt yourself."

"Why should you care?" Tanner asked without rancor or challenge, merely curiosity. "It doesn't really matter all that much."

"Oh, Tanner," Adrienne exclaimed. "You're wrong. It matters so very much. You have a choice about your life, about what happens to you. You mustn't throw that away."

Tanner shrugged. "Some choices are made for us, and the rest? I just choose not to decide. *C'est la vie,* and all that."

"It's not always that simple. Sometimes life slips through your fingers, and there's nothing you can do to stop it."

"You're not talking about me at all, are you?" Tanner turned to search Adrienne's face, surprised by the tenor of pain in her voice. But Adrienne wasn't looking at her. She was staring straight ahead at the water, her profile in the moonlight almost otherworldly—distantly beautiful, remote and untouchable. "You're talking about yourself. What things, Adrienne? What *things* can't you control?" Tanner waited in the silence, her heart pounding. *What is it? What has hurt you so much?*

"Nothing." Adrienne's jaw clenched. "I didn't mean me. I just meant that you—everyone—should value each moment."

"There's something you're not saying, Commander Pierce," Tanner continued quietly. "But you can keep your secrets...for a while." She leaned back on her arms, watching the flickering shadows play across the sand. At length, she returned her gaze to the sea. "Did you ever feel like there was something you wanted, but you didn't know what it was?"

"I think so—a long time ago." Adrienne followed Tanner's gaze, caught up in the pensive tone of her voice. Moonlight glinted on the water in broken streaks of silver. "It's been a very long time since I can remember wanting anything that badly—so badly I could feel it like an ache in my bones. Is that what you mean?"

Tanner nodded. "What was it you wanted?"

"Probably not what you're talking about," Adrienne said with a soft laugh. "I wanted a career, a future I could count on."

"And? Did you get it?"

"I thought so." In an unusually revealing moment, Adrienne said, "My parents were fairly simple people who believed that if you worked hard enough you would eventually succeed. I grew up believing that, too. I studied endless hours because I had to. I wasn't the brightest in my class, but I was the most determined. I wanted to be an engineer, and I wanted the Navy, and I wanted to be the best. It took a lot to prove myself because some people think it's still a man's world and that engineering is still a guy's field, but I stuck it out. It worked. I got my degree; I got my commission; I thought that I had everything I ever wanted."

She stared at Tanner, watching the moonlight play over her young, hauntingly lovely face. Until a year ago, nothing in her life had challenged that belief. Then suddenly, without warning, it had all dissolved. Tonight, she'd said much more than she'd meant to say. Tanner seemed to make her forget herself. "But tell me what it is you think you want."

"I don't know." Tanner ran a hand through her already tousled hair and frowned. "I can't seem to settle anywhere. I wander around, but I always seem to return to Whitley Point. I make love, but I can only sleep when I'm alone. I drink, or worse, but I only feel emptier. Nothing seems to *mean* very much to me." She sighed and looked at

Adrienne with a sheepish grin. "Pretty pathetic, huh?"

Adrienne smiled, touched by the wistfulness in her voice. "Confused, maybe. God knows, I don't have the answers. What makes life worth living is different for everyone. And sometimes it's very hard to know what those things are."

"Is that why you came to Whitley Point—to find those answers?"

Adrienne shrugged, sifting sand through her long fingers, tossing bits of broken shells into the darkness. "I thought I did, at first. Now I'm not sure. Maybe I just came here so I wouldn't have to face not knowing. It's a nice place to hide, this island. After a while, it's easy to forget that there really is another world out there."

"Was there someone you left behind...back there in California?"

"No," Adrienne said abruptly, turning her face away.

"I'm sorry." Tanner sighed. "I always seem to hit some sore spot with you. It's just that you don't seem to be the kind of person not to be involved." *You're too beautiful, too tender, to be so alone.*

Adrienne shifted slightly in the sand so that she could look into Tanner's eyes. They were warm and welcoming. There was something about this woman that made her want to talk. She felt almost safe with her. Still, she hesitated, afraid of what she might feel, afraid of what these moments with Tanner had awakened in her. She hadn't talked to anyone about the events of the last year of her life, not her friends or even her family. Because if she did, she'd have to face the pain and the fear, and she simply didn't think she could. Beside her, Tanner waited, and the honest concern in those dark eyes gave her courage.

"There was someone. A woman," Adrienne began slowly, trying to find the right words. She wasn't concerned about Tanner's reaction to her relationship with Alicia. Tanner had been clear about her own preferences and didn't seem to care who knew it. But she still couldn't bring herself to tell her all of it; she couldn't expose herself, couldn't bear the pity. "We're not together now."

When Adrienne hesitated, Tanner urged her on quietly, sensing her struggle. "Is she the reason you're on leave?"

"Not exactly. I...she left me because of something else. Something personal."

"This something...personal. That's the real secret, isn't it?" Tanner asked even more gently, "The reason that you're here at Whitley Point?"

"Yes."

"What is it?" Tanner couldn't miss the thinly veiled anguish in Adrienne's voice, and she longed to offer her some respite.

Adrienne's reply came softly. "I can't talk about it, not right now. I'm sorry." The last words came out in a choked whisper. Her eyes brimmed with tears she refused to shed, had never shed, not even in her darkest hours.

God, she is hurting so much. Tanner knew she couldn't ask Adrienne to go on. Her suffering was all too clear. Wanting so much to comfort, Tanner responded without thinking, offering the only solace she knew. Slowly, as if submerging beneath still waters, not wanting to make a ripple, she leaned toward Adrienne. Her eyes never left those troubled blue ones until their lips were but a breath apart, until at last they were so close that she had only to dip her head slightly to bring her mouth to Adrienne's. Gently, carefully, she brushed a kiss over warm, soft lips, her tongue tenderly, tentatively exploring, not daring yet to enter.

Miraculously, Adrienne did not pull away, and, feeling welcomed, Tanner didn't hurry or even touch except with her mouth. Lost in the sweet surprise of the moment, barely able to believe the tenderness of a simple kiss, Tanner let the beauty of it stream through her. A kiss like this was a new experience for her, and she felt a wonder deeper even than her first time. There had been so many others since then, and no one had moved her quite like this silent, tormented woman.

Her tongue slipped into Adrienne's mouth, the serenity of it almost more then she could bear. Moaning softly, her whole being flowed toward Adrienne and with one trembling hand, she cupped the side of Adrienne's face, feeling the racing heartbeat in the pulse just below her jaw. Rising slowly to her knees, holding the kiss, Tanner pressed closer—caressing Adrienne's neck, tangling urgent fingers in the strands of blond hair near her collar.

Desire, hot and hard, rose quickly and crashed through Tanner. Now a storm of need pummeled her; her head pounded furiously and she couldn't catch her breath. She shuddered, helpless before the onslaught, and distantly, she heard herself groan. Abruptly the kiss was lost as Adrienne pulled away with an anguished cry.

"No!"

"Adrienne..." Tanner gasped, shaking, her vision dim with need.

"Oh God...I didn't mean...I..." She reached out to touch Adrienne's arm, her hand trembling. "Please, I only wanted—"

Adrienne jumped to her feet, her eyes fixed on Tanner's flushed face. "I'm sorry, Tanner, you just don't understand. I can't...I'm sorry." She turned and ran.

"Adrienne! Wait, please. Just talk to me," Tanner called after her. "Let me explain..."

But Adrienne disappeared into the dark, leaving Tanner still kneeling in the sand.

CHAPTER SIX

Halfway home, Adrienne kicked off her shoes and gathered them into one hand, barely breaking stride. She couldn't run in the sand in them, and she couldn't stop running. She ran until her breath disappeared, and then she ran on adrenalin alone. Finally, she saw the lights from her house flickering in and out between the pines, and she stumbled to a halt, collapsing on the sand a body's length from the water's edge. Lowering her head to her knees, she wept.

Eventually, the wind dried her tears. She wrapped her arms around her knees and watched the waves rush to shore on the incoming tide. They came willingly to their destruction, deceptive curls of sweeping grace and seething power, mesmerizing in their dying splendor. She was grateful for their hypnotic beauty, because she couldn't think—not while her lips tingled from a kiss torn from them too soon, nor while her skin burned with the imprint of achingly tender fingers. She couldn't think, but she could feel. In many ways, that was worse.

She hadn't asked to be touched, but she had surrendered to that kiss as if laying down a burden she had carried for her whole life. She had closed her eyes and lowered her guard and rested in the soothing currents of Tanner's caress like a shipwrecked sailor stumbling to shore. She had been so lonely for so long, and for one sweet moment out of time, she had wanted not to be alone.

Oh my God, what have I done?

❖

Tanner sat on the beach where Adrienne had left her. If she was cold, she didn't feel it, but in some part of her consciousness, she was aware that she was shivering. Her first instinct when Adrienne fled had been to run after her. Insist that they talk. She wasn't a patient person, by nature or by breeding, and she was used to having what she wanted.

And though Adrienne had made it clear she wanted nothing from her, she almost didn't care. Something had happened here on this beach—for one brief instant they had touched upon one another's secrets. Only the pain in Adrienne's cry as she pulled away kept Tanner from going after her. Anything else she could have ignored, but not that. Pain she understood.

Sometime in the night, Sam came to curl up by her side, and she fisted her hand in the thick heavy fur, anchoring herself to the warm, living beast, searching for comfort. She was by turns angry and painfully empty. Her body held visceral memories—warm lips welcoming hers, the heat of Adrienne's mouth, the soft brush of skin against her palm. Remembering brought another wave of desire coursing through her. Not lust like the sex she had known, although her flesh cried simply to be touched, but a wild hunger to know and be known, to nourish and be filled. Fleetingly, she had felt it and, close upon it, suffered the loss like blood leaving her veins.

Tanner wrapped her arms around Sam's broad neck and waited for the sun. Eventually, with the passing of the night, she found that she could think, but her thoughts made no sense. It was so strange. She couldn't understand why this woman, a stranger among so many strangers, could have such a powerful effect on her. But it was impossible to deny. Her body still reeled from the onslaught of sensations—desire, yearning, and, something far more extraordinary, the urge to comfort. Adrienne was in pain, and Tanner wanted to make it stop. Ached so badly to banish that pain, she herself hurt.

She wasn't sure what to do. She was used to being pursued. Most often, it was her name or the mystique attached to it that was the attraction, and it was usually simplest to take the easy way out—accept the offer for a night or two of pleasure, then withdraw quickly when the situation became too intense. This time, *she* had made the offer, and she didn't want to pull away.

Frustrated, exhausted, she finally rose and walked slowly up the path that led to her bungalow. When she entered, she was surprised to find Sharon still asleep on the unmade bed. The sheets that lay twisted about her naked thighs were a testament to their fleeting passion, but Tanner couldn't remember it. She shook the slumbering woman's shoulder gently.

"Sharon, come on. It's morning already. You need to get up."

"Come back to bed," a husky voice implored.

"Are you crazy? I thought you were going home last night. Jerry will wonder where you are."

"Mmm." The blond rolled over lazily and smiled, still drowsy. "No, he won't. I'm sure he already knows where I am."

"Great." Tanner frowned in exasperation. "Just what I need—an irate husband crashing in here at six o'clock in the morning."

Sharon reached up for her with a grin. "He wouldn't do that. He knows I'll come home, as long as he doesn't interfere with my little escapades."

"Wonderful." Tanner stepped back out of Sharon's reach. "I'm glad you two have such an understanding relationship. But I'd still rather not end up in the middle of it."

"You won't, and since when did you worry about that kind of thing anyhow?" Sharon stretched leisurely, stood in one fluid motion, and moved close, threading her arms around Tanner's waist. Languorously undulating against Tanner, Sharon nearly purred. "You were so good. But you know that, don't you."

"Sharon..." Tanner protested mildly, reaching for the hands that were tugging at her shorts. "Slow down."

"I don't think so," the woman murmured, licking the side of Tanner's neck. "Last night was just an appetizer, and I always wake up hungry."

It would be so easy. In another minute, her body would decide for her, and she could surrender to the fingers stroking her bare skin, forget the longing for something—someone—else. Old habits. Immutable patterns. *Ahh...God...*

Tanner gripped the hand that had slipped down beneath her waistband and held it firmly as she twisted back out of reach, groping with her other hand at the foot of the bed for Sharon's dress. Gathering it in her fist, she held it out to the blond. "Come on. Get dressed."

"You're serious," Sharon said in surprise, studying Tanner's face. Something haunted lingered there. "Where have you been?"

"Out for a walk." Tanner flushed and looked away.

"Hmm. With that visitor from down the road?" As she spoke, Sharon slipped into the dress.

"What is that supposed to mean?"

"Nothing." Sharon shrugged and picked up her handbag. "I just noticed that you spent a lot of time watching her last night. And, if you ask me, my dear, you should forget her. She looks like a cold bitch."

"Well, I didn't ask you," Tanner responded shortly. "Now, would you mind leaving before the entire household sees you?"

"Certainly." Sharon kissed her sensuously on the lips as she made her way toward the door. "But you're a fool if you don't realize that everyone at that party knows I spent the night with you."

Tanner stared after her as Sharon slipped out the door, then pulled off her shirt and shorts and threw them on the floor. Naked, weary in more than body, she flung herself down on the bed. Her last thought before she finally slept was of Adrienne's face as she turned to run from her into the night.

CHAPTER SEVEN

Adrienne had not spoken to anyone, not even on the phone, in days. She even avoided the general store until necessity forced her to make the trip, but she hurried quickly back to her car with a bag under each arm, not even glancing in the direction of the gym that adjoined it in the tiny strip of storefronts. *Tanner might be there*, she thought, although she'd checked the lot for the silver Jag before she'd pulled in and hadn't seen it. Rationally, she knew she was being ridiculous, but she didn't care. She did not want to see her.

She still ran on the beach morning and night, but she never went north. Just heading in that direction reminded her of the night on the shore with Tanner. As if she needed a reminder. She could not get Tanner out of her thoughts, and thinking was the last thing she wanted. If she started, she'd have to think about Alicia, and her career, and her future, and she just wasn't ready. She was angry with herself—angry for dropping her guard, angry for letting anyone breach the protective barrier she had so carefully erected around her feelings.

How easily Tanner had penetrated those defenses. How easily she had come, with her dark eyes and wistful words, right into the center of Adrienne's consciousness. And there she stayed—images of Tanner's smile, memories of her hands, the soft sensuous sound of her voice would sear Adrienne with longing when she least expected it. She felt helpless to stop the memories, so she was resolute about avoiding Tanner in person.

Wonderful—you want to spend the next few months avoiding Tanner Whitley on Whitley Point. She owns the goddamned island.

Determined not to think of how gentle Tanner's lips had been against her mouth or how sweet those fingers felt threading through her hair, Adrienne read, exercised, and ate when she could remember to. Only when exhausted did she manage to sleep, and then it was fitful. And too often she dreamed. She awoke, unrested, with lingering sensations of skin against her skin and fire in her blood.

Tanner's compelling sexuality had aroused her; unwelcome and unrelenting, desire rose as unbidden as the urge to breathe. There was no good reason for it; it was obviously purely physical. And that in itself frightened her—she had not felt anything like it for so long. If there was anything she had been sure of, it was that such feelings had been obliterated by the trials of the last year. Now she wasn't certain of anything, except that she could not afford to let it happen again.

The tranquility of her solitary existence had been shattered, and with each day she grew more restless. The inactivity was intolerable, and she finally admitted that she would go mad if she didn't find something with which to occupy herself. And there was only one place where she had ever felt completely in control and completely free.

So, early one morning, she packed some gear and a lunch and set out for the marina. She parked her car in the shade on a small knoll that overlooked the bay and the marina and walked to the general store in search of Mr. Simms. She discovered him in the rear, kneeling by an open carton, unpacking cans.

"Good morning." She feigned a smile she did not feel. "I want to rent a sailboat. Who should I talk to about it?"

Mr. Simms straightened with a smile, dusting his hands off on his faded khaki pants. "That's simple enough. Just walk on down to the office and talk to Josh Thomas. He'll fix you up." He pointed through the windows to the gray-shingled all-purpose boat repair and rental building at the far end of a wooden pier with sloops and other boats moored on either side.

"Thanks."

As she walked down the pier, she smiled, a real smile this time, feeling almost happy for the first time in weeks as she imagined being out on the ocean again. When she saw Tanner's convertible parked in the lot close to the water's edge, her smile disappeared. For a minute, she considered leaving and then shook her head angrily, annoyed at her own reaction. *Enough is enough. I can't spend all summer avoiding her, and I can't keep running from her. We're both adults, and nothing happened except a slight mix-up in our signals. Seeing her won't be a problem. I hope.*

Resolutely, Adrienne pressed on, only to find the small office empty. She went back outside and began walking the length of the wooden pier, surprised that so many of the slips were full. Of course, everyone on the Point had a boat and probably most of the summer visitors as well. The location of the island was perfect for mooring if one wanted to go to the mainland for dinner or shopping. The marina was obviously another well-kept secret. Eventually, she came upon a weather-beaten, bearded man of indeterminate age who was overhauling one of the boats hoisted up in dry dock.

"Mr. Thomas?"

"That would be me," he said, looking over his shoulder at her as he continued scraping barnacles from the hull of a sloop. "Help you with something?"

"I want to rent a sailboat."

"A cat?"

"No," Adrienne said patiently. The marina manager had the look of a native about him and his distinctive New England accent confirmed it. "Something big enough to run in deep waters."

He put down his tools and walked over to her. "Sailing alone?"

"Yes."

"These waters can be tricky." He looked at her steadily. "You sail much?"

"I've sailed the Pacific for almost twenty years, Mr. Thomas, and I've crewed *and* captained all over the East Coast since I was a teenager." She answered him without a trace of defensiveness, because she felt none. He asked; she told him.

"Well," he mused, "you'll want something that'll give you a good sail then. Come on with me."

He turned out to be a charming man, although not overly talkative, but he answered her questions and outfitted her with gear once she chose a craft. He did, however, describe to her in loving detail the particulars of the boat while she filled out the paperwork.

"That's it, then, Ms. Pierce," he said finally. "She's all yours. Just be sure to keep an ear on the weather bulletins and get her in by nightfall. Summer squalls blow up quick in these waters, and this harbor is difficult to navigate in the dark."

"I'll be in well before dark," Adrienne replied with a smile. "And

I've got the radio for the Coast Guard reports." As she turned to climb aboard, she added, "By the way, isn't that Tanner Whitley's car over there?"

Josh looked in the direction she pointed and nodded. "Sure is." He laughed and shook his head. "She's been out before sunup every day for more than a week. If I didn't know better, I'd think she was out poaching lobster pots." He continued to chuckle as he walked away, leaving Adrienne alone to get acquainted with her new boat.

Adrienne sailed slowly for the first hour, getting used to the pull of the sails in the unfamiliar waters. Finally, as the wind peaked in the early afternoon, she let out her sails and made a fast run with the wind, exhilarating in the freedom and power of the boat under her. Physically, she felt wonderful, and the boat was so demanding under full sail that she didn't have time to think about the disturbing events of the last few weeks. She anchored in a quiet cove on the lee side of one of the small islands that dotted the local waters. In the distance, she could just make out the dark patch that was Whitley Point.

Famished, she opened the bottle of wine she had brought along as a treat and devoured two sandwiches in record time. After her meal, she stretched out on the deck to bask in the sun. For the first time in longer than she could recall, her mind was free from worry.

She must have napped, for the next thing she knew, the wind had grown cool, and the boat rocked heavily on the tide. To her surprise and consternation, when she opened her eyes, she discovered that the sun was already low on the horizon. Hastily, she gathered the remains of her meal and got under sail, anxious to make port before sundown. Even with a good wind, it was almost dark when she tacked into Whitley Harbor.

Josh Thomas ran to meet her on the pier and caught the towline she tossed to him. "I was getting a little worried there," he called. "It's almost dark."

"Yes, I know." Adrienne jumped down onto the dock. "I didn't intend to cut it so close, but I fell asleep in the sun. I'm sorry." She smiled at him, unable to hide her exhilaration. "God, it was wonderful out there!"

"Can't argue with that," he responded as he walked with her up toward the marina.

Adrienne cheerfully waved goodbye and started away, then

noticed the silver Jaguar parked where it had been that morning. *It's almost fully dark. Is she still sailing?* Before she could remind herself that she wasn't interested in anything about Tanner Whitley, she asked, "Oh, Mr. Thomas, is Ms. Whitley ashore yet?" She was surprised by the frown that darkened his pleasant features as he responded.

"No, and there's no telling when she will be. She's a damn fool to think she can run in these waters at night, but she does it more often than not. There's too much of her father in her. Just like him, she thinks the rules are only for other folk. If she weren't such a good sailor, we'd probably have found *her* washed up ashore somewhere, too." At Adrienne's expression of dismay, he hurried on. "I'm sorry, ma'am. I think the world of Tanner, just like I did her father. She just makes me mad sometimes. I'll try to raise her on the short-wave if you like."

"No," Adrienne said quickly. "No, that's not necessary. I'm sure she knows what she's doing." She hurried away, wanting to put thoughts of Tanner from her mind. *She doesn't need to know I was asking about her. I don't even know why I care.*

Still, as she drove home, she couldn't help wonder about Tanner, and about what solace she sought in her solitary forays onto the sea. Once in front of the house, she turned off the ignition and sat behind the wheel, hands resting in her lap. It wasn't the house she saw, but Tanner's face in the moonlight. That night on the beach, she'd heard something in the young woman's voice—something she'd recognized. A deeper longing, beyond loneliness, that stirred and frightened her at the same time. She'd seen something familiar in the depths of those dark, eloquent eyes, too—a yearning so poignant it made her want to weep.

God, why can't I get her out of my mind?

Finally, she forced herself out of the car, and, despite her lingering thoughts of Tanner and the uneasy memories of their kiss, she was aware of a thrill of excitement, too. The time on the water had awakened a long-dormant joy, a forgotten pleasure that revived and called to an essential part of her soul.

❖

Just as Adrienne gave in to a satisfying exhaustion and slept, a sailboat made its way to port in the darkened harbor. As the boat eased against the dock, a figure, silhouetted in moonlight, moved catlike to the edge of the deck and jumped down to the pier, trailing a rope behind.

"You toss me that, I'll give you a hand," a voice spoke from the shadows.

"Jesus," Tanner exclaimed. "You want to scare me to death, Josh?"

"Serve you right," he commented dryly, walking forward to take the towline from her. "You got any sense left at all coming in at this hour?"

"I could do it in my sleep," she remarked jauntily as she tied the aft line. "I was going to spend the night aboard but changed my mind." She didn't add that she'd been too restless to sleep, or that she craved something she couldn't quite name—maybe just company, a warm body in which to lose herself. She'd finally pulled up anchor and returned to shore, knowing company was one thing she could always find. "You weren't worried, were you?"

"Nope." He heard the faint apology in her tone. "Just happened to be awake and saw you come in," he lied.

"Thanks for the help then. I'll see you in the morning," she called as she walked up the pier.

"Ayuh."

He watched her headlights flash on, then heard the engine roar as he made his way back to the boathouse to close up. He could go home, now that he knew she was ashore.

Tanner hit the shore road going sixty, and by the time she reached the causeway, the silver Jag—top down, sleek as a bullet—was just a blur in the moonlight. In twenty minutes, she'd be at the local watering hole, and in an hour, she wouldn't be alone.

Funny, the prospect left her even less enthused than usual, which was odder still considering that she hadn't had sex in way too long. It wasn't that she wasn't interested; in fact, her body reminded her all too vividly at the most awkward times just how much she wanted the feel of flesh against her flesh. Except every time lately she felt the craving, she flashed on Adrienne's face. And then she remembered Adrienne's exquisite lips, and the scent of Adrienne's skin tinged with ocean salt.

Her stomach clenched and her legs trembled, and it wasn't sex she wanted; it was *her.*

Cursing softly under her breath, Tanner braked so suddenly the car nearly three-sixtied before it fishtailed to a stop on the shoulder. Hands wrapped around the wheel so tightly her fingers ached, she tilted her head back against the seat and stared up at the night sky. Nothing was working. None of the usual escapes—not even sailing eighteen hours a day—could get the image of Adrienne, the feel of her, out of her mind. And if she brought another woman to her bed, she knew damn well that when she looked down, she was going to see Adrienne's face.

"God damn it," she muttered as she started the car. She cranked the wheel hard, lurched back onto the highway, and headed for home. "God damn it to hell."

CHAPTER EIGHT

The new pattern of Adrienne's days was to arrive early each morning with her gear and her lunch and to spend the entire day on the rented boat. She swam, she read, she sailed better than she ever had. She often saw Tanner's distinctive convertible parked near the pier, but she never saw Tanner. She didn't mind, she told herself—she had no desire to see her.

With her days so full, she was able to ignore the lingering images of the two of them talking, touching, on the moonlit beach. When she would awaken from a dream with Tanner's caress still tingling on her skin, she quickly dismissed it as a natural response to her long weeks of solitude. She had been tired and discouraged, and Tanner had been there. It was nothing more than that. If some line from a song on the radio brought Tanner's husky voice to mind, she assured herself that it was just a passing fancy.

As summer approached, the weather grew warmer, the days lengthened, and Adrienne's strength returned. She felt fit and whole and nearly content. Life was as good as she dared hope it could be.

She made port one gray afternoon just ahead of a bank of storm clouds swiftly approaching from the south. It was sheer luck that she'd been sunning on the deck with the radio turned on in the tiny galley below. Through the open hatch, she'd heard the Coast Guard weather station warning of fast-moving squalls. She hadn't been that far from the harbor, but still she didn't really relax until she was in sight of the marina. By that time, the rain had started, and rising winds buffeted her sailboat from side to side. Most of the slips were already occupied with the boats of other sailors seeking shelter from the threatening storm.

Josh Thomas ran hurriedly up and down the pier double-checking tie lines and adjusting bumpers between the boats' hulls and the dock. He waved Adrienne into one of the unoccupied moorings, shouting something she couldn't hear. She tossed him her bowline, and together they secured her craft.

"Glad you're back! This one's supposed to be a beaut." He lifted his yellow slicker above their heads in a makeshift tent, leaning close to be heard over the howling crescendo of the wind. "There're gale storm warnings for small craft all up and down the coast. I sure wish the weather boys had alerted us about this before I let all the boats out this morning. Most everybody is in now though. Come on."

"Is Tanner back?" Adrienne asked as she ran beside him toward the protection of the office building, glancing automatically up toward the parking lot. Like every other day, the Jaguar was there.

He didn't answer until they were inside out of the wind. "No," he replied, shaking the rain from the slicker. "And I haven't heard from her either. She probably put in at one of the other marinas. Couple of other folks did."

Adrienne tried to ignore the sudden twist of fear. *Tanner's fine—of course she is. She knows these waters.*

"I'll put out a call," he said when he observed the worry Adrienne couldn't hide. "But I'm telling you, she can handle this."

"Thanks." Adrienne didn't argue, but as she walked to the small window and peered out, all she could see was a solid sheet of rain that obscured the boats moored not twenty yards away. *It doesn't matter what kind of sailor Tanner is; this is a deadly storm.* She doubted if she herself could have kept a sailboat afloat in this gale, and she'd raced in the Caribbean during some of the foulest weather imaginable when she'd been younger.

Josh went into the small adjoining room where he kept his short-wave radio. He returned shortly and placed the set on the desk in the main office.

"Did you raise her?" Adrienne couldn't mask the edge of anxiety in her voice.

"Nope—but that doesn't mean anything in this weather. She could be out there in the harbor and she might not hear us."

"I'm sure you're right." The reply held more conviction that she felt as she still sought valiantly for signs of Tanner in the rain. "How big is her boat, by the way?"

"Mid-thirties. Beautiful custom craft. She rebuilt it herself—calls it *Whitley's Pride*."

How like her. "That's rather large for one person to handle, isn't it?"

"Yep. It would be for most people. But then, Tanner's not most people. She's a good sailor; she'll be all right." He noticed for the first time that Adrienne was shivering from the cold. "How about some coffee?"

"Well...yes, please, if you have it. Thanks." She'd been about to refuse out of sheer habit and then decided it sounded like a good idea. It might be a very long evening. This was the kind of Nor'easter that submerged shorelines and washed out roads. She certainly was not going to chance driving until it let up, and, she admitted to herself, even if she made it home, she would probably just stay awake worrying about Tanner Whitley.

From the moment she'd met Tanner on the beach, hung over and charming in spite of it, she'd realized that the heir to Whitley Island was reckless and wild and dangerous—especially the latter. *Lord—why can't she stay out of trouble? And why can't I stop caring?* She would stay, *had* to stay, until Tanner came safely into port. She didn't question herself too closely as to why.

The winds continued with the same swirling force, showing no sign of abating, rocking the sailboats at their moorings and pounding the windows of the small office. When Adrienne turned from the unrelenting rain to glance over at Josh, he regarded her calmly, neither censure nor curiosity in his gaze. There was something about his solid presence that she found strangely reassuring. He seemed as indestructible as the rocky shoreline of his native coast. He did not question Adrienne's staying as he sat at his cluttered desk, sipping his coffee, the short-wave radio a scratchy backdrop to their silence. She did not offer any explanation.

Feeling helpless and frustrated, she asked at length, "What was Tanner's father like?"

"Charles?" Josh sat quietly, thinking about her question. "That's a hard one. How do you describe a man like Charles Whitley? He was big—about six-four, with dark hair and eyes. I imagine the ladies found him handsome—movie-star looks. He was very generous with his money, but he expected a lot from people. He expected everyone to be as determined and certain as he was. I think he was often disappointed."

"Is Tanner really like him?"

"Spitting image."

Yes, Tanner is movie-star handsome, too. She quickly pushed *that* thought away. "How so?"

"In a lot of ways," he said with a shy, fond smile. "She's got his fire—never does anything halfway. Stubborn, a little bit of a risk-taker." He frowned, not used to putting his thoughts into words. "I think she'd be a lot less angry at everything if her father were still alive. I don't think she's ever quite forgiven him for going out by himself and getting drowned. She hasn't been right since the day he died."

"Were they close?" She remembered the deep sorrow in Tanner's eyes.

Josh snorted. "That's a mild word for it. He thought the sun rose and set on that girl, and the feelings went both ways. He had her down here on his boats before she could walk, and, by the time she was ten, she could sail better than most men. Mrs. Whitley would go out with them for little cruises now and then, you know, but most of the time it was just the two of them."

His expression grew somber. "The day Charles died, Tanner wasn't with him. It was late in the season, and she was getting ready to go back to school. One of them fancy places girls go to in New England somewhere. It was a rough-looking day from the start, but he insisted. When he didn't come in by dark, Tanner came searching for him. I almost had to tie her down to keep her from going out in the launch to search. She wouldn't go home, just sat here listening to the Coast Guard station."

Pausing, he rubbed his face. "They never did find the boat. A storm had come up in the late afternoon, and he must have gotten caught pretty far out. It's hard to figure, with him being so experienced. Guess he must have been careless. Tanner kept insisting that if he had waited for her, it never would have happened." He sighed and shrugged his shoulders. "She got pretty wild after he died. She was only a teenager, but she refused to go back to school—said she didn't want to leave Whitley Point. She finished high school on the mainland with all the island kids and went away to college because her mother insisted, but I guess she was a handful there, too. Never has seemed to settle down."

God, she must have been so unhappy. Adrienne leaned against the window frame, listening to him talk in his slow drawl, her mind conjuring images of what Tanner must have been like as a teenager.

After hearing Josh's story, she thought that she understood a little bit more about the source of the shadows in Tanner's eyes.

They were both startled as the radio crackled to life. "Whitley Harbor—this is THW four-four hundred—come in, Whitley Harbor."

Josh jumped for the receiver. "Go ahead THW—this is Whitley Harbor—over." He flipped the knob on the set impatiently several times and then spoke again into the microphone. "Whitley Harbor calling THW four-four hundred. Come in, please, over."

They waited tensely while static filled the air. Then the set crackled again, followed by Tanner's garbled voice.

"I'm...bearing...two-two-zero...one...half miles...lost...sail... down...taking on water..." Her voice faded out, to be replaced by the same monotonous static.

"Damn, damn, damn," Josh swore. "I'll call the Coast Guard and give them her range and bearing. This harbor is hard enough to maneuver in the best of times. If she's got one sail down, even with the engines it's gonna be near impossible."

Tanner has come this far, surely she can navigate into the harbor. But with her boat crippled and in this wind?

"Mr. Thomas, do you have something alcoholic?"

"How about whiskey?"

"Sounds lovely."

The radio sounded the harbor's call letters, and the Coast Guard came through with a message. "Whitley Harbor, we have a small craft taking water rapidly, due east of Whitley Island, range one mile. Rescue procedures underway. Will advise, over."

Josh acknowledged the message and stared glumly at Adrienne. He handed her an ordinary drinking glass with an inch of amber liquor in the bottom.

Swirling the little blocks of ice aimlessly in the dark liquid, she continued to watch the harbor and thought about Tanner and the story Josh had told. It wasn't hard to imagine the effect Tanner's father's death must have had on her, and Adrienne glimpsed what lay behind the daughter's hidden sorrows. She could not deny that Tanner's pain called to her deeply.

So lost in reflection, she didn't immediately appreciate the dim but persistent flickering across the water. Suddenly, she realized that the steady glow was from the lights on a craft.

"Josh! There are lights out there!"

"Where?" He crowded next to her at the tiny window and rubbed at the condensation with his large callused hand. "Where?"

"There, off to the left."

"Will you just look at that! That must be her. She's dead center in the middle of the channel. She handles that boat like a lover, she does." He saw Adrienne flush and added hastily, "Beg your pardon, ma'am. Just an expression."

"I'm sure you're right, Mr. Thomas," Adrienne responded. "I'm sure she does."

Whitley's Pride materialized into view, maneuvering sluggishly, the sails badly tattered from the beating they had taken in the fierce winds. As the boat approached the pier, both Josh and Adrienne ran out, mindless of the steady downpour that drenched them instantly. Tanner was clinging to the wheel, her clothes plastered to her, looking exhausted and ready to collapse.

Josh leaned out over the water with a boat hook and snagged the towlines, guiding the boat up to the pier. As soon as it glided in close enough, Adrienne climbed aboard and rushed to the cockpit. Tanner was dazed, gasping for breath, and sagging within the confines of the safety harness that secured her to the wheel.

"Tanner, are you hurt?" Adrienne bent to untie the restraining straps.

Tanner shrugged, her expression blank. She tried to speak, but her strength finally deserted her. Released from her supports, she slumped and would have fallen if Adrienne hadn't made a quick grab for her.

Barely in time, Adrienne caught Tanner and eased her limp form to the deck. Desperate to shelter her from the wind and icy rain, she slipped an arm around Tanner's shoulders and pulled her close against her own body. Tanner shivered uncontrollably. Adrienne pushed the wet hair off Tanner's face, aware for the first time how cold Tanner's skin seemed under her fingers.

Of course. She's been exposed on the deck for hours in the freezing rain in only a light shirt and jeans. She's hypothermic, dangerously cold, and she's minutes away from going into shock—I've seen enough severe exposure cases in the Navy to recognize it.

"Josh, never mind the boat! We have to get her inside where it's warm. Can you help me carry her?"

He was beside Adrienne in a moment, and between them, they half-dragged, half-carried Tanner to the shelter of the marina.

"There's a little room in the back where I keep a cot and a kerosene heater for the winter." Josh led the way. They stretched an uncooperative Tanner out on a faded green wool blanket while she muttered in protest and tried ineffectually to push them away.

"Let me sleep," she demanded fitfully.

"Light the stove, and bring the rest of the coffee...and the whiskey," Adrienne said succinctly, ignoring Tanner's plea. She was already busy pulling off Tanner's deck shoes. She reached for another blanket from the foot of the cot and threw it over Tanner's shivering form. Lifting enough of the cover to maneuver, she stripped off the wet jeans, noting absently that that was all Tanner had been wearing. The shirt proved to be more of a problem. The wet material clung insistently to Tanner's chest, and Adrienne had to struggle to free the barely responsive woman's muscular arms. When she finally succeeded, she actually looked at Tanner for the first time.

Unprepared for what she saw, Adrienne drew a sharp breath as Tanner's body came into sharp focus. Tanner's eyes were closed now, and she looked terribly vulnerable in her nakedness. Her breasts were full and firm, falling in gentle curves toward her sides, the nipples a deep honey gold. She was tanned and toned, superbly muscled. Gazing the length of her, down the flat planes of her stomach to the slight swell of hips hidden by the coarse material of the blanket, Adrienne sensed the young woman's strength and remembered the tenderness in her touch.

Adrienne wasn't thinking at all but merely stood mesmerized for an instant by Tanner's pure and simple beauty. A soft cough and the sound of movement in the doorway jolted her abruptly back to the moment. Drawing the blanket up to cover Tanner's nakedness, she turned to face Josh Thomas and looked him directly in the eye.

"Coffee?" She didn't see any.

"Here's that whiskey and some dry duds for you," he responded, returning her gaze evenly. He held out a bundle and a half-filled glass. "They're old but they'll keep you warm. I'll have more coffee made in a minute. Should I try to get an ambulance out here? It'll be hard on a night like this—they have to come from the mainland across the causeway. It's most likely flooded."

"Call them and see what they say. We'll assume it's just us for the time being. I'll work on getting her warmed up. Thank God she's young and healthy."

"Ayuh. I'll let you know when I raise them."

Quickly, Adrienne stripped off her dripping clothes and pulled on the soft, worn shirt and trousers Josh had provided. Then, cradling Tanner's head in her lap, she brought the glass of whiskey to Tanner's lips. "Tanner, drink this." The barely conscious woman tried to pull away, but Adrienne managed to get a few drops past her lips. Tanner sputtered and coughed, protesting feebly, but Adrienne's grip was firm. *Just wake up enough to drink some coffee.*

As if on cue, Josh came in with a steaming mug. "I haven't been able to get anybody from emergency services yet. Wouldn't count on any help." He stood patiently holding the hot liquid while Adrienne tried to rouse Tanner enough to drink it. Tanner continued to shiver, her face ghostly white, the faint tinge of blue to her lips and fingers not abating. He had never seen her like this and was worried. "She's pretty well frozen."

"I know." Adrienne laid Tanner's head down softly, kicked off her own shoes, and lifted the blanket. Settling on the cot with her back propped against the wall, she pulled Tanner into her arms. "Put the coffee beside me," she directed. With her arms encircling Tanner's shoulders, she pressed the length of her body against every part of Tanner's she could reach. Instinctively, Tanner curled around her, pressing one leg between Adrienne's, nestling her face against Adrienne's chest.

Josh moved the small kerosene heater closer, then retreated to the doorway. He wasn't sure why, but he felt like he should leave them alone. "I'll be in the next room. If I hear from the EMTs, I'll let you know. Call out if you need anything."

Adrienne didn't answer. She rested her chin against the top of Tanner's head, rocking her gently, willing her to wake up. She hadn't touched another person intimately in almost a year and hadn't really expected to again. Odd—it should have felt strange, but it didn't. Tanner fit naturally into the curves of her body, as if she had been lying with her for years. It wasn't sexual, any more than looking at her naked moments before had been, but she felt something perhaps even stronger—a fiercely primitive desire to stand between Tanner and anything that might hurt her. She felt it so deeply, a stirring of passion that she had been certain she had lost forever.

"Tanner," she whispered. "Tanner."

Just when she was about to despair, Tanner stirred restlessly, mumbling incoherently at first but finally opening her eyes to peer at Adrienne in confusion. Immediately, Adrienne offered the coffee, hoping to both warm her and stimulate blood flow with the caffeine.

"Drink some coffee. It will help."

"Not now," Tanner muttered fretfully, still barely conscious.

"Come on," Adrienne insisted, "just a little."

Tanner accepted a small sip and coughed, then took another.

"That's it, good. A bit more now..." Adrienne coaxed and pleaded and ordered, murmuring encouragement as she stroked Tanner's damp face. Finally, Tanner grasped her arm weakly and pushed at the hand that held the cup.

"Please," Tanner gasped, "give me a minute. Josh's coffee might kill me before the cold does."

Adrienne laughed and hugged Tanner tightly. "Are you really awake?" She whispered the question after a few moments of watching Tanner's breathing become more regular and the color return to her face.

"I am...I think." Tanner opened her eyes, finally able to focus, and regarded Adrienne solemnly. "Or this could just be a very nice dream." For a minute there, it *had* felt like a dream. She hadn't been alone. And now she was very much aware of not being alone, in a rather more immediate fashion. She was lying against Adrienne's left side, one arm around Adrienne's waist and her head on her shoulder. Her breast, which was somehow bare, was resting very near Adrienne's hand. She glanced up and met Adrienne's gaze. Her voice was husky, from the cold—or something else—when she murmured, "Whatever this is, it's very nice."

Adrienne couldn't look away from those captivating eyes. There was so much wanting in them. Suddenly, a visceral memory of Tanner's mouth on hers churned through her belly. She remembered the heat, and the tender, almost shy stroke of Tanner's tongue over her own. A rush of arousal, completely unexpected, pulsed between her thighs, causing her breath to catch in her throat. She hadn't meant this to happen—hadn't wanted it to happen. She had only meant to help Tanner heal.

"It's not a dream, something more like a nightmare," Adrienne replied abruptly, shifting on the narrow cot to disentangle their limbs. Sliding completely out from beneath Tanner's nude body, she sat on the edge of the cot, staring at the floor, forcing her breath to quiet. She waited until she was certain her voice was steady. "You had a pretty close call, but I'm sure you'll be fine after a couple of days' rest. When you're feeling a little better, I'll drive you home."

"Can't we just stay here tonight?" Tanner struggled to keep her eyes open and sighed, pressing close against Adrienne's back. *It felt so good when you held me. Better than safe—it felt right.*

"No, we can't. You need a hot shower and a good night's sleep. Neither of which you can get here." Adrienne's fear and confusion were rapidly being replaced by anger. *God damn her for being so careless! And God damn me for caring!* She stood, breaking the contact that was rapidly becoming uncomfortable simply because it felt so good. "I'll bring my car down. It won't help for you to get soaked again. Can you get dressed?"

Tanner nodded, too exhausted to protest. She struggled into the dry shirt and pants Josh offered her from his locker and obediently waited for Adrienne to bring her car close. Once in the car, she leaned her head against the window with a weary sigh and closed her eyes. Adrienne's silence was painful after having awakened just moments before in the comfort of her arms.

When Adrienne pulled up in front of Whitley Manor, Tanner was asleep. Adrienne shook the dozing woman gently. "Tanner, come on. You're home now—it's time to leave."

Tanner stirred slowly and gazed at Adrienne, her face soft with a mixture of fatigue and need. "Will you stay with me? Please."

"No," Adrienne said gently. "But I'll call you tomorrow, okay?" She assured herself that she was offering just a simple kindness. Anyone would do the same.

"All right," Tanner murmured, getting out of the car without further protest. "Thank you for tonight."

Adrienne watched as Tanner made her way slowly around the side of the house to the path that led down to her bungalow. She hated to see her go and didn't want to think what that meant. She only knew she couldn't afford to get any closer to the lonely young woman and her secret pain. It was better to keep things uncomplicated, for both their sakes.

CHAPTER NINE

Adrienne slept poorly that night and woke before the sun was fully up. Her first thought was of Tanner, and she forced herself to attend to nonexistent household chores because the urge to call her was so strong.

She'll be fine. She doesn't need me to worry over her. And I don't need something else to worry about either.

She went for a totally unsatisfying run, plagued the entire time by her lingering concerns. Finally, at nine o'clock she gave in to her persistent worry and called Whitley Manor. The phone was answered on the second ring.

"Whitley residence—may I help you?"

"This is Adrienne Pierce. Is Tanner there, please?"

"Miss Whitley is not in right now. May I take a message for her?"

"Not in?" Adrienne exclaimed, unable to hide the alarm in her voice. "Is she all right?" She heard muffled voices in the background, and then Constance Whitley's voice.

"Ms. Pierce? This is Constance Whitley. Tanner left quite early this morning. I'm afraid she didn't leave word as to where she was going. She rarely does. Can I help you with anything?"

"No, thank you." Adrienne sighed with relief. "I was just worried that after last night she might be ill."

"Last night? I don't understand."

Just brilliant, Adrienne. Do you really think that Tanner makes it a habit of informing her mother of her misadventures?

"Oh, sorry." She recovered quickly and continued smoothly. "I gave her a ride home last night in the storm, and she was soaked. I worried she might have come down with something."

Constance laughed. "Well, I shouldn't worry, Adrienne. Tanner is rarely ill. I'll tell her that you called."

"Thanks." Adrienne replaced the receiver and stood with her hand on the phone for a few moments, wondering in exasperation why she even cared where Tanner was. *If Tanner doesn't have enough sense to take care of herself, it certainly isn't my problem.* She turned resolutely back to the task of folding laundry, determined to forget the whole thing.

She found to her supreme irritation, however, that no matter what she was doing, she kept seeing the curtain of rain, and the storm-battered craft, and Tanner, exposed and freezing, in the midst of it. It was terrifying to realize that Tanner might not have made port at all last night. Adrienne finally admitted to herself that since she was going to keep wondering about Tanner, she might as well check the marina. If nothing else, she could at least go sailing to occupy her restless mind.

The sky was unusually clear after the heavy storm, and it promised to be a beautiful day. As always, Adrienne's spirits lifted as she neared the bay and parked. Walking down the pier, she easily picked out Tanner's boat in the daylight. *Whitley's Pride* was a beautiful sloop with a polished teak hull and maroon deck. All the fittings were brass, and the central cockpit was outfitted so the skipper could single-hand all the sails if need be. She noticed several loose sheets and the remnants of the tattered jib, reminders of the previous night's perilous journey. As she walked out onto the dock for a closer look, admiring the fine workmanship, she heard whistling from below deck.

"Hello there. Anybody about? Tanner?"

Tanner's head popped up through the cabin hatch, and she grinned sheepishly at Adrienne. She looked pale and drawn, deep shadows smudging her normally vibrant eyes. But her voice was cheerful. "Hey, you. Come aboard."

Adrienne hesitated for a second and then climbed up to the edge of the deck.

"I was just about to replace the jib." Tanner climbed up from below. "She's a little worse for wear but no serious damage."

"How are *you*?" Adrienne asked dryly.

Tanner blushed. "A little worse for wear but almost seaworthy. Thanks for looking after me last night." Her expression turned serious.

"You're welcome," Adrienne responded softly before shifting her gaze away from those intently searching eyes and changing the subject quickly. "Your boat is beautiful."

"Thanks." Tanner grabbed Adrienne's hand impulsively, drawing her down into the cockpit. "Come on, let me show you how she's outfitted." She took Adrienne on a tour of the *Pride,* pointing out little modifications she had made that allowed her to handle the boat easily by herself.

Adrienne was surprised to see that the cabin was well stocked with food and wine, as well as a variety of books and CDs. The stereo system was elaborate, with speakers in both the fore and aft sleeping areas. She turned to Tanner, impressed. "It's wonderful. All the comforts of home."

"It almost *is* home to me," Tanner responded. "I can sail anywhere and just drop anchor and stay...if I want to."

"It must have taken you a long time to get it into this kind of shape."

Tanner's face clouded for an instant, and then she shrugged. "I bought her just before my last year of high school, and I've been working on her ever since. It's probably the only thing I've really accomplished since then."

There it was again, that hint of sorrow, and to hear it pulled at Adrienne's heart. Afraid to open doors she didn't want to go through, she made a suggestion instead. "Listen, how about if I give you a hand refitting the jib."

"Sure," Tanner responded, her grin returning. "But only if you promise to come for a sail with me."

"No, I don't think so," Adrienne said quickly.

"Why not?"

"Because..." Adrienne regarded Tanner for a moment, searching for an answer that made sense, and then laughed. Suddenly, she very much wanted to be out on that sailboat, in the sun, in the wind, away from her worries and her fears. "I don't know. Why not? I'd actually love to go out on her."

"Terrific. Come on, then." Tanner, her face alight with enthusiasm, grabbed Adrienne's hand again and pulled her toward the ladder. "Let's get to work."

They worked easily together, pulling down the torn sail and restringing the new one. They didn't talk much, but Adrienne found the silence comfortable. It had gotten quite warm, and both she and

Tanner were sweating. The physical exertion felt good. When they finished, she stepped back and surveyed their work with a feeling of accomplishment. She realized that she had missed that feeling—missed life having some meaning beyond mere existence.

"Ready to go?" At Adrienne's nod, Tanner grinned. "How about you handle the sails while I take her out of the harbor?"

"Sure." Adrienne quickly got used to the rigging and winches as Tanner maneuvered them efficiently out of the harbor toward the open sea. Not unexpectedly, Tanner proved to be a decisive and neat sailor, wasting none of the wind and setting the sails to full advantage. They barely spoke as the craft moved swiftly out into the ocean, cutting a clean line parallel to the coast. Eventually, Tanner steered them into a secluded cove on one of the many islands that dotted the coastal waters and dropped anchor.

"Go ahead and relax for a while," Tanner called as she headed below deck. "There are towels under the seats on the forward deck. I'll be right back."

Adrienne made herself comfortable, and a few minutes later, Tanner returned with a tray of fruit and cheese and a bottle of chilled white wine. "Brunch, anyone?"

"Great idea." Adrienne smiled in appreciation as her host spread out a tablecloth and weighted it down with plates and two glasses. Accepting the wine with a grateful sigh, she leaned back in the sun and surveyed the boat. "She sails wonderfully."

"Thanks. You're pretty good yourself. This afternoon you'll have to take the wheel."

"I'd love to," Adrienne answered instantly. "It's been a long time since I've sailed anything like this, though."

"You can handle her. Do you have your own boat?"

"Uh-huh." Adrienne helped herself to some fruit. "A bit smaller, but just right for long weekends. I used to spend as much time out on her as I could."

Tanner regarded her companion thoughtfully, very aware that personal questions could get her into trouble. The last time they had talked, it had ended in disaster, so she proceeded with caution. "What do you do—in the Navy?"

"I...I'm a civil engineer. I went to college on an NROTC scholarship and was commissioned to active duty when I graduated."

"Do you like it?"

"Engineering or the Navy?"

"Both."

"All in all, I've enjoyed the work, and I like the organization of the Navy. It's very secure—at least professionally. It has offered a lot of opportunity, despite its restrictions. And, of course, as an officer ashore, I've had a great deal of freedom. We bought a house off-base, right near Mission Bay, the first time I was stationed in San Diego. I've managed to stay basically in Southern California most of my stateside career, and we've always lived in it then. My work has been a pretty steady forty-hour week, plus the watches and the like. So, yes, both have suited me." She finished self-consciously, realizing that she had said more than she had meant to say. She had been so relaxed that she hadn't given discretion a second thought.

"Has it been a problem, being a lesbian?"

Adrienne laughed. "Being a lesbian? Or being a lesbian in the Navy?"

"You know what I mean." Tanner grinned back at her. "Were you paranoid about it?"

"Sometimes. But I did my job and did it well. So, as long as I led my own private life and avoided any scandal, no one seemed to care. There were other gays, of course, both men and women. We were discreet; we had to be. I can't say I liked that, but there aren't many situations that don't have some drawbacks."

Tanner poured them some more wine and munched a cracker. "Sounds like a pretty good life in some ways."

"Make no mistake, there's a lot that needs improving. It's far from ideal if you're gay, but I knew that going in."

"So—"

"Must you always ask so many questions?" Adrienne interrupted, laughing good-naturedly.

"Can't help it," Tanner replied. "I love details."

"I've noticed. And what about you? What do you do when you're not sailing?"

"I pretend to run the Whitley Corporation."

"Pretend?"

"I go into the corporate headquarters now and then, but it's not serious. There are a dozen suits hired specifically to keep track of the real business of running things."

"So, why do it at all?" Adrienne was genuinely curious.

"It's my responsibility—there has always been a Whitley at the helm. It's expected. I always knew that. I just didn't expect it so soon." Her voice caught and she looked away.

"I'm sorry about your father."

"How did you hear?"

"Josh told me last night."

"Oh." It was hard just getting that out. Tanner hadn't been prepared for the conversation to veer in this direction, and the memories caught her unprepared. The kindness in Adrienne's voice made it worse.

"It must have been awful for you."

Tanner stared at her, then down at her hands. It wasn't something she talked about. Ever. When she looked back at Adrienne, she found only compassion—no pity, no grim curiosity. And then the words came, almost against her will.

"We fought...the day he died. We were supposed to go out together, but he didn't wait."

"What happened?" Adrienne knew then that there was something more to the tragedy than she had been told. Tanner's hands were trembling.

"I was sixteen. I had recently stopped dating the son of one of my father's business associates—Todd Barrow. I'd also just slept with the daughter of one of the summer families." Tanner stood, walked to the rail, and looked out across the water, recalling the scene vividly. Her voice was low, rough-edged with pain. "He asked me why I had broken up with Todd. He reminded me how close our families were, and how much he liked 'the boy.' He'd never really pushed me toward anything like that before, but I think he'd always just assumed I'd end up with Todd or someone like him. Just like he assumed I'd take his place in the business someday." Tanner met Adrienne's eyes. "I informed him I wasn't interested in Todd or any other guy."

"I imagine that took him by surprise."

"To say he wasn't happy doesn't cover it. He insisted that I didn't know what I was saying, that I would change my mind. That I shouldn't ruin my chances with Todd." She blew out a breath. "He just wouldn't *listen.* I had to make him understand."

"I take it you told him about the girl?" Adrienne guessed what was coming when Tanner fell silent.

"Yeah," Tanner acknowledged with a wry grin. "Maybe a little too enthusiastically. It was my first time with a girl, and I thought I'd found God. He didn't see it that way."

"And?"

She shrugged, looking at Adrienne with wounded eyes. "He slapped me." She could still feel the blow, still remember her shock and hurt. "That was the only time he ever struck me. As soon as he did it, he looked like he might cry. He said he was sorry..." She closed her eyes, wishing she could take back the next words, just as she had wished a thousand times before. "I told him to go to hell. And then he was gone... out on the boat. He never noticed the storm. He never came back..."

Oh God. She must feel so guilty. "Tanner—"

"No need to say anything. It was a long time ago. I'm over it now." Tanner turned abruptly and began gathering the remains of their lunch, avoiding Adrienne's eyes.

Adrienne watched her in helpless silence. She of all people knew there were some hurts that words could not heal.

CHAPTER TEN

When Tanner returned from below deck, she showed no signs of her earlier distress. It pleased Adrienne to see her smile; she hoped that it was genuine. It had hurt to know Tanner was suffering.

"I should probably get back," Adrienne said. She'd only meant to go out for a sail; she hadn't expected to be so pleased with the company. Already they'd been out more than half the day, and every moment she was with Tanner, she found her more intriguing. Tanner was a walking contradiction—a quicksilver study in sudden sorrow and swift joy, a pendulum of emotion swinging wildly from light to shadow. To be with her was to be stirred, and Adrienne found the intensity unsettling. Unsettled was not what she wanted to be.

"It's too beautiful to go back," Tanner protested.

"What did you have in mind? We can't sail much further and still make it back to Whitley Harbor before dark."

"There's plenty of daylight left. But I wasn't thinking of going anywhere." Tanner grasped the bottom of her T-shirt in both hands and stripped it off, letting it fall to the deck behind her.

Caught completely off guard, Adrienne could only stare, an unwilling captive of the vision. Sunlight bathed Tanner's tanned shoulders and breasts; fine muscles rippled seductively beneath her skin as she moved. She was gloriously unself-conscious, stunning in her youthful splendor. *Oh God. She's so lovely.*

"What do you think you're doing?" Adrienne asked harshly before a fierce surge of desire struck her unawares. She had to avert her gaze or lose her sanity.

"I'm going swimming." Grinning playfully, Tanner unsnapped her shorts. "Come on—it'll wake you up."

"You go ahead." Adrienne's heart pounded as she tried to avoid looking directly at her, although it really made no difference—images of Tanner lying naked on the cot the previous evening cascaded vividly through her mind. She swallowed hard and managed to say evenly, "I'll stand guard."

"There's no one here," Tanner protested, reaching down in an attempt to pull Adrienne to her feet. "It'll be wonderful. Come on, be adventurous."

"No!" Adrienne jerked her arm away and stood up, backing away a step.

"I'll just have to throw you in, then," Tanner said teasingly, failing to appreciate the genuine note of panic in Adrienne's voice. "Let's go, Commander. Make a choice. With your clothes on or not?"

Adrienne didn't think, couldn't think. All she felt was the fear. When Tanner reached playfully for the tail of Adrienne's shirt, she just reacted. She shoved Tanner roughly away with both hands against her chest, hard enough to make her stumble backward and nearly fall. "Don't touch me!"

"Jesus, Adrienne!" Tanner grabbed the rail for balance, just barely avoiding tumbling from the boat. She gaped in stunned amazement. "What do you think I am? I wasn't going to rape you."

Adrienne stared at her, just as stunned, then turned and rushed to the bow of the boat. All she wanted was to get away, and there was nowhere to go. She grasped the rail in both hands, trembling, and struggled for composure. A few minutes later, Tanner, fully dressed again, came to stand beside her.

"I'm sorry." Tanner was sincere, although not sure exactly why she was apologizing.

"Look, don't apologize," Adrienne said quickly, her face turned away, her voice low and choked. "You took me by surprise...I'm sorry I overreacted."

"It's okay...really. Nothing bad happened." Tanner lifted her hand but was afraid to touch the woman. "You're trembling, for God's sake. I didn't mean to upset you. I was just so happy that you were here."

"It's not your fault."

"Then what is it? What's wrong?"

"Let's just go back, Tanner." Adrienne finally turned to face her, a trace of tears still on her face. She looked miserable, and that was harder for Tanner to bear than the physical rejection had been.

"Will you please tell me what I did?" She touched Adrienne's face lightly, brushing a tear away with her thumb, wanting desperately to understand.

"I don't know if I can."

"Can we try? Please," Tanner pleaded gently. "Please."

"I'll try." Adrienne sighed, too emotionally exhausted to protest further. She walked slowly back to the cockpit and sat down, wrapping her arms protectively around her bent knees. Tanner followed and sat close, but was careful not to touch her.

Adrienne watched the waves drift past the boat and searched for the right words, aware of her companion waiting patiently. There were so many things she could say, or *should* say, and yet she couldn't think of how to say them. She had never been able, in all of the last lonely and terrifying months, to express her feelings about any of it.

How could she possibly explain it all to Tanner, someone she barely knew? Yet for some inexplicable reason, she wanted to try. She wanted to tell her things that she had never told anyone. She wasn't sure why now, or why her, but it just seemed important. Turning, she met the dark eyes that had never left her face and, unexpectedly, found in them a comforting calm.

"Tanner," she kept her gaze level with Tanner's, "I have...I had... cancer. I don't know why I didn't tell you before."

Tanner's heart thudded heavily at the words, but she continued to look into Adrienne's face, wanting to understand this more than she had ever wanted anything. "What does that mean exactly?" Her voice was tight but steady. "I mean...I *know* what it means, but what does it mean for you?"

How refreshing not to be met with pointless platitudes. And how typical of Tanner to barge right in. Adrienne smiled a little, then shrugged. "That's a good question. I wish I knew the answer. No one has ever asked me before. Everyone usually thinks they know precisely what it means for me."

"Tell me what you know then," Tanner whispered.

"For me, it meant having my right breast removed." She stopped, heard the words, so final. Tanner's expression hadn't changed; she was still watching her, waiting. "And then a course of chemotherapy for insurance."

"Insurance?" Tanner's throat was dry, but she didn't think she could swallow. She was scared. More than scared—sick to the depths of her soul that something this terrible had happened to Adrienne.

"Strictly speaking, I might have done without it. When they examined the lymph nodes, there wasn't any cancer in them."

"That's a good sign, right?" Tanner was pleased that her voice sounded normal.

"Yes, a very good sign. But the doctors recommended the chemo anyhow, mostly because of my age. Believe me, they had all kinds of complicated reasons for everything, but the bottom line was better to do it now and not need it, than to wait until I do."

"Was it hard?"

Adrienne hesitated, nonplussed. Tanner was as ingenuous as a child, asking what she wanted to know with no hint of self-consciousness or embarrassment, and still she was so very unlike one—asking all the right questions because she really seemed to care. *About me.*

"It was miserable. I felt like hell most of the time. Luckily my hair didn't fall out, and I only threw up for the first few days every cycle, but I didn't have enough stamina to get through the day. I tried to work, but it was difficult for me to put in a full eight hours. I couldn't do most of the things I was used to doing." She paused for breath, thinking of those first hectic months, of how hard she had tried to continue as if her life were the same—when nothing was the same.

She pushed both hands through her hair and looked at Tanner ruefully. "My friends—my colleagues—wanted to be supportive, but most people treated me as if I might shatter at any moment. I couldn't stand their kindnesses. I just wanted them to treat me as they always had, as if I were normal. But I didn't really *feel* normal—I felt betrayed. And I had no one to be angry with, because it was my own body that had betrayed me." She took a deep steadying breath.

"Finally, I just stopped trying to go on as if nothing had changed and I could do everything I'd done before. The doctors put me back on medical leave to give me a chance to regroup and recover my strength. I thought I'd stay with my parents for a while, but that only worked for a week. Then I came here...and I guess you know the rest."

"I'm sorry," Tanner said adamantly, because it was the most truthful thing she could think to say.

"No need to be. Maybe I should apologize to you. You didn't bargain for all of this." Adrienne smiled apologetically, aware that her words had been pouring out as if a dam inside her had burst. Amazingly, Tanner still regarded her intently, her expression very serious. Most people were uncomfortable with the subject and often couldn't meet her eyes.

"Is it gone now?" Tanner's tone was soft and gentle. *Tell me everything. Tell me...tell me so I can touch you.*

Adrienne shrugged bitterly, confronting the issue that haunted her every moment, waking or asleep. "I don't know. I know the statistics, but I don't know what they mean for me. They gave me plenty of figures—two years, five years, ten. No guarantees, just odds."

"But you're okay? Now?"

"So far, so good, I think. I'm due for the big checkup soon. Every six months I have tests—chest x-ray, bone scan, some blood tests—and a mammogram on the other side, of course."

"How does this affect your status in the Navy?"

"If these upcoming checkup results are sound, and my rehab has been satisfactory, the medical board will certify me fit for duty and I can return to work. My physical strength is coming back, but I'm not sure I want to return. I may just resign. I'll have to make a decision about that soon."

"What about your lover?"

"We're separated," Adrienne said abruptly.

Tanner couldn't miss the look of pain that flashed across Adrienne's face, but she thought that there might never be another time. "Why?"

"Damn, you're persistent. We're more than separated. I left her." Adrienne shook her head in resignation. "At first, things between us seemed just as they'd always been. She came with me for the biopsy, and to the surgeon to discuss treatment, and she was there when I woke up after the mastectomy. It was only after I came home from the surgery, after I thought the worst of it was over, that I began to see that our life together had changed." Adrienne stopped, swallowing hard. She wasn't sure she could face those feelings again. She thought she could live with the fear of her cancer, but it was so damned hard to live with everything else.

"Changed how?" Tanner urged gently. She wanted desperately for Adrienne to keep talking, to allow her to get close.

"She was afraid, I think. Afraid that I might die, afraid that everything we knew, everything we had planned, might disappear. I don't think she could deal with the uncertainty."

Tanner thought she could understand that. But there must be something else. "Why did you leave? Didn't you love her anymore?"

"Did I still love her?" Adrienne asked, almost to herself. "*Do* I love her? I suppose that's another thing I can't answer in any way that makes sense. Sometimes there are things—feelings—that you don't question because you never need to. What happened to me made me look at my life, look at *us,* differently. We were friendly strangers, living more on the memory of what we'd shared than what we had together in the present." She shook her head, her expression distant. "Maybe it had been that way before I got sick, and I'd never seen it. But after...it was all I could see. She walked around me in the house as if I weren't even there. And...and I knew that she couldn't deal with the way I looked."

"Did she say that?" Tanner managed to keep her voice calm, but she felt like screaming. *You hurt so much. Too much—this is too much pain for anyone.*

"She didn't have to," Adrienne snapped, her blue eyes suddenly cold. "She couldn't bring herself to come near me. Not just in bed, but anywhere. She always found some reason to disappear any time I wasn't covered." Adrienne laughed grimly. "It made it hell trying to get showered in the morning. She pretended she just wanted to give me time to recover, to get my strength back, but I knew the real reason. She couldn't stand to look at me. When I was put on medical leave, I left her. I couldn't live that lie any longer."

She paused, waiting for some of the pain to pass. "As I said, I went home to Philadelphia for a while, until my family almost drove me crazy. They acted as if I was about to die. And that brings me at last to Whitley Point—the island hideaway. You were so right, that first morning on the beach. I'm hiding here, all right, from everything I ever knew. Probably even from myself."

"Adrienne..." Tanner said her name softly, feeling so inadequate it was like physical pain. She wanted somehow to alleviate Adrienne's sadness—to lessen the rejection and fear she heard in her voice. She had no idea how to even begin. Were there any words at all that could reach that terrible sorrow? "I wish there were some way I could help."

"Why?" Adrienne stood up suddenly. She had never meant to speak of this, and, having said the words, she felt raw and exposed. "It has nothing to do with you."

"I want to see you again. After today," Tanner said quickly, sensing her withdrawal.

"No."

"Why not?"

"It's really very simple, Tanner. I have no future, at least none that I can count on. Just think of me as another tourist, here to escape for a few months on your fairytale island. When summer ends, I'll be gone. It will make it easier for both of us." She gave Tanner no chance to reply, resolutely turning away. The conversation was over.

CHAPTER ELEVEN

Take the wheel. I'll crew for you." It was a quiet suggestion.

"Yes, okay," Adrienne responded gratefully, desperate to focus on something outside of herself until they could reach shore. She wanted to be alone; she needed time to come to grips with the storm of emotions the last few hours had unleashed.

The work of sailing gave them both an excuse to be silent. Adrienne handled the wheel with expert efficiency while Tanner rigged the sails for a fast run. When they entered the harbor, Tanner finally spoke.

"I'm here every morning at six if you would like to sail with me."

"Thank you," Adrienne replied in a tone that clearly said she had no intention of joining Tanner. She turned away, busying herself with untangling the towlines.

"Am I the reason you haven't been back to the gym?"

"How did you know that?" Adrienne looked back at her in surprise.

"It isn't important." There was no reason to tell her that she owned the place, and that she'd asked Finch every day if she'd seen her. "Is it?"

When Adrienne didn't answer, Tanner said, "Go back to the gym. I won't be there."

"Tanner..." Adrienne trailed off with a weary sigh.

"Look, it's no big deal, okay?" Tanner's tone was harsh, but it was from hurt not anger, although it sounded the same. "I have plenty of ways to occupy myself. It's no hardship on me."

At that moment, they slid up to the dock and, mercifully, Josh appeared to help them tie up. Adrienne was able to escape with little more than polite goodbyes, barely glancing at Tanner as she left.

Tanner, however, watched Adrienne all the way up the pier and continued to stare after her until the car turned onto the coast road and disappeared. She was left with an empty feeling of something only half-completed, knowing that she and Adrienne should have talked more. But when Adrienne had so thoroughly closed her out, when the pain of talking had become so devastatingly clear, Tanner had been afraid to try.

She stowed the lines and secured the deck automatically, all the while thinking of things she should have said to Adrienne when she had the chance. Now, she wasn't sure if she would ever get the opportunity. Muttering with frustration, she finally headed for her car, realizing as she climbed the slope to the parking lot that she was exhausted after the physical ordeal in the storm, too little sleep, and the emotional turmoil of her day with Adrienne. Still, she didn't look forward to an evening alone with only the memories of her unresolved past and thoughts of Adrienne's painful present for company. Though exhausted, she headed back to the boat, went below deck and showered in her tiny head, and pulled on clean clothes. This time when she headed south toward the mainland, she didn't turn back.

❖

Tanner rolled away onto her back, breathing heavily, her face running with sweat. Her head spun dangerously, making her stomach heave, and it took her a moment of focusing on the ceiling to get her bearings. A fan revolved above her head, moving stale hot air around the shabby box of a room. A neon sign blinked spasmodically on the far side of the parking lot, making the dust motes appear to dance sluggishly around the bed. She slowly became aware of a hand working at the buttons on her fly.

"Stop."

"Oh, honey, don't be like that. I can feel how wet you are right through those jeans of yours. And you *know* I'm ready to burst waiting for you to give me what I need."

Tanner closed her eyes again, felt the fingers beneath her shirt and the answering twitch between her thighs as nails played over her skin.

"You're bad hungry, baby...I can tell," a voice whispered in her ear. "Let me feed you first—then you can lick the spoon."

"I can't. I need to go." Tanner tried to sit up, but a surprisingly strong arm pushed her back. Then a thigh rode over hers, pinning her. The hand worked her fly again.

"You don't look like the shy type, but then you butch numbers always get all reluctant when you're about to give it up. Tell me you don't want my fingers on your hot, hard—"

"Let me up. Now." Tanner's voice was very clear, very calm.

For a moment, nothing happened; then a subtle shift of weight and Tanner was free. She sat up, swung her legs over the side of the bed, and tried to stand. Success. Fumbling to close her jeans, she said, "We're all done here."

"Come back to bed, baby. I like the way you kiss. You just keep kissing me like that, I'll be happy. And I guarantee you'll forget whoever's breaking your heart."

"There's money on the dresser. Take it and call a cab." Tanner checked to make sure her wallet was in her back pocket, then walked just a bit unsteadily into the tiny closet of a bathroom and stuck her head under the cold water faucet. She didn't hear the motel room door slam, but when she emerged, she was alone.

❖

Constance awakened sometime after three to the sound of a car pulling up in the drive. She was a very light sleeper, and on warm nights such as this one, she kept her windows open. She lay listening to the familiar footsteps make their way around the side of the house to the lower walkway. Surprisingly, she heard the same someone slowly climbing the outside stairs to the verandah. She reached for her robe and went outside.

Tanner was sagged into a deck chair, her feet propped up on the rail, looking worn and bedraggled even by moonlight.

"Tanner? Are you all right?"

Her only answer was a nod.

Constance sat down next to Tanner and waited. It had been a long time since Tanner had come to her like this, and she recognized it as a sign that her daughter needed company, or, less likely, that she wanted to talk. Constance tried to give comfort and, occasionally, guidance—whenever Tanner could bring herself to ask for it. Sometimes, all she could give her was a mother's unconditional love, but so many times that felt like far too little.

Tanner ran her hand distractedly through her still-wet hair and sighed audibly. "Mother?" She spoke as if they had been sitting in deep conversation for hours. "If you had known that Father would die when he did, would it have made any difference to you?"

Constance was so amazed by the raw directness of the question that she wasn't sure she would be able to answer, but she forced herself to consider her response honestly. Tanner almost never mentioned her father, and she never talked about his death. If she was bringing it up now, like this, it must be very important to her. She responded softly. "What do you mean by 'a difference'?"

"Would you still have married him?" Tanner asked pointedly, shifting in the chair so that she could see her mother's face.

"Oh, my God, yes," Constance exclaimed instantly. "I would have married him even if I knew we'd only have a month together." She smiled slightly in the moonlight. "I loved being with him. I loved being married to him. He was the one I wanted, and I wouldn't have traded that for anything."

"Was it worth the pain of losing him?" Tanner persisted, remembering how desolate she had felt when he died—*still* felt—and was barely able to imagine how much worse it must have been for her mother. She knew, too, how difficult these questions were, but she didn't care. She was drowning; she had nowhere else to turn.

"I still can't believe he's gone." Constance took a deep breath, shuddering slightly. "After all these years, I still find myself wanting him, wondering how I'm going to survive without him. But I do. Strangely enough, I not only survive, I have learned to take pleasure in life. It seems bittersweet at times, but it is pleasure nevertheless. Loving him was worth every bit of the pain of not being with him. And I can tell you something else—losing him would have hurt every bit as deeply if we had lived together two years, or twenty, or two hundred."

"So you have no regrets?"

"I didn't say that," Constance said, smiling fondly. *How like Charles you are. You can't leave anything alone until you examine it from every angle and understand it in every detail. He would be so proud of you.*

"What do you mean?"

"If I had known we wouldn't have a lifetime together, I might have tried harder to share the things in his world—the business, for one—that I never learned to care for." A soft breath. "And I think I would have told him more often that I loved him, that he was the only one I ever wanted."

Tanner swung her feet down and stood up a little unsteadily at the rail, gazing down over the dunes to the surf. Finally, in a voice so low Constance wasn't sure she was meant to hear, Tanner whispered, "I'm afraid. I'm afraid to love like that."

The wistful tone in that whisper was enough to break Constance's heart, and she went quickly to her daughter's side, slipping a comforting arm gently around her waist. "When you find someone you truly love, Tanner, you won't be afraid anymore."

Constance didn't expect a reply and, after a moment, could only watch helplessly as Tanner walked slowly down the path to her bungalow, disappearing into the darkness. Something had happened, something—or more likely *someone*—had reached beyond Tanner's pain to awaken her passion at last. Constance could only hope it was someone who would have the courage to embrace her daughter's tumultuous soul.

✣

Early the next morning, Tanner returned to the marina, hoping that Adrienne would change her mind and join her after all. Sitting on the side of the dock, she waited and watched the parking lot. Hope waned as the hours passed, and she thought about calling her. Only the fear of alienating Adrienne further stopped her. Eventually, she became too restless to sit.

"Josh," she called as she entered the marina office. "You in here?"

"Ayuh," he replied, coming out from the rear room. "What are you hollerin' for?"

She leaned against the window, hands in her pockets, and grinned sheepishly. "Have you seen Adrienne today?"

"Nope. First day she's missed in a while. Might be she'll be down later."

"Maybe." Tanner looked doubtful. "I guess I'll just go on down and finish working on the *Pride*. She took some water the other night, and I want to make sure she's tight now."

"Good idea. That was some storm. I wasn't sure I'd see either you or the *Pride* again."

"Oh, come on, Josh. You know it takes more than a storm to beat me."

"I know." He nodded sagely. "But some day, you'll take one too many chances. Me and your lady friend were mighty worried the other night."

"What do you mean?" Tanner stared at him.

"Well...she came in just ahead of the storm, late in the afternoon. As soon as she found out that you were still on the water, she plunked herself down and wouldn't budge."

Tanner had not even thought to ask why Adrienne had been there when she regained consciousness after the storm. She had been too confused to think clearly that night, and yesterday, they had had so many other things to say. But why hadn't Adrienne mentioned it, if for no other reason than to berate her for her stupidity?

"She was here all that time?" Tanner was incredulous. *She waited for me?*

"Sure was. She waited, and it was a good thing, too. She pretty much saved your butt. Mighty capable, that one." He fished around for his pipe in his pockets and finally found it under some papers on the desk. "Fine-looking woman, too."

"Now, Josh." Tanner laughed.

"I know, I know. I'm too old for her. She seemed pretty fond of you, though."

Tanner grimaced. "I'm not feeling all that likeable these days."

"I've known you all your life," he said, laughing quietly while he filled his pipe. "I can remember when you used to come down here with your daddy—you were just a little thing. *I've* always liked you."

In the decade since her father died, Josh had become the closest thing she'd had to a friend. He was honest, loyal, and completely without pretense. Most importantly, she trusted him. Tanner smiled, but shook her head ruefully. "But I'm not three anymore, Josh."

Josh puffed on the pipe until sweet cherry smoke filled the room, studying her speculatively. "What's got you all out of sorts anyhow? Adrienne?"

"Partly." Tanner looked away uncomfortably. "I make a mess of things every time I try to talk to her. I'm not sure how to handle her."

He leaned his chair back on its rear legs and thought about that, then shrugged. "Well then, don't."

"What do you mean, 'don't'?" Tanner looked at him in surprise.

"Don't try to handle her. Let her come around on her own. You can't force the wind to blow the way you want it to."

"But what if she never comes around?"

"She will," Josh said matter-of-factly, remembering the look in Adrienne's eyes when she'd held Tanner the night of the storm. "Just give her a little time."

"Time?" Tanner repeated, almost to herself. "What if there isn't any time?"

CHAPTER TWELVE

June passed, and Adrienne avoided the marina. She missed sailing, but she didn't want to see Tanner. Just thinking about her was hard—she alternated between missing the pleasant, friendly connection they had shared while sailing and fearing the even closer intimacy that had come easily, and so unexpectedly, when they had talked.

She couldn't help but wonder what Tanner's days were like and, even more torturously, how she spent her nights. She imagined that Tanner must be hurt by how they had left things and how obviously she was avoiding her, but she couldn't see that she had much choice. Tanner was so intense, so determined, and so damned...sexy.

Any relationship between them was bound to become too intimate. And as much as she fought the attraction, she knew that if she spent much time with Tanner, she would eventually give in to the temptation to touch her. And she couldn't, under any circumstances, do that.

Adrienne briefly considered leaving the island altogether, but something kept her there. She told herself it was the seclusion, and the sea, and the promise of bright sunny days and cool summer nights—and she didn't question her motives too closely. Since she wouldn't sail, she ran, morning and night, farther and farther each week. And she worked out at the gym again almost every day.

True to her word, Tanner did not reappear at the gym. Adrienne ignored the fleeting and irrational disappointment she felt each time she arrived and Tanner was not there. She was so conflicted, she could barely stand to be in her own skin. And, unfortunately, it wasn't all emotional. Maybe it was only the result of feeling healthy again, maybe it had absolutely nothing to do with the memories of holding Tanner or the sight of her naked, but Adrienne was painfully aware of a persistent desire that could not be denied. She ached for physical contact; she ached to touch—and be touched.

❖

The sun had nearly set when Adrienne prepared for her evening run on the beach. She stretched her muscles leisurely on the deck, appreciating the cool breeze blowing in from the water, a welcome relief from the sultry heat of the day. Anticipating a good run, she started out at an easy jog toward the lighthouse on the southern tip of Whitley Point. The sky exploded into a burst of color so suddenly that she nearly stumbled at the sight. Faint echoes of thunder—*thunder*?—pulsed through the night. She stopped and stared in astonishment at the strange sight.

Then she laughed out loud. *Of course! It's July fourth.*

Her days had become so solitary that the ordinary events marking the passage of time escaped her. It was too beautiful a sight to be missed, so, watching the sky, she walked on toward the lighthouse, enjoying the display that continued overhead.

As she drew closer to the source of the fireworks, she passed families on blankets on the beach, enjoying the celebration. She also smelled barbecue, which reminded her that she'd missed dinner and that she was hungry. She bought a hot dog and a beer at a makeshift refreshment stand with the money she carried in a small wrist-wallet, then settled down on the sand to relax.

Surrounded by families having picnic suppers from coolers and teenagers more interested in flirting than in watching the fireworks, Adrienne sat alone. But she still somehow felt part of the festivities as she followed the increasingly elaborate patterns of light and color brightening the night sky. At one point, she heard the distinctive sound of a motorboat approaching and looked down to the shore, wondering idly where a boat would land.

"Damn fool's going to run aground at that rate," a nearby man grumbled.

By now, Adrienne and most of the people around her had forgotten the fireworks and were transfixed by the lights on the powerful cruiser, which grew brighter as the boat sped straight toward shore. Just when it seemed inevitable that the boat would crash up onto the beach, the driver cut the engine and swung the bow around hard, bringing the boat to rest in the shallows on the very edge of the sand. Adrienne let out her breath in a long sigh. Sounds of a woman's laughter reached her as she watched several figures tumble from the boat into the surf, then stagger up onto the beach.

"Figures," the same man muttered in a low angry tone. "She thinks she can get away with anything."

"Shh!" his wife chided, glancing around in embarrassment.

"Oh, right," he hissed. "I forgot—she owns the damn place."

Adrienne recognized Tanner then as she emerged none too steadily from the water, an arm around the waist of the blond from the party at Constance Whitley's. She watched them coldly as Tanner flopped down on the sand, gasping, and pulled her companion down beside her. Tanner obviously said something to her, and the other woman laughed again. Several other partiers joined them; someone passed a silver flask, its surface shining intermittently in the glow of the continuing light show.

When the fireworks began to wind down, Adrienne stood up and dusted the sand from her legs. She was irrationally angered by the display Tanner was making of herself, and she didn't want to witness it any longer. But instead of walking away, and without much conscious thought, she strode directly down the beach to where Tanner lay in the sand and glared down at her.

"Nice entrance," she commented sarcastically.

Tanner squinted up at her, her eyes unfocused. "Glad you liked it." She held out a still burning joint. "Smoke?"

"No, thanks. Why don't you introduce me to your friends?" Each word came out clipped and sharp. Watching the blond stroke Tanner's bare thigh was making her head pound.

"Everyone," Tanner announced grandly, pushing herself up on one elbow and making a sweeping gesture with her arm. "This is Commander—no, my mistake—*just plain Adrienne* Pierce. She is living incognito here at Whitley Point. But beware...she is only here for the summer, so don't expect too much from her."

Heads turned briefly as Tanner talked, and a few people nodded in her direction before returning to their conversations. Adrienne sat down beside Tanner, ignoring the girl who clung possessively to Tanner's arm, caressing her with an indolent show of ownership.

"I want to talk to you," Adrienne said in a low voice.

"Fine." Tanner eyed her expansively. "So talk."

Adrienne shook her head. "Alone."

"What's so important right now? You haven't wanted to talk to me in weeks." Tanner heaved herself to an upright position. "And I have company tonight."

"I can see that." It was all Adrienne could do to keep her voice calm. She was furious, and she didn't want to consider precisely why. She let herself think it was Tanner's arrogance and insolent tone, but she was fighting the urge to reach out and remove the blond's hand, which was now brushing Tanner's stomach. "I'll just be a minute."

The edge of concern in Adrienne's voice penetrated Tanner's foggy brain, and she turned to her companion. "Would you mind, Sharon? Please disappear for a minute."

"Don't be long, lover." The blond kissed Tanner on the mouth, then gave Adrienne a pointedly disdainful look and sauntered away.

"So?" Tanner tried hard to sound alert. She was so tired, she thought she might pass out.

"What the hell do you think you're doing?" Adrienne hissed, her temper boiling very close to the edge. "You could easily have killed someone with that stunt. Including yourself and your friends."

"But I didn't, did I?" Tanner swayed slightly. "I was just having a little fun. I always know how far to go. Just lucky, I guess."

Adrienne felt sick and disgusted and incredibly afraid. "Tanner, for God's sake, you have to stop this. You're a mess."

"Am I?" Tanner ran a hand through her hair and pulled her wrinkled shirt into some kind of order. "I meant to dress for the party."

"Get up. You're coming with me."

"Sorry. Can't do that." Tanner stared at her uncomprehendingly. "I promised to take everyone for a midnight sail later."

"Not tonight, you're not. Not in your condition." Once she'd said it, Adrienne was determined. "Say good night to your girlfriend."

"Adrienne..." Tanner's tone was suddenly serious. "It's not what you think."

"What isn't? The fact that you're drug impaired or the fact that you're...carousing with that blond?"

"Neither...both. Ah, fuck." She rubbed her face vigorously and tried again. "Yes, I've been drinking and I smoked a bit, but we've been partying for three days. I'm more bonked than anything. Sharon... well, that's a long story."

"I'll bet. Where are the keys to that outboard?"

"In my pocket."

"Get up. We're going. They can find their own way home."

"How? This is an island."

"I don't care how. Let them swim or hitchhike or sleep on the goddamn beach—but it isn't going to be on that boat."

Tanner surrendered. She called good night in the blond's direction and got unsteadily to her feet. Sharon might have heard her, but she didn't reply. Adrienne reached out, grabbed Tanner by the arm, and led her away down the beach—double-time. Tanner didn't protest, but she had trouble keeping up with Adrienne's brisk pace.

"Couldn't we just walk instead of galloping?" Tanner gasped, stumbling slightly. "If you don't slow down, I'm going to vomit."

"We're almost there." Adrienne looked at Tanner in exasperation, but she slipped one arm around her waist and slowed to a walk. "Come on, you'll be fine as soon as you get some sleep."

By the time they arrived back at Adrienne's house, Tanner really was stumbling, her exhaustion finally wearing down even her considerable reserves. Adrienne managed to get her up the back stairs and inside to the sofa. After pushing Tanner firmly down, she started toward the bedroom. "You can sleep here. I'll get you some blankets."

"But I'm much too high to sleep," Tanner protested.

"Bull." Adrienne couldn't believe the young woman was still conscious. "You look like you haven't slept in days."

"I don't think I have. That was the whole point."

"You're an even bigger idiot than I thought. Christ," Adrienne cursed, heading for the bedroom. She needed to put a little distance between them. She knew it was madness to have brought Tanner home with her, but she had been too afraid to leave her alone. Tanner was in no shape to look after herself, at least not tonight. But if she stayed in her company now, she would say more than she meant to, and there was no point, considering Tanner's condition.

What in God's name is wrong with her? She's like Jekyll and Hyde. She wasn't like this when we talked on the sailboat...when I told her about...the surgery. She was kind and gentle. She was...wonderful.

Pulling pillows and a light blanket from the top shelf of her bedroom closet, Adrienne tried not to think further about that afternoon on the sea. She had said much more than she had intended, but Tanner had a way of making her feel as if everything about her mattered. Now, she couldn't help remembering Tanner's face the moment after she had pushed her away—the shock and the hurt. She'd hurt her then, and now...

Don't be ridiculous. That has nothing to do with this. And if it does, I can't change it. Whatever Tanner needs, it's beyond my power to provide. Adrienne sighed. *At least tonight she'll be safe.*

While Tanner waited for Adrienne's return, she lay back on the sofa, her mind racing with jumbled thoughts while her body slowly surrendered to exhaustion. For the first time in days, she had stopped long enough to realize how truly tired she was. Her body ached all over, and her head was threatening to explode. She wondered vaguely how she had gotten into this condition. Unfortunately, her recollection of the past few days was sketchy in places.

It had actually started out as just a lark. She'd been bored and restless for days; time seemed to stretch into endless hours of meaningless activity. She'd sailed, paid token visits to the firm offices on business, sat out on the deck with her mother—usually in silence—and prowled the mainland bars at night looking for company. More often than not she returned home alone. It wasn't a stranger she wanted in her bed.

Her mother made gentle overtures to conversation, but Tanner did not want to talk. What could she possibly tell her mother? That there was a woman who occupied her thoughts every moment, leaving only restless dreams and unfulfilled fantasies in her wake? That this woman was as unapproachable as a night creature on the shore? That as soon as Tanner tried to draw near, no matter how carefully, Adrienne withdrew into the shell of her silence?

She'd become more and more frustrated and angry. She'd tried everything she knew—to be sensitive and undemanding, to be patient. She was attracted to Adrienne; she admitted that. She'd been attracted to her, intrigued by her, since the first morning she had opened her eyes on the beach and seen her standing there, backlit by the sun, regarding her coolly with eyes blue as the skies. But it was more than that; she'd felt something beyond the physical when they were together. They'd understood one another—that afternoon they'd shared their secrets—and that's what she craved more than anything else. She would have waited, as long as it took, for Adrienne to trust her. But Adrienne would not give her a chance.

When a group of friends invited her to celebrate the holiday weekend with them, she'd accepted. But she couldn't seem to forget it was Adrienne she really wanted for company. She hadn't intended to lose control, but nothing helped her forget. And eventually, she just didn't care.

Groaning, Tanner put her head in her hands. She was much too befuddled to make sense of any of it. Tugging at the buttons of her shirt, she tried ineffectually to get it off. Failing that, she managed to get her shorts unbuttoned and down her legs, but the logistics of the rest of it took too much effort. She gave up and laid back, prepared to sleep exactly as she was.

When Adrienne returned, she found Tanner lying in a tangle of wet clothes. "It seems like I'm always putting you to bed," she muttered as she pulled Tanner's shoes off, tossed them aside, and extricated her shorts from around her ankles.

"Not the way I hoped," Tanner murmured.

"Sit up and help me get your shirt off."

Tanner did the best she could and pushed herself upright as Adrienne unbuttoned her shirt. The feel of Adrienne's hands glancing unintentionally over her skin set her nerve endings jangling. And when Adrienne leaned forward to strip off the garment, her T-shirt rubbed across Tanner's breasts, cool and still damp with seawater, and the unexpected contact sent a surge of excitement directly between Tanner's legs.

She was suddenly totally awake and painfully aroused. Adrienne was there next to her, nothing between them but the night, and she had waited so long, wanted her for so long. She ached to surrender, finally, to the warm shelter of Adrienne's mouth. She grasped Adrienne's shoulders in both hands, pulled her close, and kissed her.

Adrienne didn't have time to think—her body answered for her, doing what her mind had been protesting for weeks. She kissed Tanner back, hungrily, hard enough to bruise, arms tightening around Tanner's muscular back as if never to let her go.

Moaning, Tanner slid her tongue over Adrienne's parted lips, thrust her hands into Adrienne's hair, and held her head as her mouth roamed frantically over Adrienne's face and neck. She was mindless of Adrienne's reluctant efforts to move away—she only pressed closer, the rough fabric of Adrienne's shirt chafing her tender nipples, hard and erect now. She didn't care—the pain was a pleasure that awakened every cell. Her hand slid under the bottom of Adrienne's shirt, desperately seeking skin.

"No," Adrienne said instantly.

"God, let me touch you," Tanner gasped. "I'm dying here."

Adrienne managed to break the embrace and held Tanner away at arm's length. "Stop!" She tore her eyes away from Tanner's handsome face, only to find she couldn't stop looking at her breasts, her arms, her abdomen. There wasn't a single part of Tanner that wasn't beautiful.

"Please," Tanner whispered, shuddering, her dark eyes feverish with need. "Don't go away. I want you so much. I have...for so long."

God help me. I want you, too.

"I'm begging..."

"Tell me you're not drugged out of your mind," Adrienne said breathlessly. "Tell me."

Tanner took Adrienne's hand, pressed it to the bare flesh above her heart. "I swear to God, I'm not. Just please, please...let me touch you."

"No."

"Then touch *me.*" Her voice broke on the words.

Adrienne groaned softly, defeated, and lowered her mouth to Tanner's neck. She had wanted her like this since that first kiss on the beach, longed to feel Tanner yield to her touch, ached to run her hands over that golden body. It was useless to deny it now. Even if she hadn't been long past the point of rational thought, even if she had wanted to stop, she could not have. And she most desperately did not want to stop.

Caressing the soft smooth skin with her lips, she tasted the heady mixture of sweat tinged with salt. With one hand, she cupped Tanner's breast, her thumb brushing the taut nipple, drawing a gasp that sent shivers through her own body. Slowly, she kissed her way down the fragile column of Tanner's throat, feeling the pulse beat wildly under her lips, until she found the hollow at the base of her neck. She licked the tiny droplets of the sea lingering there, then moved lower to explore the curves of Tanner's breasts with her tongue.

Every time Tanner moaned, Adrienne's heart threatened to pound through her chest. Teasing her with small bites soothed with kisses, she finally grasped a nipple with her teeth, drawing it between her lips. Tanner arched her back, a strangled cry wrenched from her throat, and Adrienne closed her eyes, surrendering to the sweetness.

"You're so beautiful," Adrienne groaned, cradling both breasts in her hands, turning her face to press between them, working both nipples between her fingertips.

Tanner whimpered and pulled Adrienne's thigh between her legs, pressing hard against the unyielding flesh. "Make me come," she begged in Adrienne's ear. "I want to...so much."

"I will," Adrienne promised, feeling Tanner's pulse pounding on her leg, reveling in her heat and her need. She didn't think she could possibly feel Tanner enough, and she pressed her hips into her, hard, as her hands traveled up and down the muscular young body beneath her. Leaning up on one elbow, she kissed Tanner again, a deep demanding kiss. While she explored the depths of Tanner's warm mouth, stroking rhythmically with her tongue, she reached down between their bodies. She pressed her hips against her hand as she held Tanner's desire in her palm.

Suddenly, with a small cry of surprise, Tanner pulled her head away, breaking their kiss. She stared at Adrienne, dazed, her control in shreds. "I'm going to come," she whispered urgently.

"Not yet," Adrienne cried, wrenching herself away from Tanner's shuddering body with effort. She held herself away, breaking their contact, waiting for the storm to pass. "Wait...hold on."

"I want to...so bad." Tanner moaned, trying to pull Adrienne down against her again. "I can't wait. Please."

"You can," Adrienne soothed, running her tongue lightly down Tanner's neck to her breast again. "You can, honey. Just a little longer. I want so much more of you."

Adrienne resumed exploring with her lips, making lazy circles on Tanner's abdomen with her tongue as she shifted down onto the floor. Kneeling, knowing Tanner was ready to go off at the slightest touch, she slowly, carefully rested her head against Tanner's thighs and with both hands gently parted her legs. Tanner cried out and thrust herself against Adrienne's hand, trying to rub her swollen clitoris against Adrienne's fingers.

That motion finally broke Adrienne's control. She moaned, deep in her throat, and took Tanner into her mouth, forgetting to go slowly, forgetting to be gentle. Tanner sobbed incoherently as Adrienne took her pleasure.

"You'll make me come in your mouth," Tanner warned desperately. "Oh, I'm coming..."

Adrienne felt Tanner throb and grow harder between her lips. She couldn't deny Tanner release, and she wanted her far too much to wait any longer. She worked her faster, slipped her fingers inside, and, pressing firmly, filled her. Tanner clenched around her fingers, and Adrienne thought her own heart would stop beating. Holding Tanner against her mouth, she stroked her until the sweet torture of her caress pushed Tanner over the edge.

"Oh God...it's so good..."

Adrienne thrust in time with the contractions until Tanner's cries turned to exhausted sobs. Gently, Adrienne withdrew her hand and stretched out beside Tanner on the sofa, gathering Tanner's nerveless body into her arms. Kissing her softly on the forehead, she brushed the damp hair from Tanner's eyes. "You okay?"

"Oh yeah," Tanner managed to mumble as her entire body continued to shiver with aftershocks. "God, I'm still coming."

Adrienne's breath caught in her throat. *You're so lovely.*

Finally, Tanner roused herself enough to lift her head and kiss Adrienne on the lips, one hand caressing Adrienne's face. Her strength was coming back and with it came the hunger. Hunger for Adrienne. She pushed her fingers under the collar of Adrienne's shirt, desperate for the feel of her. "My turn," she whispered huskily.

Adrienne caught Tanner's hand in her own, stopping her explorations, but she kissed her again to soften the rejection. "Not now," she said gently.

"When?"

"I don't know. Just rest."

Tanner sighed and curled against Adrienne, desire warring with supreme contentment. She meant to protest, but sleep claimed her too quickly.

CHAPTER THIRTEEN

When Tanner awoke, she was alone. Sun streamed through the screens, directly into her face. Shielding her eyes with her forearm, she waited for her head to clear. She had a pounding headache, but otherwise, she seemed to be in one piece. Finally, she tentatively opened her eyes, wincing again at the bright light, and looked around.

Her clothes lay spread out over a chair. With that one reminder, all the events of the past evening came back to her in a rush. Suddenly, her skin burned hot, the feel of Adrienne's hands a tangible memory, and a pulse thudded heavily deep within. She sat up quickly, ignoring the flash of pain in her head, needing to see Adrienne. Needing to be certain it was real.

"Adrienne?"

The answering silence was not a surprise.

She's not here, you idiot. She's off somewhere—thinking something rational, no doubt. As if there is anything rational about this. And when she gets back, she'll probably try to convince me that last night was an accident that should not have happened. Yeah, right.

Tanner swung her legs to the floor, ignoring the sudden lurching in her stomach. In her own way, she was just as frightened as she suspected Adrienne probably was. Adrienne had run from her not once, but twice, and if she did again, it would be unbearable. Somehow, she must convince Adrienne to let her in, to give them a chance to learn to trust each other, but she was at a loss as to how to begin. There was so much she wanted to say to her, but every time she tried, she was met with the cold wall of Adrienne's fear. She knew that more had changed, or been lost, for Adrienne in the last year than she herself had ever considered—a lover, a career, a lifetime of plans. The thought was staggering. How could she ever hope to replace any of those things?

"Maybe I can't," Tanner muttered to herself as she got up unsteadily to search for the bathroom. "But I'm going to make her listen to me, make her understand how I feel about her. She's not disappearing on me again. Not this time."

She turned on the cold water full blast and stepped into it, shivering as the icy pinpricks assaulted her. The shower cleared her head, but it didn't cool the blaze in her body. She hadn't been touched like that in so very long. She'd had sex, and she'd pleasured others, but rarely had she welcomed—or wanted—anything in return. Giving herself to Adrienne, being taken by her, left an afterimage of passion carved into her soul. The desire was still so fresh she ached, ready to come from the memories alone. Bracing both hands against the wall, she lowered her head and let the cold spray sluice down her neck and over her shoulders. She needed a minute before she could trust her hands on her skin. It wasn't her own touch she wanted.

❖

Adrienne walked slowly up the beach toward the house a little after eight. She'd left at dawn, gently disengaging herself from Tanner so as not to awaken her. It had been hard, moving from the warmth of her body into the chill morning air, and Tanner had looked so lovely asleep that she'd hated to leave her. But she'd known she had to; she couldn't seem to think clearly with their skin touching, with the whisper of Tanner's breath against her neck.

To her utter surprise and dismay, her body seemed to want to continue the activities of the previous evening. Lying with Tanner in her arms, she'd grown heavy with desire. She wanted to touch Tanner again, make her shout her pleasure again, make her cry with the sweetness of it. And she could not deny the insistent, throbbing ache in her own body. That pulse-pounding need, more than anything else, propelled her from the sofa. Too much had happened too quickly, and she needed to sort it out.

Now as she returned, she was no closer to understanding any of it. Oh, she understood her desire. How could she not? Tanner, beautiful to behold and seethingly sensual, was impossible to resist. But Adrienne was too old to believe that desire was an end in itself. She had known desire, infatuation, lust—whatever one called it—more than once in her life, but she had rarely acted upon it. Hers had always been a reasoned, predictable existence.

Inexplicably, Tanner had been able to overcome all of Adrienne's natural reluctance with the force of one simple kiss. That kiss had tormented her, but it was Tanner herself, with her impossible charm and her unexpected insight and her wild, passionate spirit, that Adrienne found completely irresistible. Tanner upset the carefully constructed balance of her life, and, at this point, she needed all of her control. She wasn't at all sure what she would say if Tanner was still there when she returned. She wasn't even sure what she wanted to say. All she knew was that she was very frightened.

The sofa was empty but Tanner's clothes were still there and the door to her bedroom was ajar. The sound of the shower running drew her to the open bathroom door. Had she thought about it, she would have known better than to follow the sound, but by the time she realized her mistake, it was too late.

The frosted doors of the shower ran with rivulets of water, but Tanner's shape within was clearly discernible. Even if it hadn't been, Adrienne would have been able to see every glorious curve and plane of her. She'd had her hands and her mouth and her tongue on that body just hours before, and she knew the sight, the scent, the taste of it. Those indelible impressions had marked her, claimed some critical part of her, and the merest reflection of the woman through misted glass made her thighs tremble with wanting. She feared if she stayed another instant she would have to touch her, or touch herself, because she was about to explode into a million fragments. She did the only reasonable thing. She fled.

❖

Tanner pulled one of Adrienne's old shirts off a hook behind the bathroom door and slipped it on. It barely reached to the tops of her thighs, which was good enough. She walked out onto the deck to wait. To her surprise, Adrienne was already there, leaning against the deck rail, looking gorgeous in a cotton short-sleeved shirt and shorts. Never had she seen a woman look so sexy. Smiling shyly, Tanner said, "Hi."

"Hi, yourself." Adrienne smiled back, trying not to look at the expanse of skin left uncovered by the shirt that Tanner had closed with only two buttons. "How are you feeling?"

"Depends. A little stupid and embarrassed, a lot grateful, and very crazy."

Adrienne laughed, throwing up her hands at the same time. "What on earth are you talking about?"

"Well, I feel stupid about my behavior the last three or four days. I'm not sure of the exact number because I'm not sure what day it is today. Very embarrassed that you saw me when I was so completely wrecked. And grateful that you dragged me away." She took a deep breath and looked directly at Adrienne, continuing in a tumble of words, "And then, I'm crazy about you."

Adrienne looked away uncomfortably, turning to gaze out over the dunes below. Her voice was low, but Tanner heard her. "I can't tell you how angry you make me when you do those things to yourself. And it scares me, Tanner. You could injure yourself, or someone else, and I can't believe that it does you any good emotionally. But I also know that no one can stop you or change you. You'll have to do that yourself. But I won't pretend I can tolerate it for a minute. I can't."

It was a risk, but Tanner took a step closer until she was beside Adrienne at the rail. Their hands were close enough for their fingers to touch, but neither of them closed the final distance. For so long, she just hadn't cared—not about herself, not about anything. It had taken meeting Adrienne, recognizing her own sorrow in Adrienne's eyes, to make her care. "I understand," she said quietly. "Believe it or not, I've been trying to clean up my act."

"Ah...that boat ride last night..."

"I know. I know how it looks." Frustrated, Tanner ran a hand through her hair. "Give me a chance, okay? I'm working on it. I just need a little more practice."

Adrienne did smile at that. "You are so special, Tanner. I'm glad if you're beginning to believe it." She shrugged helplessly. "I have to admit—I find you quite impossibly irresistible. But..."

"But?" Tanner raised an eyebrow.

"I don't want a repeat of last night's events," Adrienne said flatly, finally shifting enough to meet Tanner's eyes. "I won't pretend I didn't enjoy it. You know better than that. I was swept away, or off my feet, or whatever. I couldn't say no to you—I didn't want to. But I need that to be the end of it. It can't happen again."

"Last night was the best thing that ever happened to me." Tanner's voice was remarkably calm, when what she wanted to do was shout and rave. She had no doubt that Adrienne meant what she was saying. She even thought she understood some of the reasons. Understanding didn't mean she had to accept it, though. "I don't want it to end."

"Oh, Tanner!" Adrienne cried in exasperation. "Don't make this any more difficult than it already is."

"Tell me that you don't want me." Tanner spoke softly, her ebony eyes searching Adrienne's face. She leaned forward until their bodies nearly touched, so close that she could see the tiny beads of sweat on Adrienne's forehead. "Because I want you. I hurt, I want you so badly."

"Don't." But Adrienne's expression softened. She couldn't help it, looking at Tanner—the wind-ruffled hair, those liquid eyes, that impossibly beautiful mouth. Taking a deep breath, she steadied herself, determined to remain resolute. "Wanting isn't the point. Not for me at least. Lust has nothing to do with it. I don't have room for this sort of thing in my life. You are a desirable woman, Tanner. I'd have to be dead not to notice. But I still don't want to be involved with you."

"It's more than wanting, and I can't stop." Tanner rested her hand on Adrienne's waist, her lips only inches away.

"I don't care what you *think* it is." Adrienne stood absolutely still, more afraid than ever because her hands shook from wanting to touch her. Her voice was but a strained whisper now. "I don't *want* you to want me. I don't want you to feel anything for me. It doesn't work for me anymore. I really don't have the need for it anymore. Can't you see how one-sided it would be?"

Tanner didn't reply. She simply put her arms around Adrienne's waist, pressed against the length of her, and slipped her tongue into Adrienne's mouth. She kissed her thoroughly, letting the kiss answer for her. Finally, breathing unevenly, she leaned away to study Adrienne's face.

"I don't believe you," she gasped, trying to calm the storm rising in her depths. She had to do this right. "I can feel your body respond to me. If you can't feel it, it's because you don't want to. Now, I'm going to kiss you again. Only this time I'm not going to stop, and you're going to kiss me back."

"Are you always so brave?" Adrienne murmured, unable to take her eyes from Tanner's lips.

"No," Tanner breathed. "Only when I'm desperate." She insinuated one naked thigh between Adrienne's legs and moved slowly against her, thrilling to the answering surge of Adrienne's hips. She groaned. "Yeah. Just like that."

"Tanner..."

"Just...just shut up..." Her lips met Adrienne's and they both moaned. When she started to feel dizzy from lack of oxygen, she broke the kiss, gasping, but immediately moved her mouth to the suntanned triangle of skin beckoning from Adrienne's open collar, savoring the warmth and sweet taste of her while she caught her breath. When Adrienne grasped her hips and pushed a thigh hard between her legs, Tanner thought her head would come off. She usually wasn't so quick to reach such a critical state of arousal, but somehow Adrienne could bring her to the edge with just a touch. Already, she felt the first faint twinges of orgasm. If she wasn't careful, it would end the same way it had the night before. And this time she wanted Adrienne more than she wanted anything else. "Easy." She groaned against Adrienne's neck. "I need...a minute."

Adrienne, eyes closed, didn't seem to hear. She shifted until Tanner's back was against the railing and, breathing rapidly, continued to thrust, the bare skin of her leg growing wet with Tanner's arousal.

"Adrienne," Tanner pleaded, holding her away with both hands. Her limbs shook so badly she had to hold on tightly to keep from falling. *Oh, I'm not sure I can hold off.* Her throat was so tight she could barely make sound. "Please...wait."

Adrienne opened her eyes, startled and confused. "Why are you stopping me? You're about to come...I can feel how hard—"

"I don't want to come. I want you. Come inside to the bed."

Adrienne wanted to refuse, but she didn't have the strength. She wanted Tanner so desperately, she couldn't think. She ached to hold her, taste her. And she couldn't deny any longer her own urgent need to be touched. Her body was imploding; she had no other choice. She had to go with her or start screaming.

When Tanner tugged on her hand and led her toward the double doors to the bedroom, Adrienne didn't resist. Only when they reached the threshold did she hesitate, suddenly afraid. She didn't think she would be able to bear it if Tanner turned away from her in revulsion or looked upon her with pity.

"Tanner," she whispered. "I'm not sure I can do this."

"Yes, you can." Tanner kissed her, very gently, then drew her forward. "*We* can."

Tanner stopped by the side of the bed. "Lie down," she murmured. "Watch me." Slowly, she unbuttoned her own shirt, watching Adrienne's expression. As she let the fabric slide off her shoulders, she saw Adrienne's gaze drop to her breasts. Her nipples hardened as if the look were a caress. "Okay so far?"

"Oh God, yes." Adrienne's voice was honeyed granite—soft with desire, harsh with need. "Get over here."

Tanner laughed. Naked, she eased herself up onto the bed, then moved above the reclining woman until she straddled Adrienne's hips with her thighs. Slowly, she pulled Adrienne's shirt from her shorts and pushed it up to her ribs, exposing her abdomen. Spreading her fingers, she placed her thumbs on either side of Adrienne's navel and spanned her middle, pressing gently, then stroked her softly from rib cage to the top of her shorts. "Anything you want..." It wasn't a question.

"Whatever *you* want," Adrienne murmured, mesmerized by the sure steady caresses that sent her blood racing.

Tanner leaned forward to kiss her, breasts swaying as she moved.

Adrienne gazed at them and gasped, "Oh, yes." She moaned and captured both breasts in her hands. Running her thumbs over Tanner's nipples, she raised her head to claim one with her lips.

"Uh-uh. Not yet." Tanner pulled back a little, pushing Adrienne gently back against the pillows. "Don't make me crazy," she ordered with a smile. "There are a few things I want to do first." Shifting until she sat astride Adrienne's bare stomach, she rocked her hips slightly, knowing that Adrienne would feel the wet hardness between her thighs. The exquisite friction made her head swim. "Can you tell how much I want you?"

"Do that for another minute or two," Adrienne groaned. "I...dare you."

"You know I wouldn't last," Tanner murmured and began to unbutton Adrienne's shirt. Adrienne stiffened at the touch, but Tanner merely whispered, "It will be all right. I promise."

"No one has done this since..."

Tanner stopped what she was doing but did not move her hands. She stared at Adrienne, her eyes fierce. "*I* want to be the one. I want to be the only one."

Adrienne tried to fight the terror, her gaze locked onto Tanner's face. The truth would be revealed in those expressive eyes. *God, if she flinches, if she looks away.* She was barely breathing. If she had been physically able, she might still have fled.

Tanner waited, obsidian eyes boring holes in Adrienne's defenses.

In a whisper, Adrienne said, "Yes."

Carefully, Tanner slipped her fingers under the collar of Adrienne's shirt, parted the garment, and gazed down. Adrienne's left breast was not large, but it was round and youthfully firm. The nipple was small and taut, a deep rich rose. Where her right breast had been, a faint red scar, narrow as a pencil line, extended from under her arm nearly to the center of her chest. Her well-defined chest muscle was obvious just underneath the skin, very much like a man's chest, except there was no nipple. Tanner wanted to touch her there, but she feared it might hurt her. She never wanted Adrienne to hurt again.

Adrienne watched Tanner's face, trying to read her reactions. Tanner's expression had grown serious, but she didn't appear shocked. She seemed to be studying her. Relieved and reassured, Adrienne didn't mind.

At last, Tanner raised her eyes to meet Adrienne's. "Will it hurt you if I lie down on top of you?"

"No." Adrienne laughed softly and shook her head. "I...I want you to."

Tanner lowered herself slowly until her breasts were touching Adrienne's chest and their legs entwined. Sliding her hands up Adrienne's lean arms to her shoulders, she let her weight rest on her. "Okay?"

"More than okay." Adrienne held her tightly, feeling their bodies cleave. After a few moments, she whispered into Tanner's hair, "You feel so right."

Tanner only moaned softly in response, pressing her face to the long curve of Adrienne's neck, reveling in the wonderful sensation of being so close to her at last. She was still acutely aroused, throbbing in fact, but she was in no hurry. She wanted to remember every second of this first wondrous joining.

"Tanner?"

"Hmm?"

"I still have my shorts on."

"Oh," Tanner groaned. "That was suave of me."

"Could we take them off, please? I'm getting a bit...congested."

"Not if it means I have to move," Tanner replied in a husky voice. After a moment, she rolled onto her side and sighed in mock exasperation. "If it must be done, I'll do it." She loosened the snaps and zipper with one hand, managing to kiss Adrienne at the same time. Finally, she reached down and pushed the garment lower until Adrienne could kick it away.

"Come here," Adrienne demanded and pulled Tanner against her, suddenly feeling terribly exposed now that she was nude.

"In a minute." Tanner leaned on one elbow and gently encircled Adrienne's breast, finding the nipple with her thumb and forefinger. She could almost hold all of it in her hand.

"That's nice," Adrienne whispered softly, then gasped as the pressure on her nipple intensified. "Ahh...very nice."

"Uh-huh," Tanner agreed. She put her lips where her fingers had been, teasing and pulling with her tongue, her hand resting now on Adrienne's chest just below her collarbone. The muscles there tightened as Adrienne's excitement grew. Tanner took her time. Inching down Adrienne's body, she alternately licked, kissed, and lightly bit until finally she was stretched out between Adrienne's legs, her face resting against Adrienne's stomach. She blew softly across the surface of Adrienne's sweat-slick skin, smiling to herself as muscles twitched beneath the surface.

"Tanner," Adrienne murmured hoarsely, restlessly stroking Tanner's cheek with one hand, "I need you to touch me."

"Soon?" Tanner teased.

"Now...before I come apart."

Intoxicated with the rush of power, Tanner dipped her head, brushing fleeting kisses on Adrienne's inner thighs, then higher. She'd waited forever, it seemed, and it was so much more than she had imagined. She was certain her heart had stopped beating, and she knew she wasn't breathing. As Adrienne moaned, Tanner kept up the slow steady rhythm, drawing her tongue, then her fingers, over Adrienne again and again, teasing in and out of the slick folds. When Adrienne thrust trembling hands into Tanner's hair, Tanner followed the silent signals, increasing the pressure on Adrienne's clitoris and entering her at the same time.

Adrienne gasped and tugged Tanner's face away. "Come up here. I want to hold you."

"I want to make you come," Tanner protested softly.

"Believe me, I *want* you to make me come." Adrienne smiled, her eyes nearly closed. "In a minute. It feels so good. I don't want it to end."

Tanner moved up, slipping her thigh between Adrienne's. Settling on top of her again, she supported herself on her elbows so she could see Adrienne's face. "Oh, man," she moaned as the sudden touch of skin against her own engorged clitoris made her twitch. "Bad idea."

"Why?" Adrienne asked innocently, her smile one of heady satisfaction. She lifted her hips, watched Tanner's eyes go wide. "In trouble, are you?"

"Oh, yeah. Big time." Bracing her arms, Tanner began to thrust downward as Adrienne matched her rhythm. "You're beautiful."

"No...you...are." Adrienne's lids fluttered and her eyes, glazed with need, sought Tanner's. Clinging to one another, gazes fused, they drove one another higher—each thrust faster, more erratic—as they sought release. Adrienne struggled to keep her eyes open, wanting to see Tanner's face as she climaxed, but she couldn't last. Arching her back, she dug her fingers into Tanner's shoulders as every muscle clenched. Her passion, long denied, finally exploded, and she cried out, a thousand nerve endings bursting simultaneously.

Tanner held her tightly, trying to absorb every sound, wanting to memorize every tremor in Adrienne's body. So precious, so special, so..."Oh fuck," she cried in surprise as her clitoris twitched, lengthened, and went off in one endless spasm. "Oh God..."

A century later, Adrienne stirred enough to slide partway out from under Tanner's weight. Tanner slept where she had collapsed, her face buried in Adrienne's neck. Adrienne looked down at Tanner's hand, tanned and strong, lying across the ravaged plain of her chest. For the first time, she didn't hate the thin red scar.

CHAPTER FOURTEEN

Tanner next awoke in the late afternoon. It was warm in the room, and she felt lazy from the heat and the aftermath of love. She lay with her eyes closed, enjoying the feel of the woman beside her. It was rare for her to awaken with a lover, and she wanted to savor the pleasure before conversation and activity broke the spell. Because this was Adrienne, and every second was a gift.

She opened her eyes eventually, but didn't move, marveling at the sensation of Adrienne's chest rising gently under her hand with each breath. Adrienne was turned slightly away, curled on her side. Blond hair, partially covering her face, fluttered gently against her cheek on the breeze from the open door. There were tiny freckles on her shoulders from the sun, and downy hair on the sides of her cheek. Tanner felt a surge of tenderness, so intense it nearly choked her. She wanted to protect Adrienne, to keep her from harm, as if such a thing were truly possible. She wanted her feelings to be enough to shield Adrienne from further injury. She sighed at her own foolishness, but part of her clung to the desire nevertheless.

At the moment, Tanner couldn't see the scar on Adrienne's chest, but she remembered every detail of it. She had never truly understood before what that kind of surgery meant. Of course, she'd heard about it and read about it, and it had become such a common topic that it had seemed familiar—until today, when she'd finally *seen.* It wasn't horrifying or ugly. The strangest thing was the absence of the shape she was used to.

Women's breasts had always been a source of beauty to her, long before she had begun to love women sexually. She remembered when she was small, watching her mother naked. Her mother's breasts had fascinated her. They were so intriguing to look at, moving in a mysterious, magical way as her mother walked. She could recall looking down at her own flat chest and trying to imagine what it would be like to have such wonderful things on her own body. Now she tried to imagine what it would be like *not* to have them.

Indeed, Tanner rarely thought of her breasts as separate parts of herself. They were just there, like her arms and her legs. Would losing one be like losing an arm? Would she feel unbalanced, like a stranger to herself? She tried to imagine how she would feel letting someone else see her like that. Despite all her self-confidence, she was always a little insecure that a lover would find her less than perfect. How would she cope with knowing that she truly was less than physically whole? She wasn't at all sure she would have the courage to find out.

And there was Adrienne, sleeping peacefully beside her. She had risked much, exposing more than her body when she'd allowed Tanner to touch her. Tanner was grateful and humbled that Adrienne had trusted her. She cuddled closer, stirred by a new respect for the woman who had gone through so much and was still willing to risk more.

Adrienne stirred and sighed softly, turning toward Tanner in half-sleep. Her hand trailed softly over Tanner's hip and up to her shoulder. Nestling her face against Tanner's breast, she gently kissed her there. Tanner extracted her arm from between them and settled Adrienne's head in the crook of her arm.

"Hello."

"Mmm—hi," Adrienne replied, burrowing her nose against Tanner's nipple.

"Are you waking up?" Tanner laughed and kissed the top of Adrienne's head.

"No."

Tanner smoothed the hair back from Adrienne's temple, kissing her softly again. *God, I feel good.* "You know, I don't think I've eaten for at least a month. I may perish right here in a few minutes."

"That would be criminal," Adrienne responded, raising her head to run her tongue over Tanner's lower lip.

"Can I take you out to dinner, then?"

"How about room service?" Adrienne joked. She really didn't want to face the world. Or to allow reality to dispel this brief moment of peace.

"Impossible to get that kind of help out here."

Adrienne looked at Tanner, who smiled back, her face still dreamy with satisfaction. She sighed. "I suppose we must get up then."

"Just for a little while," Tanner said, kissing her yet again. "I have to refuel, I have to tell Richard to pick up the boat, and I need clean clothes."

"And I have to shower." Adrienne was coming fully awake at last. "I'm downright indecent."

"I like you indecent."

"Really?"

"Oh, yeah. Most definitely."

Adrienne sat up abruptly, turning her back to Tanner as she swung her legs over the side of the bed. She reached for a robe on a nearby chair. "I'd better go shower."

"In that case, I'll come with you." Tanner moved to get up.

"No," Adrienne said sharply.

Caught off guard by the abrupt tone, Tanner hesitated for a second and then sat up. She wrapped her arms firmly around Adrienne's waist from behind, holding her fast, preventing her from standing. "I want to."

"You don't give up, do you?" Adrienne leaned the back of her head against Tanner's shoulder and sighed.

"Nope."

"Has it occurred to you that your seeing me naked might make me uncomfortable?"

Tanner tightened her hold, rubbing her cheek softly against Adrienne's temple. "Does it?" she asked quietly. "I saw you this morning. You were beautiful."

Adrienne suddenly remembered them together, saw Tanner's hands and lips on her body, her face tender and gentle. "No. It doesn't make me uncomfortable."

She reached for Tanner's hand and pulled her along to the bathroom.

❖

The water was cool at first, and they both gasped as it struck them. Adrienne shampooed Tanner's hair and, while her eyes were closed, took advantage of the opportunity to look at her unobserved. Her gaze wandered over Tanner's sleek torso to her strong legs, lingering for a long moment on the dark wavy hair at the base of her smooth belly. Adrienne acknowledged the quick flush of desire, shaking her head in self-reproach.

You're acting like a horny seventeen-year-old. This is going to get completely out of hand if you don't keep your head. It's going to be tough enough as it is to convince Tanner that this can't get serious. Jumping on her every time you look at her is not going to help. You can't possibly become involved with anyone—and certainly not a young, wild heartbreaker like her.

She was startled by the touch of Tanner's hands on her waist.

"That feels great," Tanner murmured with a sigh, lulled by the steady gentle pressure of Adrienne's strong fingers in her hair. She liked being guided by Adrienne's touch, comfortable to surrender to her direction. She knew that Adrienne was studying her, and she was pleased. It was a new experience—wanting this much to be wanted, wanting this much to please. Their lovemaking had been wholly satisfying, but arousal was still just a breath away. Desire simmered hot beneath her skin, and she wanted Adrienne to burn with her.

Adrienne sensed Tanner's body grow soft and somehow fuller under her hands as she turned her slowly in the warm spray of the shower. She watched the rivulets of water run in curving trails over Tanner's face and down onto her body. Pushing the wet strands of dark hair back from the strong planes of Tanner's face, she traced the carved cheekbones and stubborn jaw with her thumbs.

Swiftly, Tanner turned her head and captured Adrienne's thumb in her mouth and sucked gently.

"You're bad," Adrienne whispered. She had to have her again. *One more time. God, just one more time.*

She didn't even stop to think. In a single fluid motion, she backed Tanner against the shower wall and lowered her head, pulling a nipple into her mouth. Her thumb still between Tanner's lips, she splayed her fingers along Tanner's jaw, holding her head against the glass.

"Do it hard," Tanner moaned softly.

Alternately sucking and licking, Adrienne worked first one nipple and then the other until Tanner's hips twisted against her thigh, until her arousal was hot on Adrienne's skin. "Don't even think about getting off like that. You'll have to wait."

"Please," Tanner whispered.

"No." *God help me, I want to make her beg.*

Adrienne kept Tanner pinned to the wall and went back to tormenting her nipple, lost in the exquisite feel of it in her mouth. With her other hand, she circled the tiny hollow just above Tanner's buttocks, then brought her hand to the front, smoothing her palm down the flat plane of Tanner's abdomen, brushing her fingers through the wet curls below.

"What are you doing to me?" Tanner sobbed, her neck arched under Adrienne's hand. "Nobody ever did this to me before."

"Oh, yeah? Used to being in charge, are we?" Adrienne smiled to herself as she pressed one finger against the base of Tanner's clitoris. Tanner's knees buckled and Adrienne held her up.

"Patience, honey, patience." Adrienne's teasing voice, deep with excitement, was barely recognizable to her own ears. When she stroked lower between Tanner's swollen lips, she found the wetness that was not from the water streaming over them. She lingered, fingering her softly, reveling in the power she had to pleasure this glorious young animal.

"Oh please," Tanner begged. Quivering with arousal, eyes blind with need, she gripped Adrienne's wrist and thrust into her palm. "I can't stand it—you've got to let me come."

"Go ahead," Adrienne whispered huskily, her lips pressed to Tanner's ear. She parted warm folds, sliding deeply in and slowly out, her thumb pressing the length of Tanner's clitoris with each stroke.

Tanner stiffened, her breath coming in short hoarse gasps, and then Adrienne was moaning too as muscles clamped and spasmed around her fingers. Somewhere, a pulse beat wildly against her hand. Focusing, matching her movements to Tanner's inner rhythm, Adrienne tightened her hold on the woman in her arms. Faster, harder now—some instinctive sense guiding her—she pressed inward, deeper. And then there was only Tanner, crying her name, clinging to her, coming.

"Don't. Don't come out," Tanner managed to gasp when she could breathe again. They swayed, locked together for a long time, until finally Tanner took a deep breath and grinned sheepishly. "Adrienne, you destroyed me. I'm going to fall down if I don't drown first."

"I doubt you'll drown." Adrienne laughed. "You survived more water than this in that gale storm, remember?"

"That wasn't quite the same thing." Tanner circled Adrienne in her arms, holding her close. "I hadn't just been ravished then." A flicker of almost-pain flashed across her face as Adrienne slipped out. The loss echoed somewhere deeper than her flesh. "I have never felt anything like that before."

Neither have I. I've never done anything like that before. Adrienne cleared her throat and hoped she sounded nonchalant. "We're going to lose the hot water."

Tanner sighed and stepped back. "Well, let me have the soap, then."

Adrienne looked at her, puzzled, but did as she asked.

With the soap in one hand, Tanner reached around Adrienne's body with the other and held her still. She worked the lather into swirls over Adrienne's chest and belly. Lowering her eyes, Tanner continued the soft circular motions as she traced the contours of the firm muscles under her hands. Laying the soap aside, she gathered Adrienne's breast in her hands and ran her fingers gently over the nipple. She followed the curve to the center of Adrienne's chest and placed her palm gently on the flat surface where Adrienne's other breast had been. Tenderly, she continued to work the lather into the pink scar with care.

Adrienne stiffened slightly, and Tanner tilted her head back to look at her. Adrienne was watching her with a question in her eyes.

"What is it?" Tanner asked.

"You really don't mind about this?" Adrienne glanced down at her body.

"Of course I mind," Tanner replied instantly, her eyes blazing. "I mind very much that you've been ill and that you were hurt physically and emotionally. I mind that you had to live through it and that you still have to live *with* it now. God, I mind that I can't change it or help it."

"Oh, Tanner, you have helped." Adrienne stopped the rush of words with her fingers against Tanner's lips. She pulled her close, embracing her fiercely. "Every time you look at me and still want to touch me, you help. You've helped me to feel whole again. I never thought I would want to touch anyone or be touched, ever again. You have no idea what you've done."

"I *hate* what happened to you," Tanner whispered, tears mixing with the water that streamed from her face.

"It's all right." Adrienne kissed her, murmuring the comfort she herself had longed to hear not so long ago. "Really, it's all right."

❖

After Tanner walked home and changed, she picked Adrienne up and drove to a restaurant, one of the locals' favorites, just across the causeway on the mainland. The maître d' greeted Tanner with polite familiarity and showed them to a secluded table that overlooked the inlet between the coast and the island. Whitley Point was visible across the water, and, gazing at it through the picture window, Adrienne was reminded of the true isolation of her summer hideaway.

"Let's have champagne with dinner," Tanner suggested. "Any requests, or do you trust me to choose?"

"Are we celebrating something?" Adrienne smiled at Tanner's lighthearted mood.

"I am," Tanner replied, glancing at her watch. "I'm celebrating the best...let's see...eighteen hours...I've ever had." She looked at Adrienne with a satisfied grin on her face, and her meaning was clear.

Adrienne blushed and turned back to the window. The last of the sailors and fishermen were bringing their trawlers into the inlet; the setting sun cast the sky in colors that artists dreamed of painting. The scene was almost too idyllic for Adrienne's comfort. She realized how easily she could be drawn into the languorous life of the island and exactly how much she longed to do just that.

The last few hours with Tanner seemed like magic moments, lived outside the reality of the life she had previously known. She had needed so badly to escape from the torment and uncertainty that had plagued her since leaving California. For those hours with Tanner, she had. She'd felt like her old self again, confident and wholly alive. She'd forgotten for the first time in nearly a year that her life was no longer hers to do with as she wished. How simple it would be to wander into that void wrapped in the comfort of Tanner's arms and the timelessness of life on Whitley Point.

She sighed, knowing she could not allow herself the luxury of this line of thinking much longer. She would not use Tanner in that way—taking from her with nothing to offer in return. It was folly and she knew it.

"What are you thinking?" Tanner was quietly solicitous. "You look sad."

Adrienne found Tanner's expressive eyes intently searching her face. And she did not want her to see the truth. *Oh, how I want you.* Her voice came out harsher than she meant. "Don't lose your head over this, Tanner. I'll be leaving here soon."

"What? Why?" Tanner steadied her voice with a calm she did not feel. She'd been expecting something like this. It was too much to hope that Adrienne would simply accept what had happened between them, not after she had resisted it so determinedly for weeks. *For that matter, I haven't shown her much reason to trust me.*

"You said it yourself when we first met." Adrienne looked directly at Tanner, her cool blue eyes betraying none of her anguish. "I'm hiding. I have been for the better part of a year. I can't stay here just because I feel safe by the sea and protected by the seclusion. In the end, even the beauty of this island, and you, cannot change what might happen to me. I have to get on with my life, whatever there is left of it." She saw Tanner pale and added tenderly, "I'm sorry. I don't mean to sound morbid, but I have to be realistic."

"What's so realistic about leaving one place for another just because you happen to be happy here?" Tanner couldn't temper her anger. "Is it only realistic when you feel miserable? Is there some reason that you think you don't deserve to be happy?" She didn't even try to conceal the bitterness in her tone. Adrienne had given her a glimpse of happiness, an image of peace, and she couldn't just let it disappear without a fight.

"I can't talk to you rationally about this." Adrienne gestured out the window to the placid scene below them, frustrated because she had let things go so far. It wasn't Tanner's fault and she knew it, but her anger was directed at the young woman nonetheless. "You live in your own world, literally, with its own special rules. My God, Tanner, do you even know what it means to go without anything?"

"*Yes,* I know." Tanner flinched, her face flushing. "I know what it is to be without purpose, without dreams, without one honest feeling from one day to the next. I know what it means to wake up in the morning and wonder if there's any point to it. And I know how to forget those feelings with alcohol and drugs. Do you think you hold a monopoly on unhappiness?"

"Oh, don't...I'm sorry." Adrienne reached quickly across the table and grasped Tanner's hand. "I didn't mean to attack you. It's not you I'm angry with. I want to enjoy tonight with you. You *have* made me feel wonderful, and I'm grateful."

"For God's sake, Adrienne! I don't want you to be grateful." Tanner shook with anger, but she did not release her grip on Adrienne's hand. "I just want you to accept what's happening between us for what it is. You touch me somewhere no one ever has. You take away the pain. You give me something special, and you make me want to give that back. I want to know you—I want to hold you, and laugh with you, and just *be* with you. I think it's called love." She shrugged and fell silent. It was that simple to her. She knew what she felt, and that was all that really mattered.

"I can't love you, Tanner, and I don't want you to love me," Adrienne said quietly. "I don't have anything left to love you with. I'm tired; I have nothing to offer you. I don't even have a tomorrow to count on." She slumped slightly, suddenly very weary. Too much had happened; too many memories had been awakened. And she could still feel Tanner's hands on her. When she looked at Tanner, her blue eyes were desolate. "Please don't make me hurt you, Tanner. Please."

Tanner signaled the waiter, who appeared instantly at their side.

"Yes, Ms. Whitley?"

"A bottle of your very best champagne, Daniel. And then we'll order." As he nodded and moved away, Tanner turned back to Adrienne and said calmly, "You may choose not to love me, but you can't stop me from loving you."

Adrienne closed her eyes briefly, still holding Tanner's hand. She couldn't fight with her any longer, and she couldn't walk away, no matter how much she knew she should. Not tonight, not with Tanner looking at her with what could only be love in her eyes. Tomorrow... tomorrow she would sort this out.

CHAPTER FIFTEEN

When they returned from the restaurant, Tanner got out of the car and came around to Adrienne's side. "Can I come in?"

Adrienne shook her head. "I'm sure that you don't believe this, but you actually need to sleep. And so do I."

"We'd sleep...eventually."

"That's what I'm afraid of—the eventually part." Adrienne couldn't help but smile. Tanner's grin was disarming, and the way she looked—hips leaning against the side of the Jag, arms crossed over her chest, a dangerous glint in her eye—she was walking, talking sex appeal. Saying no to her took Herculean effort, but it wasn't just sleep that Adrienne needed. She needed to step back from the maelstrom of emotion that being with Tanner had stirred. She was in danger of drowning, and drowning could sometimes be mistaken for salvation. "Go home."

"Okay, I'll call you," Tanner murmured, brushing her lips against Adrienne's cheek. "Tomorrow."

"Don't." Adrienne only managed a whisper. "Give me some time."

"How much time?"

"I don't know."

"Will you call me, then?" Tanner worked to hide her sudden anxiety.

"I don't know. Please go home, Tanner."

As Adrienne stood on the steps of her rented home, watching Tanner walk around the front of the car with her characteristic saunter, she wondered why she was letting her go. All she really wanted to do was take her inside and undress her...slowly, and lie beside her in the silvery moonlight, and explore every rise and hollow of her body. She wanted to kiss away the frown lines that had formed between her brows when she'd told her to go home. She wanted to make her cry out again when her body could no longer contain her passion. Perhaps more than anything else, she wanted to hold her while she slept.

The roar of the powerful engine leaping to life nearly propelled Adrienne back down the steps.

No. I won't be that selfish. Tanner is young, too young. Her emotions might be sincere, but she's so restless and so passionate—desperate to fill the emptiness of her life with something meaningful. And she has mistaken the respite from her terrible loneliness for love.

She'll move on from this brief encounter, as she should. She'll discover someone who can match her own vitality and relentless spirit. It can't be me. I have no joy left to offer her, and I won't take with nothing to give. I'd surely come to hate myself, even if Tanner didn't. It's madness to even consider getting involved.

So Adrienne watched Tanner hurtle away in her sleek silver sports car and took desolate comfort in the rightness of her decision.

❖

A week passed, and Adrienne soon discovered that there was sometimes very little comfort in doing the right thing. She was surprised, but reluctantly grateful, that she had not heard from Tanner since that night.

Nevertheless, when she awakened each morning, she longed to feel Tanner beside her. She ached to see the softness of her face as she slept and to watch those dark eyes blaze with passion when they touched. She wanted Tanner's warmth, and her intensity, and her desire. She tried to force the many images of Tanner from her mind, but she failed. No matter how she tried to occupy her thoughts, she could not escape her memories and cursed her own weakness even as she longed for Tanner's presence.

In desperation, she ran on the beach until she was exhausted, but still she searched the dunes for Tanner's familiar form. So, when she saw the Jag pull up in front of her house early one morning, her heart leapt. Despite her determination to forget the young woman who haunted her waking hours and restless dreams, she hurried out onto the front porch as Tanner stepped from the car.

"Hi," Tanner called, a devil-may-care grin on her face. She leaned against the fender in her familiar pose—black hair tousled, denim-clad legs crossed, a white T-shirt stretched tight across her chest. She looked every inch the dashing, dangerous creature she was.

Adrienne's stomach tightened with an unmistakable message. Hoping her voice sounded steadier than she felt, she replied, "Hi."

"I'm going sailing. Want to come?"

"Oh, yes. Let me get some things together," Adrienne replied instantly, steadfastly ignoring the warning bells clanging in her head. She quickly reentered the house before she had time to change her mind. Just the sight of Tanner was enough to make her forget all the careful rationalizations of the last week. Rushing about gathering her gear, she felt better than she had in days.

Tanner waited, her heart pounding, wondering if Adrienne had any idea how nervous she was. She didn't want to make a mistake now. She had tried to give Adrienne the time she requested, hoping each day that she would call. When the call never came, Tanner finally broke under the agony of waiting. She couldn't let Adrienne just drift away, not when she was everything Tanner had ever wanted.

She hadn't been able to think of anything except this tender, vulnerable, strong woman since the minute they'd parted. She'd slept that night, only because her body had finally given out on her. But, since then, she couldn't sleep, she couldn't eat, she couldn't even sail. Her body was on fire, she wanted Adrienne so much. She ached to touch her, and nearly lost her mind remembering how Adrienne had touched her. She had never before wanted anyone to take her like that, and now she couldn't stop wanting it. The sun rose on sleepless night after sleepless night to find her staring out the window, longing to hold Adrienne in her arms.

She'd fretted around the house so much that her mother had finally confronted her when she'd come upon her out on the verandah that morning, staring moodily at the sunrise.

"Good morning, darling." Constance sat down beside Tanner and sipped her coffee.

Tanner turned, surprised to see her mother so early, and smiled wanly. "Hello, Mother."

"Have you had coffee?"

"Not yet."

"May has some ready in the kitchen."

"I'll get some in a while."

Constance sighed. "I love having you around the house, Tanner, but this is hardly like you. If you're not sailing, then there's something very wrong." She spoke softly, and the affection in her tone was clear. "Is there something I can do? I hate to see you like this."

"Does it show that badly?" Tanner laughed ruefully.

"I'm afraid it does, sweetheart."

"Would you think me very foolish if I told you that I was in love?"

"Quite frankly, I would be delighted." Constance regarded her daughter seriously for a moment. "It appears that there is some difficulty, however?"

"Oh, man. What an understatement. Difficulty. Yeah, that's it all right—and not just one—that would be too simple." She sat forward in the chair, resting her head in her hands.

"Who is it?"

"Adrienne Pierce."

"Ah, our lovely summer visitor."

"Yes." Tanner winced, because the summer was already half over.

"Can you tell me about the problems?"

"Not exactly. Not now...it's Adrienne's...it's something personal."

"I understand." Constance hesitated, then said gently, "Tell me what you can."

"I think it's a matter of trust." Tanner was hesitant. "I have a feeling she doesn't think I can weather a storm, let alone a hurricane, if one comes up."

Constance laughed softly and reached to stroke her daughter's arm. "Well, sweetheart, she simply doesn't know you well enough yet."

"But how do you convince someone to trust you?"

"Well, you don't. I believe that trust develops slowly, as you face difficulties together and see them through. For some people, Tanner, trust is more than just a matter of faith, especially if they've been disappointed in the past. I'm afraid it often comes down to time."

"Time!" Tanner responded angrily. "Must everything take so much time? I don't even know where to begin."

"You might begin by letting her know that you aren't going to disappear simply because everything isn't easy at the moment."

Tanner jerked, her mind suddenly clear. Her mother was right—Adrienne expected her to disappear, to give up in the face of her resistance. And she'd let Adrienne's fear keep her away, not just this time, but every time. "What an idiot," she whispered to herself.

Feeling more like herself than she had in days, Tanner leaned to kiss her mother's cheek, then took the stairs down to the path to her bungalow on the run. She had no plan—only her love and the determination to prove herself.

Tanner looked up as she heard Adrienne's front door closing. "Hi," she said again, searching Adrienne's face for some hint of welcome.

Adrienne stepped down off the stairs and kissed her on the mouth, quickly but without any doubt that it was more than a friendly greeting. "Hello," she said, then turned and headed around to the passenger side of the car.

Tanner stood rooted to the spot for a second, slightly weak in the knees, and then vaulted for Adrienne's door, grinning triumphantly.

✣

"Did you miss me?" Tanner asked as she took the car smoothly around a turn.

"No." Adrienne slipped her hand onto Tanner's thigh and turned her face up to the sun. "But I missed this car."

"She's at your disposal, whenever you desire." Tanner's voice was husky, and her leg trembled beneath Adrienne's fingers.

"I'll remember that." Eyes closed, she murmured, "Watch the road."

Minutes later, Tanner swung into the parking lot at the marina. "Adrienne," she asked softly, "are you asleep?"

Adrienne opened her eyes as Tanner leaned toward her. The look in Tanner's unguarded eyes was like nothing she had ever seen—tender, almost reverent. "No," she answered around sudden tears, "just dreaming." She sat up quickly, reaching for the door handle. "Come on, let's catch some good wind."

Josh Thomas came out as they hurriedly stowed their gear, but they didn't linger to chat. Tanner assured him that they would radio if for any reason they put in at a different port later in the afternoon, and then they quickly set sail.

This time Adrienne maneuvered them deftly out of the channel. Tanner moved effortlessly around the boat, adjusting the sails and luxuriating in the pleasure of being out to sea again and, much more than that, in the pleasure of being with Adrienne. She thought that perhaps she loved Adrienne best here, on the sea, sharing the thrill and freedom of the sailboat racing over the water, seeking the serenity of some secluded cove where they could be alone.

When they were well underway and Adrienne had set a course for one of the undeveloped islands, Tanner leaned back against the bulkhead to watch Adrienne at the wheel.

Adrienne enjoyed the attention. Although a few weeks earlier such scrutiny would have made her very uncomfortable, now it didn't bother her. In fact, she felt unaccountably self-assured, at ease in her body. The spray off the bow blew onto her, drenching her cotton shirt. She wore no bra, and she knew that Tanner would notice the asymmetry of her chest beneath the wet material. She wasn't worried. Tanner, after all, had seen it before.

Instead, she basked in the pleasure of Tanner's appraising glance until she became aware of a different kind of discomfort. A look from Tanner, at least one that went on for more than a few seconds, was very much like a caress. A persistent stirring was beginning to make itself known between her thighs as she imagined Tanner's hands on her, and she glanced at Tanner sternly.

"Stop it."

"What?" Tanner slouched a little more, her arms spread along the top of the rail, her legs parted insolently, her grin infuriatingly confident.

"You know *what,"* Adrienne replied, trying desperately to hide a smile. "I'm navigating here."

"Okay, okay. I was just looking."

"No...you weren't."

Tanner merely laughed. And when they were well out from shore, she stripped off her T-shirt and tucked it into her back pocket.

Adrienne watched her fondly, envious of her utter lack of self-consciousness. Even before the surgery, she had seldom been that uninhibited physically. Tanner was completely different—her body was a totally integral part of who she was—and Adrienne found her sensuousness entirely natural, as well as heart-stoppingly erotic. And she could no longer continue to divide her attention between the wind, the waves, and Tanner's breasts.

"That's it," Adrienne announced, when Tanner stepped out of her jeans. "I'm finding a place to drop anchor."

"What took you so long?" Tanner indolently smoothed lotion over her chest. She laughed at what sounded like a snarl from Adrienne, then stretched out on a bench and closed her eyes. The sun on her bare body was wonderful, but it was nothing compared to the heat from Adrienne's eyes, watching her undress.

After Adrienne brought them into the lee side of a small, uninhabited island, she dropped anchor and stood for a moment just savoring the view. She wasn't looking at the sea. Tanner had obviously fallen asleep, because she hadn't stirred even when the boat came to a stop. She lay on her back on a padded bench seat, one knee partially raised against the rail, an arm dangling by her side. Her sleek muscular body was covered with a light sheen of perspiration, and she literally glowed in the sunlight. Even her breasts were deep amber gold. Had Adrienne not seen the slight rise and fall of her chest with each breath, she might have thought Tanner a statue cast in bronze.

With the boat secured, Adrienne stepped silently across the deck and knelt at Tanner's side. With one finger, she traced the line of her cheek, lingering on the edge of her jaw, then resting lightly on Tanner's neck. She held her breath, marveling at the strong steady pulse that seemed so close to the surface. Just looking at Tanner made everything within her grow still, her desire so thick it slowed the blood in her veins. This was not the passion of wild abandon, some momentary escape from reality; this was a hunger so profound she feared her pores would open and bleed if she didn't touch her.

She took one of Tanner's breasts into her palm, squeezing lightly as her thumb circled the dark nipple. Tanner murmured in her sleep but did not awaken. Smiling, Adrienne pressed her face against Tanner's breast, her mouth finding the nipple, drawing it in. She teased with her tongue until she felt the nipple grow hard between her lips, then moved to the other. Tanner's breath quickened at her ear. With one hand, she stroked Tanner's belly, tracing her ribs, then circling her navel, pressing hard enough to make the muscles tighten in response. When she reached the crisp moist triangle of hair nestled between Tanner's legs, she brushed lightly through it. Tanner's legs twitched, and Adrienne heard her gasp.

She's awake, and she's letting me have her. So trusting, so brave. God, what a gift.

Delving deeper, Adrienne discovered warm pools shimmering in sunlight, and breathlessly, she submerged her fingers in them. When she carried the sweet liquor to Tanner's clitoris, Tanner whimpered and lifted her hips—a wordless invitation to enter. Still Adrienne delayed, pressing, stroking, teasing, until her own head threatened to explode. At last, she moved easily into Tanner's welcoming depths, and Tanner's responsive body instantly enclosed her fingers.

But it wasn't mere entry Adrienne desired; she wanted to reach for Tanner's soul and hold it, if only for an instant. Carefully, judging her pace by Tanner's breathing, she pressed deeper, allowing the engorged tissues to relax, feeling Tanner's body slowly surrender and accept more and more of her. Once fully surrounded, Adrienne rocked slowly, choreographing her movements to the beat of the pulsing tissues around her hand. A flood of moisture accompanied by a low groan from Tanner soon rewarded her. Almost there...

"Adrienne..." The word a plaintive plea.

Adrienne lifted her face reluctantly from Tanner's breasts, nearly blind from the intensity of being inside her. Tanner's pupils were huge, glassy with need, and a high flush suffused her face and neck. Adrienne had never seen a more stunning woman.

"Are you all right?" Adrienne could barely whisper, her throat so tight her voice was foreign to her. "Am I hur—"

"Take all of me," Tanner gasped. "Do it now."

Adrienne nearly wept. Rising on her knees, she crushed her lips to Tanner's mouth, her kiss as hard as her hands were gentle. Forcing Tanner's lips apart with her tongue, she plunged into her mouth with ravenous strokes, her hand echoing tenderly inside.

The force of Adrienne's hunger and the rhythmic motion of her thrusts caught Tanner by surprise, the orgasm crashing upon her before she could draw a breath. As her body clamped down convulsively around Adrienne's hand, her hips nearly bucked off the bench, and she finally found air to scream. It was a cry of surrender and victory, a combination that only love could forge.

❖

When Tanner opened her eyes, she was alone on the deck, mysteriously covered by a huge beach towel that hadn't been there before. *Adrienne.* Smiling, she stretched. Her limbs still felt like jelly, but at least she could feel them all. She remembered gasping through the tumultuous climax, fearing that she might literally die. *Man, I would have died happy.* Then she flashed back to Adrienne's face just before Adrienne had made her come. *She'd looked at me as if I were some kind of miracle.*

Suddenly, all Tanner wanted was to find her. She stuck her head down through the hatch, but the cabin was deserted. Clambering up onto the bow to look around, she heard splashing. Adrienne was swimming.

"Hello there," Tanner called.

"It's wonderful." Adrienne waved and smiled. "Come join me!"

Tanner dove gracefully off the bow and made a smooth arc through the water to surface near Adrienne, who was effortlessly treading water. She flung her head back to clear the water from her face and reached for Adrienne.

"Hey, you. I missed you." Tanner grasped Adrienne's waist and attempted to kiss her, succeeding only in pulling them both under.

"Idiot!" Adrienne coughed and sputtered water and finally laughed. "Not out here."

"Why not?" Tanner gently pulled Adrienne against her. Treading water to keep their heads above the surface, she slipped one leg between Adrienne's and the other around her, supporting her. Adrienne fit neatly into the bend of her body, and Tanner finally managed to kiss her.

"If you don't stop doing that to me," Tanner chided when the kiss ended, "I'm going to start feeling outclassed."

"Doing what?" Adrienne feigned innocence, but her heart hammered with the memory of Tanner arching under her, calling her name.

"You know damn well what—making me come until I pass out."

Adrienne smiled, leaning her forehead against Tanner's. Her blond hair fanned out around Tanner's face, gently stroking her cheeks. "You make me want things I can't even put words to," she murmured.

"Words don't matter. I can feel it," Tanner answered. "Come up on deck with me. If I do what I want to do here, we'll both drown." She slipped her legs free and swam toward the boat, one hand clasped in Adrienne's.

Tanner spread the towel in the sun on the broad bow and pulled Adrienne down on it beside her. She kissed the salt from Adrienne's lips, then moved languorously down her neck, alternately licking and kissing the remains of the sea from her skin. Unhurriedly, Tanner kissed Adrienne's chest, her navel, her inner thighs, losing herself for long moments in the sea scents, immersing herself in Adrienne's essence.

"Remember I'm older than you," Adrienne murmured, eyes closed, drifting in the heat Tanner kindled with her tongue. "I can't take too much teasing."

"Aren't paybacks hell?" Tanner laughed against Adrienne's flushed skin. Relenting when Adrienne groaned, she rested her cheek at last in the crook of Adrienne's thigh and tasted her. Then she forgot that she had intended to go slowly. It was too good, too wildly wondrous, and following the dictates of Adrienne's body she took claim with her hands and her mouth, effortlessly, without thought—speeding up, slowing down, now harder, now softer—guided by the ebb and flow of blood and breath and muscle.

Adrienne fisted her hands in Tanner's hair, opening to her, swelling and throbbing while her blood rushed to meet Tanner's lips. As Adrienne's thighs tensed, Tanner wrapped her arms around Adrienne's hips, feeling the storm breaking. She was not disappointed as Adrienne's fingers clenched, her hips lifted, and she shouted Tanner's name.

Continuing her soothing strokes until Adrienne quieted and the tremors stopped, Tanner then crawled up to gather her lover into her arms. Sighing, she pulled Adrienne's head onto her shoulder. "God, you're wonderful."

"*You're* marvelous," Adrienne whispered when she found her breath. She snuggled close and curled her hand in Tanner's hair. "And I know you could tell."

Tanner kissed her forehead lightly and murmured, "I love you."

"I don't suppose there's any use in trying to talk some sense into you, is there?"

"None at all."

CHAPTER SIXTEEN

For a few idyllic weeks, Adrienne surrendered completely to the storybook world of Whitley Point—immersing herself in sun-drenched days on the sea and starry nights making love. She made no plans; she wanted none. She and Tanner dined out; they explored the mainland shops; they shared the memories of their pasts and their childhood dreams. She refused to think of anything beyond their precious moments together. Being with Tanner was all she knew and everything she needed. Tanner. Attentive, passionate, beautiful Tanner.

Tanner, for her part, exulted in Adrienne's happiness. She had no need of plans beyond the next moment with Adrienne. Never having tried to define her future, she was not bound by the limits of any particular vision. For her, each day of loving and being loved was a miracle and more than she had ever dared imagine. Adrienne made no promises, spoke no vows of love, and Tanner sought none. She needed no words to affirm what was obvious. When she and Adrienne made love, when they walked hand in hand on the moonlit beach, when they listened to one another's silences, Tanner found the peace she had always sought.

Then one afternoon in early August, reality walked uninvited into their lives.

Tanner stood on the bow as Adrienne brought the *Pride* smoothly into her berth. Josh Thomas waited on the dock to catch the towlines. He looked up at Tanner and said low enough that Adrienne couldn't hear, "Somebody up at the office looking for Adrienne."

"Who?" She was instantly uneasy at the concern in Josh's voice. He was obviously unhappy about something, and it was rare for him to take notice or comment upon anyone else's business.

He simply shrugged.

Tanner shaded her eyes with one hand and stared up at the marina. When she saw a man in a Navy uniform coming down the dock toward them, her stomach did a slow roll. Whoever he was, whatever he wanted, he was a part of Adrienne's life before that summer—before her—and that scared her. When she turned to Adrienne, it was plain that she had seen him, too. Her face was pale, and the hand that rested on the rail was white with strain.

"What's going on?" Tanner inquired urgently, disturbed by the stillness that had settled over Adrienne. "Who is he? Adrienne?"

Adrienne started slightly, then shook her head ruefully. "The past has finally caught up with me. You're about to meet my friend and fellow officer." She squeezed Tanner's hand firmly, aware of the worry in her voice. "Come on."

Hands clasped, they stepped off the boat and down onto the dock, waiting side by side for the clean-cut middle-aged man in the pristine white uniform to join them.

"Well, hey. Finally tracked you down." He smiled warmly as he held out his hand. "How are you, Adrienne?"

"Really fine, Tom." Adrienne returned his smile and took his hand. "What are you doing here?"

"I had some duty in Washington this week, and since I had a few days' leave coming, I thought I'd detour here before heading home."

"I see." She didn't believe him but saw no point in arguing. He'd tell her his reasons soon enough, and this wasn't the place to discuss what they needed to resolve. Not with Tanner standing uneasily by her side.

Actually, she had been anxiously anticipating some contact from the Navy. She hadn't expected Tom, but considering that they had been close friends for many years, she wasn't all that surprised. "Tom, I'd like you to meet a friend of mine—"

"Hold the introductions for a minute, Adrienne," he interrupted. "There's someone with me." He gestured with a nod back toward the office.

"Damn it, Tom," Adrienne exclaimed when she saw the woman, also dressed in Navy summer whites, approach. "What are you trying to pull?"

Tom had the grace to look embarrassed but did not lower his gaze. "It was her idea. We were both in DC for briefings, and when I told her I was coming here to see you after, she wanted to come along. There was no way I could not bring her."

By then the second officer, a stylish dark-haired woman in her mid-thirties, had reached them. Her eyes were fixed on Adrienne's face. "Hello, Adri," she said softly.

Adrienne stared for a moment into those hazel eyes she remembered so well and then turned aside coolly. She grasped Tanner's hand. "Tanner, I'd like you to meet Commander Tom Hardigan and Lieutenant Commander Alicia Ames. This is Tanner Whitley."

Tanner nodded to them both, wondering how quickly she could get Adrienne out of there. She wasn't exactly sure what was going on, but she could sense Adrienne's tension, and she wanted to talk with her in private. Another thing was certain—she wasn't leaving Adrienne alone with them, especially not with Lieutenant Commander Ames. An awkward silence ensued as Alicia continued to stare at Adrienne while Tom Hardigan stared out to sea, apparently trying to memorize the position of each sailing craft at its mooring.

Tanner was first to speak. "Excuse me, Adrienne, but we'll need to hurry if we're going to be on time for our dinner engagement."

Alicia Ames's eyebrows rose slightly as she abruptly shifted her scrutiny to Tanner.

"You're right." Adrienne quickly hid her surprise, realizing almost immediately that Tanner was offering her a polite, albeit temporary, escape. "I'd almost forgotten about it."

She forced a smile and started up the pier, Alicia and Tom following after a slight hesitation. "I'm sorry," she continued as the group climbed up to the parking lot. "I didn't expect you, and we're a little short on time right now. Where are you two staying? We should get together and talk...sometime."

"Well, actually, we haven't booked accommodations yet." Tom glanced at Alicia uncomfortably.

"Well, I suppose you could stay at my place tonight," Adrienne offered reluctantly. *After all, they are my friends.*

Tanner was secretly seething. The last thing she wanted was to have Alicia anywhere near Adrienne, let alone in Adrienne's house. She spoke up quickly.

"Actually, Commander, Lieutenant Commander—we would be happy to accommodate you at Whitley Manor. We have several guestrooms at the ready that never get enough use, and my mother and

I would be delighted to have you. I think those arrangements should be suitable?"

Adrienne looked at Tanner in amazement, almost not recognizing the cool, patrician tone in her voice. But, of course, she reminded herself, Tanner was the Whitley heir, with all that that entailed. She had indeed been raised to assume that position although it rarely showed in her manner. Even Tom and Alicia seemed to recognize that there was no way they could politely refuse Tanner's offer.

"That's a very generous offer, Ms. Whitley." Tom looked at Alicia, who smiled somewhat thinly.

"Thank you. Commander Hardigan and I are grateful for your thoughtfulness. We can follow in our car." Alicia addressed the remarks to Tanner, but she was looking only at Adrienne, a question in her eyes. *Who is this young woman? And what is she to you?*

"Fine." Tanner did not miss the touch of sarcasm in Alicia's voice, nor the way the pretty officer regarded Adrienne, but she held her temper for civility's sake. Taking Adrienne's arm, she urged her toward their car. What she wanted to do was point the Jag south and keep going until they had left everything, and everyone, behind. But Adrienne couldn't run from the past, or the future, any longer—and so neither would she.

Alicia's eyes followed the two women as she and Tom walked toward their black rental car. "She looks well, doesn't she?"

"Better than I've seen her look in a long time," Tom concurred. "This place seems to agree with her."

"I can certainly see why." Alicia had to admit that Adrienne had obviously come to some sort of terms with her life. She looked marvelously fit, and there was no mistaking the look in that handsome young woman's eye. If this was what it took to bring Adrienne out of the despondency that had threatened to stifle her for the last year, she was glad. Despite everything that had happened, she couldn't erase the memory of the good things she and Adrienne had once shared. She hoped that Adrienne hadn't forgotten either.

Settling back in the passenger seat of the car, she contemplated her next move. Adrienne and Tanner Whitley, ahead of them in the convertible, looked for all the world like a happy couple, but she was certain that Adrienne could be made to see reason. Levelheadedness had always been Adrienne's mainstay, and surely she could see that her future was back in San Diego.

CHAPTER SEVENTEEN

What the hell is this all about?" Tanner gunned out of the marina parking lot with Alicia and Tom trailing in their rental car. Her voice quivered with anger despite her best efforts to stay calm. Her hands on the wheel were clenched tightly, the tendons taut beneath her tanned skin. "What do they *want?"*

"Obvious, isn't it?" Adrienne sighed, rubbing her eyes briefly, trying to dispel the tension. "They're here to take me back, I would imagine."

"That's ridiculous! You're not some escapee—you didn't go AWOL or anything. Tell them to go the fuck away."

"Tanner, slow down. We're going to end up in a ditch." Adrienne grasped Tanner's hand, alarmed by her anger. *God, why didn't I see this coming? And now, Tanner is involved too—just what I had wanted to avoid. Back when I still had some sense left.*

"Don't listen to them," Tanner said through gritted teeth. *We've been so happy. Don't allow them to make you forget that.*

"These are my friends, two of the most important people in my life." Adrienne moved closer on the seat, placing her hand lightly on Tanner's thigh. "I understand how you feel. I'm angry, too. They should have called, let me know they were coming. But I can't just send them away."

Tanner slumped slightly behind the wheel. "I know...I'm just frightened."

"Of what?" Adrienne asked gently.

"You said it. They've come to take you away. I'm afraid you might go."

"Oh, Tanner..." It broke her heart to hear the anguish in Tanner's voice and to know that she was the cause of it. "You've always known I would leave. Don't make it any more difficult."

"No," Tanner said fiercely. "I haven't always *known* that you would leave. You said yourself that you were undecided about the Navy. For some strange reason, I thought what has happened between us would make you change your mind."

"I can't stay here indefinitely."

"Why not, Adrienne? What about us? What about what we have?" She turned to Adrienne, her eyes wounded. "Do you want to leave just because you have something to stay for now?"

"This isn't the time for this, Tanner." Adrienne bit her lip, because Tanner was right. The truth was she was more afraid to stay than she was to leave. If she stayed, she would have to make decisions, about Tanner, about the Navy, and about the future. Future—a word that still terrified her. She'd have to make choices, choices she was afraid to make. *Do I even have a future?* Suddenly, she felt that what she was doing was somehow wrong. She had let Tanner ease her loneliness. *No, I've let her heal me. I've let her give me her strength and her joy, and now I don't know how I'll survive without them. Without her.*

"This has to be the right time," Tanner persisted, pulling through the gates of Whitley Manor. "They're here now. We're out of time."

"Please, can we at least talk later, when things have settled down a little?" *I need more time with you, a few more moments to live on, before I can let you go.*

Tanner heard the plea in her voice. Heart aching, she answered quietly, "Yes, later."

❖

Tanner made introductions all around, and Constance Whitley welcomed the unexpected visitors graciously. She directed May to take Tom and Alicia upstairs to the guestrooms, then smiled at Adrienne. "You're staying, of course, Adrienne?"

"Yes, thank you."

"Wonderful." Turning to Tanner, Constance asked, "Could you mix us a pitcher of martinis? And I think I'd like them strong—your father's recipe."

"I'll be right back," Tanner murmured to Adrienne, brushing gentle fingers over her hand as she passed. She almost couldn't bear the separation.

Constance watched Adrienne's gaze follow her daughter from the room, and the expression on her face warmed Constance's heart. "I'm pleased that your friends are staying here. It will give you a chance to talk with them...on neutral territory."

Adrienne, taken off guard by Constance's insight, laughed and felt her burden ease slightly. "We might need a referee. How did you know?"

"I can usually forecast the weather in my daughter's eyes, and right now there's a storm brewing. In addition to which, I don't imagine two Navy officers travel all the way across the country for a simple chat."

"No," Adrienne admitted with a sigh. "It's anything but simple."

"Come," Constance said gently, grasping Adrienne's arm. "Let's talk out on the verandah."

They walked to the far side of the wide porch. Below them, the top of Tanner's bungalow was just visible in a stand of windswept trees near the shore. Standing side by side, they silently watched the sky turn a brilliant red as the sun inched toward the water's edge. Finally, Constance asked quietly, "Is there anything I can do?"

"You must understand, Ms. Whitley—"

"Constance, please."

"Constance...Tom and Alicia have come here because they care about me." Adrienne studied her face, so like Tanner's, wondering where to begin, and wondering how much she already knew. "There is no mystery, really. I've been on extended medical leave for some time, considering my options. And they hope to convince me to return to San Diego...and the Navy. It is a decision I have been avoiding all summer and, honestly, before that really. Under other circumstances, I would be delighted to see them."

"Do you want to return to the Navy?" Constance asked quietly, without the slightest hint of criticism.

"I miss it." Adrienne sighed. "This summer has been wonderful, but I can't continue to live this way. I must make some plans. I must work, now that I know I can. The military is a life I'm used to and I have obligations to fulfill. It's just that there are some...difficulties... which I need to resolve."

"Tanner has been happier these past weeks than she's been in years. She and her dog don't seem to be residing on the dunes much these days. You've been very good for her."

Adrienne stared at Constance, at a loss for words.

"Forgive me if I'm acting like a mother," Constance continued quickly. "Tanner doesn't discuss the details of her private life with me, but she is very much like her father, and I could read his moods rather well. He was a wild sort of man—quick to anger, unsettled in many ways—but he was a man of passion, and he loved deeply. It was a kind of love one could depend on. I have always known that Tanner would someday find someone to love, and when she did, it would be as he did—intensely, instinctively, and with honor. I hope that you consider Tanner in your decision."

"Constance," Adrienne began, moved by Constance's compassion, "there are some things you may not realize. Tanner is young; she has a lifetime ahead of her. She deserves a future as bright as her spirit, and I...I don't think that future is with me." Adrienne's voice faltered, and she had to look away, her own words tearing at her soul. *God, how it hurts to say it, even when I know it's true.*

"There are not many things on Whitley Point I don't know, Adrienne," Constance said softly, placing her hand gently on Adrienne's arm. "I hope you'll forgive him, but Admiral Evans has been a dear friend of mine for many years. He spoke to me, in confidence of course, but I am aware of your difficulties."

Adrienne grimaced bitterly. "Then you must know how little I have to offer Tanner."

"Time is an elusive element. Sometimes an hour with someone you love very deeply feels like a lifetime." Constance spoke softly, lost in memory. "It seems to me now, looking back, that I loved Charles for an eternity. Measured in years, it was not long, but the emotions we shared sustain me still. I would not change the choices I made in my life because things turned out differently than I had hoped. I believe that in that way, at least, Tanner is like me."

"Yes," Adrienne agreed, thinking of the past weeks, and her time with Tanner. Moments at once eternal and tragically fleeting. A shadow in the corner of her eye caught her attention, and she turned to see Tanner leaning in the doorway, watching them. *The pain is back in her eyes again. Because of me.*

"You two look very serious," Tanner said, crossing the wide porch toward them. She'd heard the last of her mother's quiet words. For the first time, Tanner realized what the last ten years had been like for her, and she was embarrassed that she had never given her mother's loss, or pain, much thought. As she contemplated the agony of losing Adrienne, she could imagine her mother's anguish so much more vividly now.

Tanner drew close to Adrienne and took her hand. "Hey," she said softly.

"Hey," Adrienne replied, wanting nothing more in that moment than to take her away and kiss the sadness from her eyes.

"Have you made the drinks, love?" Constance asked, her face alight with the pleasure she always drew from her daughter's presence.

"All done." Tanner met her mother's clear brown eyes, her throat tight with long-ago tears. "I hope I've succeeded in repeating the secret Whitley recipe."

"You are your father's daughter, Tanner." Laughing, she slipped her arm around her daughter's waist. "Some things are inborn. Let's test the theory, shall we?"

❖

Seated on her mother's left, across the table from Adrienne at dinner, Tanner watched Adrienne and Alicia talking together. Both Tom Hardigan and Alicia had changed into civilian clothes. Tom was a trim, athletically attractive man who would have fit well in a corporate boardroom, while Alicia appeared softer and almost seductive in her silk blouse and slacks. Tom Hardigan quickly engaged her mother in conversation, questioning her on the island's development and the Whitley family history, and Alicia responded to Adrienne's queries about friends and colleagues in California.

Tanner wondered how much remained of the life, and the love, Adrienne and Alicia had shared together. They were obviously still close, and the connection bothered her. She'd never cared enough about a woman before to be jealous, but she felt it now, and most of it stemmed from fear—fear that she could not give Adrienne what she needed, fear that Adrienne would leave her, fear that what she had to offer was not as strong as the pull of the life Adrienne had known. By the time the meal was ended and Constance and Tom retired to the verandah, leaving Adrienne, Alicia, and her alone at the table, Tanner was ready to snap.

"I can certainly see why you've grown so fond of this place, Adrienne." Alicia leaned back in her chair, indicating with her hand the sweeping panorama beyond the wall of windows in the dining room that overlooked the ocean. Her gaze, however, was fixed on Tanner. "The island—like its inhabitants—is very beautiful."

"Yes," Adrienne said softly, looking from Alicia to Tanner. "Quite extraordinarily beautiful."

"Adrienne, I'd love for you to show me the beach. You know how much I enjoy watching the sunset with you." Noting the flush that stole over Tanner's cheeks, she added with a thin smile, "Would you mind very much if I took Adrienne away, Tanner?"

"Not if Adrienne doesn't object." Tanner stood up slowly, her eyes coldly meeting Alicia's hazel ones. Her voice, when she spoke, carried a threat of warning. "But just for a while."

Adrienne and Alicia were silent as they threaded their way across the dunes toward the beach. When they reached the water's edge, they stood watching the waves break, their bodies buffeted by the wind.

"I'm glad to see you and see you're doing so well," Alicia said softly, slipping her arm through Adrienne's. "I've missed you these last months."

"I've missed you, too." Adrienne stared straight ahead, watching the sun turn to blood and disappear into the sea. "Don't antagonize Tanner, Alicia. She's not to blame for any of this."

"She doesn't look like she needs your protection," Alicia observed. "She's got that 'angry young man' look about her. But I imagine you've tried to tame that."

"No," Adrienne said almost to herself. "I would never want to."

"You know why I've come, don't you?"

"You're both rather obvious," Adrienne responded, beginning to walk, Alicia still clasping her arm.

"Oh, we both want you to come back, of course. But, it's more than that. I want you to come home."

"Come home?" Adrienne stopped abruptly, finally facing her. "To you?"

"Yes, Adri." Alicia smiled wistfully. "I want you to come home—with me, to me." She hurried on before Adrienne could protest. "Oh, I know I've acted badly. I didn't know how to cope, so I made a mess of things. I've done a lot of thinking in your absence. I think I can do better now. I'd like you to give me another chance."

"Alicia, nothing has changed," Adrienne said gently to the woman she had loved. "I'm still the same. I haven't miraculously been made whole again."

"But *I've* changed." Alicia stepped close to Adrienne, her hands gripping Adrienne's arms. "I still love you. I always have. I want us to be together again. I *know* we were good together. I haven't sold the house—you could come back. We still have our plans."

"Those things may never happen now," Adrienne said harshly, knowing it was time to say what had never been said between them. "I may not be able to do all the things we once planned. I may not have the time."

Alicia shook her head stubbornly. "But we have memories, Adrienne. We have a past together. History together. Don't turn your back on that. No matter what happens, you would be with someone who knows you and who cares about you."

"Memories," Adrienne said softly. "Oh, yes, we have memories. Don't think I've forgotten, Alicia. I haven't. I never could. But I'm not sure I want to spend the rest of my life, however long that may be, hiding in safe memories."

"Don't you love me anymore?" Alicia tilted her head up, her lips close to Adrienne's.

"Love you?" she whispered, her voice breaking. They had loved together, grown together, struggled together, and finally come to a harsh parting. "Of course I love you. How could I not love you? I know you like I know my own skin—there's a part of my heart that will always belong to you."

"But you don't love me in quite the same way any longer, do you?" Alicia stepped back and studied Adrienne's face intently.

Adrienne was silent for a moment. "No," she said at last. "I don't."

The finality in Adrienne's voice shook Alicia, but she knew if she relented now it truly would be over. "Do you love this girl so much it can erase everything we've been to each other? Everything we've shared?"

"No one could ever make me forget," Adrienne said, meaning it. "But I love her. I do love her. I'm sorry if that hurts you, Alicia, but it's the truth. She makes me feel things I didn't think were possible any longer. I can see forever in her eyes." She realized as she said it that it was all true. It was the first time she had admitted those feelings to herself.

"That's not very fair to her, is it?" Alicia persisted harshly. "You know as well as I do how tenuous forever might be. Especially for you."

Adrienne recoiled, stung by the words that she couldn't deny. She looked out into a night sky so black even the stars were obscured. Her heart ached for some respite. "I know it's selfish of me to want her. I *know.* But she makes it so easy to love her. When we're together, tomorrow doesn't seem so very important."

"Not to you, perhaps. But what about her? She'll get over you if you leave now, but the longer you stay the harder it will be if..." Alicia stopped, unable to say it. She finished quietly, "What will happen to her then?"

"I don't know." Adrienne's voice was hollow. "I haven't wanted to think about it."

"Let her go, Adri...for her sake. I can accept that you feel differently about me now. I don't care. I am so lonely without you. I can live without the passion, but I can't live without you in my life. We could be happy together, even without the physical things. We have friendship; that hasn't changed. Come home where you're safe, at least. Let Tanner get on with her life."

Adrienne clenched her hands, her fingers ice cold while the night rolled in off the ocean. *Leave Tanner? How can I leave Tanner, when she's the only thing that means anything to me? But how can I ask her to risk her future on me, when I might not even be able to share it with her? Alicia cares for me, and she's prepared for what might happen.*

"Just think about it, Adri. Think about her, if not me."

"Perhaps you're right. I don't know; I can't decide now. Give me time."

"Of course, love. I'll wait." Alicia smiled in relief and took Adrienne's hand. It was a beginning.

❖

Tanner lay awake in the hot, heavy darkness, the pain in her chest growing larger with each breath. When she finally heard steps on the stone path to her bungalow, she closed her eyes, waiting. *Let it be her.*

Adrienne entered softly, then closed the door carefully behind her, snapped the lock, and crossed the room to the bed where Tanner lay naked in the humid August night, outlined in moonlight, more beautiful than any painting. She looked down at her, wanting to commit each detail to memory. Undressing quickly, she lay down beside her, pressing close. Slipping an arm around Tanner's waist, she nestled her face in Tanner's hair and kissed the base of her neck. Tenderly, she cradled one breast in her hand.

"Are you all right?" Tanner whispered.

"I am right this minute."

"Then stay here. Always."

"Shh. Just let me hold you tonight."

Tanner remained motionless, feeling Adrienne's tears fall on her own cheeks. Helplessly, she willed peace for her with all the strength of her love. Long after Adrienne's tears had stopped, Tanner lay awake, wondering for which of them Adrienne had cried.

When Tanner awoke, Adrienne was gone. She ached where Adrienne's hands had lain, missing the touch of her, excruciatingly aware of how empty her days would be without Adrienne beside her. She had always known what she risked in loving Adrienne. It had never mattered. She didn't want a guarantee; she wanted Adrienne—now, today, tomorrow, and for all the tomorrows they might share.

She rose and threw on her clothes, ran out into the bright sunlight, and hurried south. Over each crest of windswept sand, she searched the shore for Adrienne's familiar figure. She scrambled up the path to Adrienne's house and knocked hard enough to shake the door in its frame.

The house was empty, and when she walked around to the drive, she saw that Adrienne's car was gone. She considered going to look for her but knew it was pointless. She'd said all she could, tried everything she knew. Adrienne had chosen to fight her demons alone.

CHAPTER EIGHTEEN

Adrienne sailed out to the quiet cove where she and Tanner had spent so many afternoons swimming, talking, making love. She dropped anchor, climbed up onto the bow, and, arms wrapped around her bent knees, watched the clouds stream across blue skies so perfect it was painful. She followed the waves as they dwindled into soft tongues of froth along the shoals, her thoughts of nothing but Tanner.

Every now and then she smiled at some memory. She missed her, especially here on the ocean, where Tanner was in her element. Indelible images of her—moving about shirtless, diving into the cool clear waters, climbing out with a shake of her wild hair, her smile brilliant enough to eclipse the sun. They'd often sat for hours, Adrienne content just to hold her hand, doing nothing more than listening to her breathe. Tanner had been her joy.

The months since she had first arrived on Whitley Point had been magical, more than she had ever hoped to have again, and in many ways more than she had ever known before. Tanner's love had come at a time when she had forgotten how to dream, and for those brief weeks together, she had been blessed. She was, indeed, a lucky woman. Finally she turned the craft toward home; her decision was made.

When she drove up the familiar lane toward the house she now considered home, she knew Tanner would be waiting. She climbed slowly up the outside steps to the deck, rehearsing what she would say. She found Tanner sitting in a lounge chair in the sun, her head back, one arm curled over her face to shade her eyes.

"How long have you been here?" Adrienne brushed the tousled hair back from Tanner's forehead, her fingers lingering for a moment. Tanner's face was pale, and her hands trembled where they lay on the arms of the chair. "Tanner?"

"All day," Tanner said quietly. She stood up, and they moved to the railing, facing the ocean, standing close together as they so often had. Only this time, they did not touch. "You're going to leave, aren't you?"

"Yes," Adrienne responded softly.

"Why?" Her voice broke on the question. She hadn't meant it to.

"I want to go home, Tanner. I want to go back to Alicia, to the life I knew." Adrienne didn't look at her, choosing her words carefully. She wanted to leave no room for argument. She knew she had to convince Tanner beyond any doubt, and she knew only one way. "That's where I belong; it's where I've always belonged. This summer has been like a fantasy—a wonderful fantasy—but it's ended for me. It's over."

"Do you love Alicia?" Tanner swallowed, suddenly dizzy, and gripped the rail hard to steady herself. Her arms shook, and she was afraid her legs wouldn't hold her.

"Yes. I...love her." She said the words she had planned to say, closing her heart to the anguish in Tanner's face.

"And me?"

Adrienne could not answer while she looked into Tanner's wounded eyes. Lowering her head, she stared at her hands on the rail, holding it so tightly her nails dug into the wood. "I care for you, Tanner, you know that. But, it's not love—it's passion, perhaps, but it's not the kind of love I need to live on. I'm sorry."

"I see." Tanner shuddered as if she had been struck. She had been so wrong. All this time. She forced out the next words slowly to keep from screaming. "Will you call me before you go?"

"It would be best if we said goodbye now," Adrienne answered, her voice low. Tanner closed her eyes, swaying slightly, and Adrienne very nearly relented at that moment. She wanted so badly to hold her and to heal the hurt she had created. "You should go home now, Tanner."

"No. You can't mean this," Tanner gasped. It was too much. She grasped Adrienne's arms, tears streaming unheeded down her face. "Adrienne, please. I'm begging you...please. I need you. Don't do this to me."

I have to stop this! Adrienne stepped back firmly, breaking Tanner's hold on her. "Go home, Tanner. Please, it's over. Just let it go."

Tanner stared at her for a moment, barely able to breathe, and then she took the stairs two at time down to the beach. In a moment, she was gone. Adrienne slumped against the rail, exhausted. She had done it. And now she must leave—quickly. It would kill her to see Tanner again.

❖

From the balcony, Constance saw Tanner running hard up the beach and then heard the door of her bungalow slam. A few moments later, the Jag careened down the drive and roared off into the night. Saddened that Tanner was once more alone with her pain, she despaired that she could not comfort her.

When she ventured out on to the verandah a few minutes later, she found Tom Hardigan there, elbows on the rail, a faraway look on his face.

"Am I disturbing you?" Constance asked quietly.

"No, of course not." He shook his head, smiling ruefully. "I was just thinking...or trying to."

"I have a feeling Adrienne will be going back to California with you and Alicia." Constance moved to stand beside him, comfortable in his presence, which might have surprised her if she hadn't been distracted by thoughts of Tanner.

Tom inclined his head in agreement. "I used to think that was the best thing for her. Before I came here, at least. Now, I'm not so sure."

"How so?"

Tom's eyes met hers. "The Whitleys are very charming—both mother and daughter."

"Thank you, Commander Hardigan." Constance smiled faintly, but her voice was edged with anger. Her worry over Tanner prevented her from exercising her usual emotional restraint. "But in this situation, charm hardly seems enough. Tanner is involved, and she's suffering."

"Forgive me," he replied seriously. "I've known Adrienne a long time—well before she and Alicia met. We've been friends since our time together at CECOS. We've seen each other through a lot. This year has been incredibly difficult for her, as I'm sure you know, but I've never seen her quite like this. She looks better right now—stronger, healthier, more *alive*—than anyone could have foreseen several months ago. And I apologize if I seem presumptuous, Mrs. Whitley, but I do not believe it is just the salt air that has brought about this transformation.

Leaving here may be much harder than she imagines."

"You're right, of course. Things have been very difficult for Adrienne, too." Constance sighed. "I respect her for her concern about my daughter's future, but I'm afraid her perspective is slightly off balance. Tanner will most definitely *not* be better off without her."

Tom frowned. "I'm not sure Adrienne is going to do well, either. I'd hate to see her lose her desire for life again. At least Tanner is young—she'll get over it, I imagine."

"No, Commander, you're wrong. Tanner will survive, but she will not get over it. That is *not* the way the Whitleys love." She said the last words with finality.

Tom Hardigan studied the elegant woman beside him, marveling at her serenity and deep understanding. "Does she take after you?"

"Only in appearance." Constance laughed. "She is her father, through and through."

"He must have been quite a man," Tom said, meaning it.

"Oh, he was that." Constance looked at Tom thoughtfully, sensing an unspoken question. "My husband has been dead ten years, Commander Hardigan. In that time, I have never thought of another man. There have been a few who were...interested. A part of my heart, my life, my dreams will always belong to him, though. Most men find that intolerable, and I am not good at deceit."

He nodded, his eyes never leaving her face. "But, if a man, knowing this to be true, were to desire your affection...in a serious way...you might consider it?"

Constance laughed. "I might consider it, Commander."

"Well, I am very glad to hear that."

"Will you do me a favor, Tom?" she asked softly.

"Of course."

"If Adrienne is not happy...if, in fact, she is wrong in this decision, will you at least try to talk to her—for Tanner's sake, and mine?"

"If it comes to that, I may be able to do more than just talk to her."

❖

It was dark by the time Tanner reached the mainland. She drove north on the coast road to one of the bars where she was not likely to meet anyone from the island. It was not crowded, and she was relieved.

She wasn't looking for company; she just wanted to forget.

She took a seat at the bar and ordered a scotch, which she swallowed down quickly, then signaled for another with a practiced motion of her hand. The bartender refilled her glass and moved away. A few couples sat in the shadows at small scarred tables, talking in low voices and slowly sipping drinks. Someone played sad '50s ballads on the jukebox, and a woman in a cutoff sweatshirt and jeans danced with a much younger woman, the two of them barely moving in the middle of the room. They looked lonely, even in one another's arms.

Tanner stared at her reflection in the long mirror behind the row of bottles opposite her. She recognized the face as her own, but it resembled a mask, strained and brittle. About to shatter. She felt that way, too—on the verge of disintegrating. Her thoughts were all of Adrienne, and all of them hurt. The dawn without Adrienne on the beach, the sea without Adrienne on the *Pride,* the night without Adrienne in her arms. She couldn't make sense of it, despite how hard she tried. She replayed Adrienne's parting words, but she couldn't understand them either. *Not love me? How can that be? How could she have touched me the way she did and not love me? I couldn't have been that wrong. I just couldn't.*

She sighed and drained the glass again, then lifted it in the general direction of the bartender. "It doesn't matter what I think if she doesn't want me. And she doesn't," she muttered under her breath.

"Talking to yourself now, baby?" asked a woman beside her.

"Yeah." Tanner turned and appraised the vaguely familiar face. "Seems like it."

"Haven't seen you around much lately. Someone must be keeping you pretty busy."

Tanner didn't answer, intent on her drink.

"You don't remember me, do you, baby?"

"No. Should I?"

"We had fun a while back—not as much fun as I wanted, but maybe we can make up for that tonight." She pushed her leg against Tanner's thigh and her breast into Tanner's arm. Lips close to Tanner's ear, she whispered, "You're a great kisser, and I didn't get enough of those lips last time."

"Not tonight," Tanner said gruffly, concentrating on the glass she turned between her hands on the bar top.

"You alone, sugar?"

"Yes," Tanner answered hollowly.

"Then what's the problem?" She curled her hand around Tanner's forearm, stroking lightly with one fingertip. "So am I. And I already know what you like. Why don't we find a place to get reacquainted? So's I can remind you."

Tanner stared at the intruding hand, wondering why she couldn't feel the caresses on her skin. "No, thanks. I'm not looking for anything tonight."

"You've got to be kidding. You were about to come out of your skin last time, and I bet you're in bad need tonight. Now, don't be shy... I'll take care of what's hurting you."

"No, sorry, you can't." Tanner left a twenty-dollar bill on the bar and got up to leave. "Nothing is going to make me feel better."

She didn't rush on the way home; she drove slowly and carefully. There was nowhere to go in a hurry. When she finally reached Whitley Manor, it was well after midnight, and the entire house was dark. She went through the front door and climbed slowly to the second floor. Her legs felt like stone, and she wasn't certain she could make it.

At the familiar room at the end of the hall, she pushed open the door and entered quietly. She hesitated, wondering why exactly she had come as she stared at the sleeping woman. "Mother?" She spoke softly, almost afraid to intrude on the stillness.

Her mother stirred slightly.

Tanner averted her gaze from the naked profile exposed to her. "I'm sorry," she whispered, turning to go.

"Tanner?" Constance called softly. "What is it?"

"May I talk to you?"

"Of course, my sweet." Constance reached for her robe and covered herself quickly. As Tanner approached, she arose from her solitary bed and reached out in the darkness for her daughter's hand. "It's too warm in here. Come outside."

Once outside on the moonlit deck, Constance asked gently, "What is it, love?"

Tanner leaned against a column, steadying herself. "I'm so frightened." She worked to keep her voice even.

"Tell me why." Constance slipped an arm around her daughter's firm waist, pulling her close.

"It's Adrienne," Tanner continued, struggling with tears. "She's going to leave." Her voice broke suddenly, and she swallowed a sob. "I don't know what to do. It hurts...so much."

"I'm so sorry, Tanner," Constance whispered softly, wishing there were some way she could shield her from the pain. Instead, she said the very thing that she knew would hurt her daughter even more, because she believed it needed to be said. "Perhaps she needs to go. Perhaps it's best."

"No," Tanner protested wildly, her fists clenched at her sides, her entire body rigid. "It isn't. It can't be."

"Tanner..." Constance began slowly, wanting to spare her feelings but knowing she needed the truth. "Adrienne apparently needs to return to the familiar, to a world she trusts. To stay here, she would have to give up everything else, including her career. Not everyone is brave enough to begin something new in the face of uncertainty. You may have to let her go, if you love her."

"No...I won't believe that. I can't." Tanner shook her head violently, tears finally escaping her control. "Adrienne is *alive,* and she loves me. She says she doesn't, but I don't...I can't believe it."

"Tanner, love doesn't solve all problems." Constance sighed, seeing so much of her husband's stubbornness in her daughter. "No matter how pure, sometimes passion doesn't answer all of a person's needs."

"Adrienne needs me and I love her," Tanner insisted. "I have enough faith for both of us. If only she would trust me, I know it would be all right."

"I think Adrienne is concerned for you, sweetheart. She doesn't want to disappoint you."

"Disappoint me?" Tanner pulled away angrily, unable to bear the words. "Why? Because she can't offer me what I don't want anyway? I'm not asking for promises—none of us can really keep them. I want her *now,* today. I can't offer her any more than that, and I don't ask for any more in return." She turned away, her chest heaving with the effort it took not to break completely. "Why can't she see that? I do understand—I don't care about tomorrow—I care about today!"

"Tanner," Constance said, stroking her daughter's shoulder, trying to calm her, "when I first met your father, I was engaged to another man. That man was kind and gentle and considerate. I thought marriage to him would be warm and comfortable. Then I met Charles. He was wild and impetuous and filled with passion for life, and for me. That nearly frightened me away. I was afraid of not being able to love him enough. You are very much like him, Tanner. And I think Adrienne is afraid of what might happen to you if she is unable to return the intensity of your love in kind."

"But she already has returned it," Tanner said quietly. "In more ways than I could ask." She was silent for a while, thinking of how her mother must have felt when her father died. She forced herself to consider Adrienne's death. *Could* she bear it? "How did Father finally convince you to trust him?"

Constance laughed softly, her face alight in the glow of the moon. "He was never a patient man, Tanner. What he wanted, he went after, and he usually got. He was also the most sensitive man I've ever known. When I was with him, I felt so alive. He made me want to explore the world, conquer all my fears. In the end, he didn't have to do anything. He waited, he loved me, and he allowed me to make up my own mind. I chose him because any other sort of life seemed too dull to contemplate."

"Were you still afraid?"

"Yes, but I was more afraid not to love him."

"What if Adrienne refuses to see that what we have is real and right?"

"I don't know." Constance sighed. "Tanner, do you love this woman, truly love her, knowing that she might not live to share your life with you?"

"With every beat of my heart."

"Then, my sweet one, I'm afraid you must wait."

The rental car was gone from the driveway the next morning.

Tanner burst through the French doors to the dining room where her mother was sitting with her coffee. "Where are they?" she demanded breathlessly.

"They left just after dawn."

With a gasp, Tanner lunged for the door.

"Wait!"

Tanner didn't reply. She was already running down the path to the beach.

Adrienne's house appeared like so many others when they were closed for the season. The shutters were locked, the few pieces of deck furniture stored away. Tanner dashed up the rear stairs to the deck and rattled the bedroom door.

"Adrienne? Adrienne! It's Tanner. Open the damn door!" When she got no reply, she raced around to the front. Despite the fact that Adrienne's car was gone, Tanner was sure she must still be there. She took the front stairs two at a time, ready to break the door in if needed. It was then that she saw the envelope taped to the door, the initials *THW* scrawled on the front in a bold hand.

Tanner stared at it for a long time, not wanting to touch it. If she didn't open it, didn't read it, perhaps it wouldn't be true. Maybe Adrienne had just gone for a walk on the beach or out for a sail. She always went sailing when she needed to think.

Finally, when her heart stopped beating as if it would break loose and fly from her chest, she took the envelope in a trembling hand and sat down on the front stairs. She held it while the sun revolved into afternoon, until she couldn't feel her heart breaking—until she knew that Adrienne was not coming back. At length, she took a deep breath and slid out the single sheet of paper.

"My darling Tanner,

Forgive me for being a coward and saying goodbye like this, but I knew if I phoned you, you would ask me to stay. Anything I said to you in explanation would only hurt you more. Accept that I don't have the courage to remain here with you, as much as a part of me longs to. I want you to know that had we met under different circumstances, nothing could have forced me to leave you. I hope you'll try to forgive a soul less brave than yours. You have brought me great joy, and I wish you all the happiness you deserve.

Adrienne."

CHAPTER NINETEEN

Tom Hardigan drove down the now-familiar coast road to Whitley Point with a light heart. From San Diego, he had been courting Constance Whitley at a slow gentlemanly pace for over six months and managed to visit Whitley Manor once or twice a month on long weekends. He and Constance spent time exploring the nearby coastal towns, visiting maritime museums, and discovering small out-of-the-way antique shops. It was pleasant time they both enjoyed.

Their evenings spent at Whitley Manor were filled with quiet dinners, moonlight walks, and conversation. Their nights were decorous—Tom slept in the guestroom in a different wing from Constance's bedroom. He did not mind. He enjoyed Constance's company more than any person he could remember, and he wouldn't conceive of offending her in any way.

She had been honest with him, and he knew if she were to love him, it would grow out of their friendship. He found her lovely, and he desired her, but most of all, he wanted her to remain in his life, in whatever way she chose.

He turned onto the back-bay road once he reached the island and drove north. Briefly, he considered turning off at the marina but decided against it. He knew that Tanner avoided his company. She seemed to stay away from the house purposefully while he was there, and he doubted that she would welcome an impromptu visit from him.

Thinking of that, his lighthearted mood was momentarily deflated. They had never discussed it, but he thought that Tanner somehow held him responsible for Adrienne leaving. It wasn't true, but there was no way he could convince her of that. Not that he would try. She was much too bitter for him to even broach the subject. He felt for her, but the thought of seeing Constance made it impossible for him to be gloomy for long.

As he turned into the drive, his spirits soared. He carried his travel bag up the broad stairs and rang the bell.

May answered and smiled a greeting. "Mrs. Whitley is in the garden, sir. You know the way?"

"Of course. Thank you." He walked through the house and down the rear steps to the garden, where he found Constance uncovering a cluster of early-blooming crocuses. "Hi," he said, bending to kiss her cheek. "Bit cold still for gardening, isn't it?"

She turned quickly, her face alight with pleasure. "Hello." She returned his kiss, her own placed quickly but firmly on his lips. "Yes, I'm rushing things, but I am always so happy to see spring arrive, I couldn't help it. Did you have a good drive from the airport?"

"Wonderful, as usual. How have you been?"

"Nothing changes here, Tom, you know that." She shrugged, her voice surprisingly melancholic. "I attend the local social functions—the benefits, the charities—and I entertain at the appropriate times. Sometimes, it seems rather silly for me to continue to play the society matron when those times have passed. If Charles were still here, as head of the Whitley family—the true Whitleys, you understand—it might be different."

"I'm sure," he agreed. It always surprised him that he didn't mind more when Constance spoke of her late husband. Sometimes he felt as though he and Charles had been friends in another lifetime. "Are you getting just a little bored?"

"Perhaps," she answered honestly. "You know, Tom, Tanner loves this island, this place, much more than I ever did. Like with Charles, it seems to be in the Whitley blood. I have often thought of simply moving back to the mainland—Washington, perhaps—and leaving this place to Tanner." She pulled off her gardening gloves and slapped them absently against her thigh. "I have some distant relatives there, and Tanner is much more the heir to this island than I. I've always believed she has what it takes to guide the corporation the way Charles would have wanted it."

Tom followed her up to the house, listening intently. "Why haven't you tried it then—at least on a trial basis—say six months out of the year or something like that?" He went directly to the bar and busied himself mixing drinks as he talked. "God knows, the winters here are beyond brutal."

"I don't suppose you have any ulterior motives for prompting me, do you, Commander Hardigan?" Constance looked at him with a rare grin on her usually tranquil face.

"Well, I am in Washington for meetings and the like quite often." Tom flushed as he hastily stirred the martinis. Suddenly very serious, he continued, "And there has been some discussion of my being permanently posted to Washington sometime late this year."

"I see." It was Constance's turn to blush.

Tom hoped it was from pleasure at the news that he would be closer—perhaps much closer. He brought her the martinis, sitting beside her on the couch. "But you haven't answered my question. Why haven't you tried it?"

"I considered it this winter. As you say, the winters can be desolate here on the coast. But, truthfully, Tom, I didn't want to leave Tanner. Not then."

"How is she? Is she...better?" He didn't usually inquire so directly, because he knew that Constance guarded Tanner's privacy ferociously. Only once had Constance ever broken that confidence—she had been so worried about Tanner during those first few weeks after Adrienne left that she had finally called him to ask if he thought Adrienne's decision was final. Reluctantly, he had informed her that it appeared that way.

They had talked for a long time, that first call, and by the time they finished, she seemed calmer, and he had promised to stop by the next time he was in Washington. He had been visiting regularly ever since, and Constance never spoke of that night again.

"If you didn't know her, you'd think she was fine." There was a disconcerting note of desperation in Constance's voice. "She *acts* perfectly normally. In fact, she seems to have settled down. She's not dragging strange girls home with her any longer; sometimes, I almost wish she would. She seems so lonely." She took a deep breath. "The drinking and the drugs she thought I never knew about have stopped. And she has taken more of an interest in business. A few months ago, she negotiated development rights to the harbor and personally took over management of the marina from the corporation. She has plans to run it herself and has been talking about creating an international yacht club there."

Tom was impressed. "I'd say it sounds like she's turned her life around."

"Oh, Tom, that's just it. It does seem wonderful, until you really look at her. She never smiles anymore. She never seems to sleep, and I have no idea when she eats. Josh Thomas and a few sailors at the marina are the only people she ever sees. And when I look into her eyes, all I see is pain. It's worse than after Charles died, and I wasn't sure she'd survive that." Constance's voice broke and she took a moment to collect herself. "I'm afraid she's lost something vital, Tom—her spark, her joy—the most wonderful things about her are gone. It's as if her passion for life left the day Adrienne did."

Tom was alarmed. Constance was close to tears, and he'd never seen her lose control in any situation. Moving closer, he slipped his arm around her waist. "I don't know if it will do any good, but I'll talk to Adrienne."

"I hope she's ready to listen," Constance rested her head on his shoulder, "because I'm afraid Tanner is never going to recover."

"You wouldn't object if I talked to her, would you? About something else?"

"No, of course not. Is there something we should discuss?"

"No," he replied, kissing her softly. "Not just yet."

❖

Early the next morning, Tom drove down to the marina, assuming that he would find Tanner there. True to form, she hadn't returned to Whitley Manor the night before. On his way down the pier toward the office, he noticed that construction was underway on what looked like the foundations of several buildings. He thought approvingly that the plans looked good—the harbor needed modernization, and, judging from the layout of the new structures, a great deal of thought had been put into the planning. The same concern for preserving the environment that permeated the entire island was evident in the work progressing around him. Tanner had clearly inherited her father's love for this island. Constance was right; her daughter was born to it.

As he approached the marina office, Tanner came striding up from the construction site. He noted immediately how thin she was. She'd always been trim, but now she looked gaunt. Despite the cold, she wore only khaki work pants and a light blue denim shirt, the sleeves turned up to her elbows. She had a sheaf of architectural plans rolled under one arm. Even though she'd obviously been outside a great deal, she was pale and her face was drawn and tight. She did not smile when she saw him.

Nevertheless, he continued toward her and held out his hand. "Tanner, good to see you. How are you?"

"Busy." Tanner regarded him for a moment, expressionless, then took his hand in her firm grasp.

"I can see that. It looks very impressive." Tom searched her face for some hint of her true feelings but found no clue in her hooded gaze. Her eyes were as still and hard as stone. He decided to say what he had come to say and then leave her in peace. "Can you spare me a minute? There's something I'd like to talk to you about."

Tanner regarded him steadily, wondering just why she resented him so much. She knew in her heart that it was not his fault that Adrienne had left her. Still, the sight of him reminded her of all she had lost, and she couldn't forgive him for currently being a part of Adrienne's world. He, at least, could see her, talk with her. She shrugged.

"Sure." Instinctively, she headed for the water, her only source of comfort. When she couldn't stand the confines of the marina office or her own barren bungalow, she sailed. Even though every time she stepped onto the *Pride* she was reminded of Adrienne, it was the only place she could think of her without pieces of her heart bleeding. Only there, on the water—the place where they had been so happy together—could she find any relief from the pain. She leaned against the rail at the edge of the cove, and Tom joined her.

"I want to talk to you about your mother," he began quietly.

"What about her?" Tanner stared straight ahead, but the muscles in her jaw bunched.

"I'm going to ask her to marry me."

"You can't be serious." Tanner gaped at him, sure she had heard incorrectly.

"Oh, but I am—very serious."

"Why are you telling me?"

"Things have been rocky between you and me since..." He hesitated but couldn't find any easy way to say it. "Since Adrienne left. I wanted to clear the air." He met her gaze steadily. "I love Constance, Tanner. I want us to live together, share our lives together. Weekends now and then are not enough."

Tanner winced. His words were arrows directed at her very soul. A weekend. She would be so grateful for just a weekend with Adrienne. But, that was over. Adrienne was gone.

"And Mother? Does she feel the same way?" The look of uncertainty that flashed across Tom's handsome features surprised her.

"I don't know. She cares for me, I think." He spoke slowly, almost to himself. "And I think she's lonely here on Whitley Point."

"Lonely? But—"

"Wait, I didn't mean she's unhappy," he said quickly, raising a hand to interrupt Tanner's protest. "She loves you, and she loves the island, too. There's no doubt of that. But I think the main reason she's stayed on the Point these last few years is because you, and this place, remind her in so many ways of your father. And she loved him so much that she didn't want to part with all that remained of him."

"He's dead," Tanner said in a low voice, knowing how precious memories could be when that was all that was left. "She'll always have the memories, no matter where she is."

"Yes, I know." He squared his shoulders, unconsciously adopting a formal military stance. "But she deserves more than memories; she deserves a chance to live again. Maybe without all the passion she knew with Charles, but at least with someone who cares for her, someone who cherishes her. And I do."

"Even if she still...loves him?"

"Even then. I knew about your father long before I fell in love with your mother."

Tanner didn't know what to say. This honesty and sensitivity astounded her, and she realized that she didn't know the first thing about Tom Hardigan. All he had been to her was a painful reminder of Adrienne. She thought about her mother, quietly bearing her grief with dignity all these years, somehow always there when Tanner had needed her. She swallowed hard and nodded.

"She *has* seemed lonely. I've seen the signs, but I never wanted to admit it. I've never been much company for her. I was either running from the past or wrapped up in my own private unhappiness. Lately, since Adrienne..." Her voice faltered; it was difficult to say that name without something tearing inside. She looked at Tom, trying to find the words that came so hard. "Lately, it's been worse. Do you really think she would be happy away from Whitley Point?"

Tom smiled at that. "Not for long, I don't imagine. Constance is more of a Whitley than she realizes. I hope to be stationed in Washington, DC next year. And if Constance agrees to marry me, we would never be all that far from Whitley Point...or from you."

"You don't have to worry about me," Tanner stated quietly. "I have everything I need right here."

Tom seriously doubted that. It wasn't hard to see the emptiness in her eyes or to hear the bitterness in her voice. He wanted to offer some comfort but knew that there wasn't any. None that he could give. "So you don't have a problem—"

"There's nothing that needs to be settled between you and I, Tom." She laughed suddenly, a spark of her old self reappearing for an instant. "But I think you'd better present your case to my mother."

"You're right." Tom grinned back. "Now that I have your permission, I can ask her."

"You *are* crazy."

"You bet," he said quickly.

Suddenly Tanner's face grew still. "Tom, how is Adrienne?"

"If you ask me, and no one does, I'd say lousy." Tom hesitated a moment and then decided to be totally honest. "She's living in an apartment near the base. She and Alicia seem friendly—that's only natural, I guess—but I don't know what's happening between them. Adrienne doesn't talk to me about it, or to anyone else, I imagine. She's back to full duty and doing fine—better than ever really—but that seems to be the only thing she cares about."

He'd probably already said more than he should have, because Tanner was very pale and visibly trembling. Her torment was so sharp, so clear, it hurt him to look at her.

"She isn't...sick?" Her voice was a pained whisper.

"Not as far as I know. She looks fine physically, but there's something missing. She's going through the motions, Tanner, but I think she was wrong to go back to San Diego. I'd say she left her heart and soul right here on Whitley Point."

Tanner closed her eyes, struggling to bury the pain. She was overjoyed that Adrienne was well, but it hurt so much to think of her being with Alicia, she was dizzy.

"Tanner? Are you all right?"

"Yes," she whispered, gripping the rough-hewn railing along the dock for support, struggling to contain the anguish.

"I think she misses you." Thankfully, when Tanner finally looked at him, he was heartened to see something hard and determined force its way through the wounded confusion.

"Tom," she asked urgently, "what should I do? If I thought she'd come back, I'd fly out there tonight. I've wanted to, so many times. I went so far as to buy the tickets once, but she said...she said she didn't want me. She said she didn't..." She faltered for a second. "She said she didn't love me."

"God, Tanner. I'm sorry." He tried to imagine how hurt Tanner must feel and didn't really want to know. "I think Adrienne truly believed that leaving you was the right thing to do...for you. Remember, she met you when she was just barely beginning to recover, and everything in her life was turned upside down. I think she was afraid she would die, and you would be alone."

"I *know* what she was afraid of." She drew a sharp breath, the thought of anything happening to Adrienne so agonizing she felt weak. "What I don't understand is how she could think that living without her now, knowing that she is on the other side of the country and won't even see me, could be any worse."

"I don't know either," he replied sadly, thinking that he had let Adrienne down. She had sacrificed a chance for real happiness, and he had stood by watching, doing nothing. *I'll ask her. It's about time somebody did.*

❖

After Tom left, Tanner finished up the work plans for the next day and left notes for Josh with instructions for the contractors. She considered sleeping on the *Pride* that night, as she usually did when Tom was visiting, but then decided there was something more important than her own lingering discomfort with him. Something she should have done weeks ago. She went directly into the main house where Tom and her mother were having a cocktail.

"Mother," she said after a brief hello to Tom, "could we talk for a minute?"

Both Tom and Constance looked surprised, but Constance rose immediately. "Of course, sweetheart. Let's talk in the living room. May has a fire going in there."

Once they were out of Tom's hearing, Tanner turned to her mother. "Mother, are you happy here?"

"Happy here?" Constance repeated, startled. "Why, of course I'm happy. This is my home."

"That's not what I meant. I meant, are you *happy* here?" She sat in one of the chairs in front of the fireplace and regarded Constance seriously. "Is this the life you want? Enough of a life?"

"I love the island; I always will." Constance studied Tanner for a moment, no longer seeing the reflection of her husband, but the strong, forthright woman her daughter had become. "But I must admit, I do get lonely. Sometimes, I think my life ended when your father died."

"No! That's not true. You can't let it be true. You're alive, and Father is gone. You owe it to yourself to make a life for yourself. You deserve that."

Constance tilted her head and smiled almost shyly at Tanner. "And do you think I should make that life with Tom Hardigan?"

"That's only for you to say." Tanner shrugged. "But he does seem to care for you." With another sigh, she admitted, "And I like him."

Suddenly serious, Constance asked, "And what of the island? There are still many things here that need looking after. The corporation and its managers are not the same as a Whitley."

"I know that. That's not a problem you need to worry about. I can take care of things here." Tanner straightened her shoulders and reached for her mother's hand. "It's the one thing I've discovered I'm good at."

"And you, Tanner? Who shall look after you, sweetheart?" Constance asked softly.

"I don't know. It looks like it's just going to be me."

Constance held her daughter's hand tightly, hoping fervently that Tanner was wrong.

CHAPTER TWENTY

Look at these, will you, Josh?" Tanner indicated the drawings she had spread out on a drafting table inside the marina office.

"What you got there?"

"The plans to remodel the pier and dredge the center of the channel so the big boats can dock. If we're going to have a world-class marina, we need room for large cruisers as well as sailing boats. And you know what that means—restaurants and private shoreside accommodations. The whole nine yards."

"I don't know how you sold this idea to the locals." He gave a shake of his head as he peered at the newest specs.

The financial developers, of course, were delighted to see a move toward modernization on Whitley Point. The long-time inhabitants, however, had been worried at first that such changes would ruin the serenity of their island. They'd been reassured when Tanner presented the designs for the new installations. She'd been adamant about preserving the integrity of the shoreline, much as her grandfather and father had insisted that the island's habitat be protected when housing construction on the island had first been considered. She won their trust.

"Yeah. Just in time, too," Tanner said with a grin. She'd already purchased a base fleet of sailboats, due to arrive in just a few weeks, which she intended to lease for charter.

"You're gonna have to ride those contractors if you want this done by summer."

"That's no problem. I'm not going anywhere."

The work was challenging, and she felt for the first time that her energies and her talent were being put to good use. She'd assumed more of the financial management of the project, as well as having the final say over all the design plans. It was a job that could quite easily consume all of her time, and it nearly did. And that was exactly what she wanted. Being totally involved with work was the only way she could keep her mind off Adrienne, even if just for a little while.

Tanner thought of her constantly, a continual ache that never abated. As winter had turned to spring with no word from her, she tormented herself with questions. Would Adrienne tell her—would anyone tell her—if Adrienne were ill? What should she have said to make Adrienne stay? What could she say now to change her mind*? Please, come back. I'm dying without you.* She was worn thin with the unrelenting loneliness and worry, but still she worked day and night and at least took some comfort in exhaustion.

"Tanner?"

"Hmm?" She realized that she was drifting again and tried to focus on what Josh was saying. "Problems?

"Hell, no." Josh studied the designs the draftsman had constructed to Tanner's specifications. "I'm saying, I like it—I sure do. I thought you'd have a time finding mooring space for the big boats, but you did it. It's going to be dandy."

"I'm glad you approve." She smiled at his obvious delight. "I can't make a move without your consent, now that you're my new general manager."

Josh beamed, a happy man. "Remember, eight, nine months ago, I said I always liked you when you were a little whippersnapper?"

Tanner nodded, remembering what had prompted the conversation—the big storm and her nearly fatal journey to port in the *Pride*. God, it seemed like a lifetime ago that she had awakened, soaked and almost frozen, to discover herself in Adrienne's arms. She saw herself as she must have seemed then—so arrogant and foolhardy. *So fucking blind to the things that really mattered.* She shuddered and pulled herself away from the memories.

"I remember."

"Well," he said thoughtfully, "I think I can say with fair certainty that I like you even better now. You're a fine person, Tanner Whitley."

"Thank you, Josh," Tanner said softly. "Coming from you, I almost believe it."

Josh studied her quietly, aware that she suffered from some deep hurt in her soul. He also knew why and that there wasn't much anyone could do for it. He looked past her up the pier and whistled low.

"Well, well—here comes the Navy again." He muttered something that sounded like, "Always bringing trouble."

Tanner wheeled around, instantly concerned when she saw Tom Hardigan coming down the pier. She was certain that her mother had mentioned he wasn't expected again until next week. Heart pounding, she hurried outside and up the dock to meet him.

He looked uncharacteristically solemn. "Tanner, I—"

"What is it?" she cried, her stomach in knots. "What's wrong? Is it Adrienne? Is she all right?"

"Slow down a minute." He held up a hand, his face suddenly alight with pleasure. "Why don't you ask her yourself?"

"What are you saying?" she whispered, suddenly finding it hard to breathe.

"I brought company." He gestured over his shoulder.

Tanner looked beyond him to another figure, then grabbed for a nearby railing to steady herself, suddenly so dizzy she thought she might fall. She blinked to clear her vision. Adrienne walked slowly down the pier toward her, just as Tanner had prayed she would a thousand times. "This can't be," she murmured, her voice a wistful plea.

"Believe it, Tanner." Tom quietly excused himself, knowing she didn't hear him.

Tanner remained riveted to the spot, afraid to move lest the spell be broken. *Please, let this be real. Please.*

Adrienne stopped a few steps from Tanner, searching her face for some sign of welcome. What she found nearly broke her heart—pain and bewilderment and an uncertainty that she had never before seen in Tanner's eyes. She looked haunted, pale and trembling. Adrienne's breath caught in her chest. *Oh my God, have I done this?*

"Tanner," she said when she could swallow around the lump in her throat. "I know it's been too long...I'm sorry..."

"There's nothing to be sorry about." Tanner's voice came out raw and harsh, shot through with tears. *What does this mean? Why have you come?*

"There is. I hurt you—"

"Don't." *Don't give me hope, Adrienne. Are you just here to say hello? Will you leave again with Tom in two days? Do you even know that that will kill me?* "I understand why you left."

"Do you?" Adrienne suddenly wondered if she herself even

understood, seeing Tanner now, like this. The reasons that had been so clear to her eight months ago crumbled in the sure knowledge of the hurt she had caused. *Can you ever forgive me? Does it even matter to you now? Do you feel anything for me besides anger?* The thoughts made her ache.

"Why are you here?" Tanner was desperate to make sense of what was happening.

"I needed to come east for some meetings..." Adrienne faltered and fell momentarily silent. "We need to talk. I need to talk."

"Can you stay...for dinner?" Tanner was cautious, afraid to make any assumptions.

"I'd like that. Actually, Tom has spoken with Constance already, and we'll both be staying there." She wasn't sure if that news pleased Tanner or not. Searching for some way to ease the awkwardness, she hurried on. "Would you show me around the marina? Tom's told me of some of the changes you've been making."

"Of course." Tanner, still too shocked by Adrienne's sudden appearance to do anything else, led the way.

They walked around the harbor, Tanner quietly pointing out the renovations under way and describing her plans. Adrienne was impressed, both by the scope of Tanner's design and by the determination she displayed. The wild young successor to the Whitley dynasty had obviously found her focus in the time they'd been apart, and Adrienne was glad for her.

"It's wonderful. You must be very proud."

"I'm...content with it. If you want to come inside, I can show you the scale models." Suddenly shy, wondering what they were doing, talking as if they were strangers, Tanner added, "If you like."

"Yes." Adrienne followed her into to the office.

Josh Thomas looked up as they entered and rose stiffly from behind the desk. He eyed Adrienne coldly, nodded, and left the room.

Adrienne raised one eyebrow and followed his retreat with her eyes. "Guess I'm one of his un-favorite people."

"Sorry." Tanner looked uncomfortable. "Josh is a little protective of me."

"He has a right to be. I can see why he finds you special." She wanted to touch her then, not for Tanner, but for herself. Seeing her was like seeing the sun after a long cold winter and remembering what spring felt like. "Tanner—"

"Here it is," Tanner said hurriedly, indicating the drafting board with a mock-up of the fully developed harbor. She did her best to explain the plans, but her mind was on Adrienne standing so close that she could smell her distinctive scent. She was afraid if she looked at her she would have to touch her.

Adrienne tried to listen attentively but found her mind wandering instead to the curve of Tanner's neck as she leaned over the table, to the slight smell of the sea that clung to her, and to the way the muscles moved beneath the skin of her forearms. Sighing, she stepped away, afraid she might take Tanner into her arms right there in the office.

"Tanner? Would you mind if we saved the rest of this for another day? I'm tired. It was a long flight. I think I'd like a shower and a meal."

Tanner risked glancing at her then, and for the first time noticed that Adrienne was thinner than she remembered, and there was a hint of shadows under her eyes. Her heart lurched with sudden fear. *Is she ill again? Is that why she's here?* Her anxiety made her almost breathless. "Adrienne, are you all right?"

Adrienne looked startled for a second before she understood. Impulsively, moved by the near-panic in Tanner's eyes, she pulled her into her arms and whispered against her ear, "I'm more than all right. All of my latest tests were absolutely normal. The doctors tell me I'm in perfect condition, okay?"

Tanner closed her eyes in relief, then had to break the embrace. She couldn't bear the closeness—it hurt, being near her now. "Yes. Okay. But you are a little thin."

"I've missed you," Adrienne whispered, placing one hand on Tanner's cheek.

"We should go." *Or I'm going to lose it right here.*

"Yes." Adrienne let her hand drop reluctantly. "We should."

❖

Tanner took the shore road home, driving slowly. They were both quiet. Adrienne was torn between watching the scenery, just realizing how much she had missed the island, and watching Tanner, who was even more captivating. Tanner for her part was still trying to absorb the reality of Adrienne's presence, vacillating between euphoria and terror.

When they reached Whitley Manor, they found that Tom had already arrived. He and Constance met them at the door.

"Adrienne," Constance said warmly. "I am so glad to see you. You remember May—she'll show you to your room upstairs."

"I need to get cleaned up before dinner," Tanner said as Adrienne departed, then left quickly for her bungalow.

"Tom?" Constance lifted an eyebrow. "Did you have a hand in this?"

"Well, a small one perhaps. I *did* talk with Adrienne. When she admitted that she was miserable, I told her that she wasn't alone in her feelings. I suggested that...ah...she was a fool to let Tanner go."

"Thank you. I've been praying for this."

Tom cleared his throat. "I have some news of my own, Constance."

"Oh?"

"I've been cleared for a transfer to Washington later this spring. I'll be posted there permanently."

"But that's wonderful, Tom." Constance laughed with delight. "I'm so happy for you."

"I was hoping you'd be happy that I will be close to...Whitley Point."

She answered softly, "Oh, but I am."

Adrienne coughed to announce her presence and crossed the room to join them. "Forgive me for eavesdropping, but I couldn't help overhearing. That's great news, Tom."

"Thanks." Tom accepted the congratulations graciously. He looked from Adrienne to Constance and continued, "I have some other news as well. Papers crossed my desk a few days ago which concern you, Adrienne."

"Oh?" she said as she reached for coffee from the serving table. "I'm not being court-martialed, I hope."

"Far from it. You were recommended for an award for your exceptional work on that project you recently completed. Your Navy Commendation just came through."

Adrienne looked stunned. "This is a surprise."

"Your work has always been noteworthy, and it's finally getting the attention of the higher-ups. You're on the fast track for promotion with this recognition, Adrienne. And you deserve it."

"Deserve what?" Tanner said as came through the door from the rear deck to join them.

Missing Adrienne's motion to silence him, Tom continued unperturbed. "Adrienne's getting an award for her work."

"Congratulations," Tanner said softly, looking at Adrienne.

"Thank you." Adrienne shrugged. "It's really not that big a thing. I'm sure my life will proceed pretty much as it has." She smiled slightly. "But I'm pleased."

"Well, so am I," Tom said emphatically. "In fact, if you don't mind talking business for just a few minutes, Adrienne, there are a couple of more things I need to review with you." Glancing apologetically at Constance, he added, "I promise, this will be the last business until Monday morning."

"Don't make promises you can't keep, Commander," she warned lightly, but she was smiling as Tom and Adrienne walked into the adjoining room.

"What are you thinking?" Constance gently rested her hand on Tanner's arm.

Tanner started slightly at the touch, then shrugged. "I was thinking about Adrienne's career. It sounds as if it's going great. I'm sure she'll never want to leave the Navy now. I'm happy for her, I really am. But I...I had hoped..." She looked away. It was too hard to think about Adrienne leaving again.

"Don't make any assumptions, Tanner. She's here. Give her a chance to tell you why. And it's time for you to tell her what *you* need, and what you want."

"What about you, Mother? Are you in love with Tom?"

"Oh, Tanner. I don't know if *in love* is the right term for it. I've grown very fond of him. He's a marvelous man, quite sensitive and gentle. I do miss him when he's gone. In many ways, yes, I love him."

"Have you slept with him?"

"Tanner Hughes Whitley! One does not discuss one's sexual life with one's children."

"Who says? I know you must have sexual feelings. Certainly mine are no secret."

"That's no reason to discuss them before dinner."

"Why not?"

Constance studied Tanner for a moment and then she laughed. "I actually don't know."

"Well? Have you?"

"No."

"Want to?"

"I don't know that either." Her mother sighed wistfully, her eyes clouded with memory. "You may find this hard to believe, but your father was the only man I ever made love with. I feel odd thinking of another man that way."

"Odd," Tanner asked gently, "or guilty?"

"What do you mean?"

"Father is gone. You wouldn't be unfaithful to him if you love someone else, desire someone else. You're alive—you have a right to your life. You've honored his memory for a long time. It's all right to move on. And, if you ever decide to leave Whitley Point, that will be all right, too. I love it here; I doubt I'll ever leave. And I'll be fine."

"I want more than that for you, Tanner," Constance said adamantly. "I want you to be happy."

"Happy?" Tanner responded as if the concept were new to her. Then she heard Adrienne's laughter in the other room. "Maybe... someday."

CHAPTER TWENTY-ONE

The Whitleys and their guests sat in the living room after dinner, but the conversation bordered on strained. Both Adrienne and Tanner, seated next to one another on the sofa but carefully not touching, repeatedly lost the thread of the discussion or lapsed into silence. Finally, Adrienne acknowledged her mental absence.

"I'm sorry. I think I'm more tired than I realized. If you will all excuse me, I'm going to call it a night." She glanced at Tanner. "I'll see you in the morning?"

"Yes," Tanner replied quietly. "I'll be here."

Once alone in bed in the guestroom, however, Adrienne couldn't sleep. Tanner was so near, and for the first time in months, she allowed herself to think about being with her. Touching her. She hadn't been able to think about it before—the ache ran so deep, if she had let it surface, she wouldn't have been able to function.

She had crossed the country because Tom had goaded her into admitting that she was absolutely miserable and that her existence was little more than a mockery of life, but she hadn't made any real plans. She'd only known that she must see Tanner again. Now, with her a hundred yards away, she hesitated. It would be folly to go to her without making the decisions she had avoided for many months, and, even more frightening, she wasn't entirely sure of her welcome.

Tanner had changed in the months they'd been apart. She seemed older, more settled, than the previous summer, and that wasn't a bad thing. But it was plain to Adrienne just how much she had hurt Tanner by leaving her, and now she feared that Tanner's passion for her had been destroyed by her betrayal. As she lay awake in the still room, tossing and turning, she heard soft footsteps in the hall. *Tanner!*

But it wasn't. She listened, heart pounding...then plummeting, as the footsteps passed by her room. A door opened down the hall where

Tom was sleeping, and she heard first Constance's voice, then Tom's deep one. A lock clicked shut, and the house was silent again.

At a little after three, Adrienne got up and threw on a robe over the T-shirt and Navy athletic shorts she'd worn to bed. It was an unusually warm night for early spring, and she stood on the small deck outside her room, thinking. She considered her life in California and found it acceptable. *Acceptable. Is that all I want from life?*

She finally admitted how dark her days had been without Tanner and how the slightest hint of tenderness in Tanner's eyes still made her heart soar. She thought of Tanner now, sleeping nearby, and of how much she wanted her. And then she stopped thinking and listened to her heart, at last.

❖

Tanner was not asleep. She was naked in the warm room, the shutters open to admit a faint breeze that carried promises of spring. Her mind was on the woman who had filled her dreams every night for months, and who, miraculously, was now here. Afraid to think what it might mean, unable to think of anything else, she twisted in the rumpled sheets, her body aroused, her mind in turmoil. She didn't hear the footsteps outside until the door to her room opened. Holding her breath, her body tense, she rolled onto her side, watching the shadow in the moonlight, and waited.

"Tanner?" Adrienne called softly.

"I'm here."

"I know it's late. I couldn't wait." Adrienne crossed to the bed and sat on the side, facing Tanner. She reached out and tentatively stroked her cheek. "I have to talk to you; I couldn't wait until morning. I've been going crazy..."

"Not now," Tanner rasped, pulling Adrienne close, groaning at the touch of their bodies after so long, her restraint vanishing in the face of desire too long denied. She silenced Adrienne's faint protest with a kiss. It was not a gentle kiss—she had been without this solace for far too long, and when she finally pulled away, she knew they'd both be bruised. "Please, I don't want to talk. I need to touch you...I need to so much...I'll die if I don't."

Adrienne groaned, instantly insanely aroused. "God, yes." Her words were lost into Tanner's mouth, her blood already singing with the distant beat of wild joy.

Tanner pulled at Adrienne's clothing, pushing the robe from her shoulders, then grasping the T-shirt and stripping it off over her head. She pulled Adrienne down onto the bed and fell upon her, ravenous, grasping her breast and forcing the nipple into her mouth.

Adrienne cried out, a frenzy of excitement building between her thighs, and held Tanner's face to her, wanting to be swallowed whole. The teeth on her nipple only made her clitoris pound harder. Arching her hips, offering herself, she urged desperately, "Hurry."

"Help me." Tanner groaned as she fumbled at Adrienne's shorts, her lips still on Adrienne's skin.

Adrienne slid both hands between their bodies and pushed her shorts down. "Inside." The frantic tone in her voice was foreign to her. She was afraid she would start screaming if she didn't feel Tanner, have her, take her soon. Adrienne's mind was white noise and blazing need, and she was going to fly into a thousand pieces. *Tanner... nowpleasenow.*

And then Tanner was there, moving on her, moving in her—reaching only the places she could reach, touching her as only Tanner could. Fingers digging into Tanner's shoulders, thighs clenched around her arm, Adrienne gasped. "Tanner...you're making me come..."

"Oh, yeah," Tanner cried, her forehead pressed to Adrienne's chest, her hand driving hard—needing to have her, claim her, keep her. "Oh yeah...come...come now."

"Oh God," Adrienne whimpered brokenly as everything inside her started to dissolve. "I love you so much."

Tanner didn't even see it coming. The feel of Adrienne tightening around her fingers and the sound of her choked sobs as she climaxed blew through her like a seismic crash, and all she could do was shout in surprise as orgasm engulfed her. Then she was clinging to Adrienne, shuddering, helplessly moaning her name.

❖

Adrienne woke alone. She turned and tried to focus on the bedside clock. Five forty-five. She reached for her T-shirt, then found a sweatshirt and canvas deck pants in a bureau next to the bed and pulled them on, too. They were too loose and a bit short, but she didn't care. They were Tanner's, and she needed some piece of her right now. She hungered for the feel of her, starving for her, as if she'd just crawled out of a cave after hibernating all winter.

She stepped out into a cold dawn and went to find Tanner. She knew where she would be, and the knowing hurt. Two hundred yards below the bungalow, the surf pounded angrily to shore, resisting imminent death with impotent fury.

Tanner sat in the shelter of a dune, her forearms crossed on her raised knees, hair blowing wildly in the wind, watching another cycle of the tides.

"Aren't you cold?" Adrienne lowered herself to the sand beside the young woman. "It's a bit early in the season for just jeans and a T-shirt."

"I'm okay."

"Tanner," Adrienne said quietly, "I don't want to be one of the women you can't spend the night with after making love."

"Is there going to be another night?" Tanner finally looked over, her voice tight with anger and pain.

"I want there to be."

"When? How?"

"I don't know," Adrienne admitted. "All I know is that living without you wasn't really living at all. When I learned I had cancer, I thought dying was the worst thing I had to fear. These last several months, I've discovered that living a lie is far worse, and pretending that I could forget you was the biggest lie I've ever told myself. Without you, only my work meant anything at all, and even that isn't enough. I need to see you—whenever we can manage."

"No."

"Last night...I thought you wanted me, too." Adrienne's heart pounded with sudden, terrible fear. "Am I wrong? Have you met someone else?"

"Jesus, no! I can't go to sleep without wanting you. I wake up lonely and struggle through the day empty, bleeding inside, because you're not here." Tanner ran her hand through her hair, shaking her head in disbelief. "Last night, didn't you *feel* what loving you has done to me? You own me—I touch you and I'm lost, drowning in you, gone. There hasn't been anyone since you. There could never be anyone else."

Adrienne took Tanner's hand tentatively, pressing warm lips to her palm. "What is it then? I know I can't make any promises. I still don't know what will happen to me next year, or the year after. But we could be happy for now—"

"It's not enough, Adrienne." She hated the words, but she had to say them. Even if it meant losing Adrienne forever, she had to say them. "I love you. A night, a few days now and then, it isn't enough. Making love with you and then watching you go—I'll die a little every time you leave. I just can't do it."

Adrienne sat for a long time studying Tanner's face, and when she spoke, her voice held tears. "Until last night, I never said the words, but I always felt them. I love you, Tanner. I've always loved you. More than I ever thought possible. I left you last summer because I was afraid I couldn't love you enough, that I didn't have enough—physically or emotionally—to give you. I felt selfish...how much I needed you. And I *still* need you just as much, actually more, but it doesn't frighten me any longer. Living *without* you frightens me. Let me love you today, Tanner, please."

"No. You don't understand," Tanner said stubbornly. "Today is not enough, Adrienne. I thought it was once, but I was wrong. I want every one of your days, every tomorrow. I want a lifetime."

"What if..." She hesitated, then pushed on, forcing herself to ask. "What if a lifetime with me isn't long enough?"

"A lifetime will never be long enough," Tanner whispered. "It's the promise of one I want."

Adrienne linked her fingers through Tanner's and pressed close to her side, listening to the ocean roar and the gulls cry. Alone in California, she had walked through her days frozen, numb to possibility and joy. Now, the touch of Tanner's hand warmed her in a place far deeper than mere flesh.

"I can promise you a lifetime of tomorrows," she said finally. "Every single one I have."

CHAPTER TWENTY-TWO

"Don't you think we're expected at breakfast?" Adrienne asked when Tanner pulled her down onto the bed, preventing her from dressing.

"Our absence may be noted, but I don't think that where we are or what we're doing is much of a secret."

"Ah," Adrienne commented dryly, nestling her cheek in the curve of Tanner's shoulder. "So everyone will just assume we're down here screwing. I see. I wonder if Tom will be embarrassed."

"I hope so. How do you think I've felt with him pining after my mother for the last eight months?" Tanner grumbled, shifting so that Adrienne's thigh fit between her legs.

"I don't think he's pining any longer."

"Huh?" Tanner raised her head so she could see Adrienne's face.

"I believe there was a midnight assignation—initiated by your mother, I might add—just last night."

"No kidding?" There was a note of appreciation in Tanner's voice. "Well, good for her."

"Good for both of them," Adrienne murmured, running her hand down Tanner's chest and over her stomach. The muscles in Tanner's abdomen tightened under her fingers, and a swift surge of wonder mixed with pure unmitigated lust swept through her. "You are marvelous."

"Hmm?" Tanner was concentrating on Adrienne's fingers. *God, they seem to be connected directly to my nerve centers.* Her breathing had already started to hitch.

"But you're way too thin. Great muscles, but I'd prefer that you had a little padding here and there, too."

"I'll work on it." Tanner kissed Adrienne's temple, then began to trace her fingers along the curve of Adrienne's flank toward her hip.

"And look who's talking. You haven't been getting enough sleep—I can tell. You need a vacation, Commander."

"I'll be fine now."

"Yeah, me, too," Tanner whispered, rolling over on top of her. She kissed Adrienne, lingering to suck gently on her lower lip, reveling in its softness. She sighed, head spinning. "Breakfast will have to wait. I have eight months of missing you to make up for."

"Take your time." Adrienne drew Tanner's hand between her legs. "I'm not going anywhere."

Tanner closed her eyes, savoring the words.

❖

When Tanner awoke again, the sun was high and the room was aglow with late morning light. Adrienne was pressed close, her head on Tanner's shoulder, her hair a golden sheet across Tanner's breasts. She didn't think she would ever tire of waking like this, of feeling the wonder of holding her, of having her, each time she opened her eyes. Carefully, she stretched her cramped muscles, not wanting to awaken her sleeping lover.

Nevertheless, Adrienne stirred and sighed. Wordlessly, she caressed Tanner's shoulder and brushed her cheek across one soft nipple. "I love you."

"I love you, too," Tanner whispered.

"Mmm—what a lovely way to wake up." Adrienne pressed her lips against Tanner's nipple and teased it with her tongue. She smiled contentedly when she heard Tanner's sharp intake of breath. "You know," she said between bites, "I love to make love to you. I love to make you crazy. Never...never have I wanted anyone like this."

"Ahh...Jes...wait." Tanner attempted to sit up, despite the fire Adrienne's mouth on her breast had kindled between her legs. "Adrienne," she pleaded, "wait. You know I can't think when you do that."

"So?" Adrienne chuckled, running her fingers along Tanner's thigh. "What's the problem with that?"

"This is where we started a few hours ago." She captured Adrienne's hand and stilled it with her own.

"Uh-huh. And as I recall, I never got to the part where I make you beg." Adrienne moved her hand back between Tanner's thighs, higher this time, moaning in the back of her throat when she found her hard and wet. "But I will this time."

Tanner groaned, her hips jerking with a will of their own. "I don't want to come..." She gasped at the brush of fingertips. "I mean—I do... God. Just not...right...now." She struggled into a sitting position.

Adrienne, suddenly displaced, was left staring at her. "I want you right now," she insisted throatily, leaning toward Tanner again. "And you are about one minute from liftoff."

"Yeah." Tanner grinned. She grasped Adrienne's arm and held her away. "Maybe less." When her head stopped pounding and she thought she could ignore the insistent twitches that signaled an imminent meltdown, she managed, "But I want to talk...first."

"This better be good." Adrienne growled.

"I don't want to wait another month or more to be with you again."

"Neither do I." Adrienne, suddenly completely serious, swung her legs over the side of the bed and sat up, holding Tanner's hand firmly. "I don't even want to wait two weeks."

"I was thinking, this morning out there on the beach," Tanner began hesitantly. "One ocean is pretty much like any other." She ran her thumb back and forth across the top of Adrienne's hand. "I could... move to California. If you wanted."

"No."

Tanner stiffened. "I thought—"

"Wait," Adrienne interrupted, lifting Tanner's chin in her hand so that their eyes met. "You're not leaving this place. Whitley Point is your home—more than your home. It's your touchstone. You need to be here."

"But—"

"God, you're impatient! One of your completely infuriating and more irresistible traits." Smiling, Adrienne kissed her because she couldn't help it, then leaned back again. "There's something else I haven't told you, because I'm not certain yet. There's a good chance that I can have a transfer to the East Coast if I like. I'm due for rotation, and there are some positions available that will set me up for my next promotion—including one about thirty miles north of here."

"Oh." Tanner remained still, but her heart was racing. "Do you want to transfer here?"

"It depends," Adrienne responded contemplatively.

"On what?"

"It snows a lot, for one thing."

"We have fireplaces for that, very romantic, too." Tanner caressed Adrienne's forearm. "And parkas—"

"Oh, yes, now *that's* very sexy."

"I think we could work something out to keep you warm." Tanner lifted her palm and brushed it along the curve of Adrienne's breast. "What else?"

"I hate living on base, for another."

"I'm sure we could find you something suitable around here," Tanner said, the caution back in her voice. "Something on Whitley Point, maybe?"

"Yes, that might be good...close to the marina that way."

"Absolutely."

"I heard there's this knockout new owner down there—dark, handsome, unbelievably sexy. Quite a good sailor and magic in bed."

"I'll have to kill her," Tanner muttered, tugging Adrienne back down beside her. When she finished kissing her, she asked impatiently, "How soon?"

"I don't know, honey. I'll need to go through channels. There'll be paperwork—the usual military red tape."

"By summer?"

Adrienne laughed softly. "You don't want much, do you?"

"I want it all," Tanner replied, her gaze steady and calm. "And I don't want to be without you one day longer than absolutely necessary."

"I'll call in every favor I can." Adrienne smoothed her palm over Tanner's chest, then cradled her breast. "I want to be here with you as soon as I can, too. I need to make up for these last eight months."

"No, you don't," Tanner assured her. "We're done with the past, okay? Both our pasts."

"To the future, then?" Adrienne breathed as her mouth came down on Tanner's.

"To the future," Tanner murmured when she could think again. "And speaking of that...about the living arrangements..."

"Well, there was one particular place I had in mind." Adrienne's eyes were on Tanner's, her expression shimmering with love. "That is, if you're willing to take a chance."

Tanner gathered Adrienne into her arms and kissed her. "I never pass on a sure thing."

EPILOGUE

Adrienne turned into the drive with a sigh of relief. It had been a long day, full of meetings, site reviews, and a late afternoon rush to complete the final draft for a project she headed. She was glad to be home. As she approached Whitley Manor she smiled. *Home.* It had taken her several months to get used to the idea that this *was* her home. After almost a year, she couldn't imagine living anywhere else. She and Tanner had moved into the main house when Constance relocated to Washington the previous month.

She reached the door just as the housekeeper opened it. "Hello, May. Is Tanner home yet?"

May rolled her eyes and pointed upstairs. "Packing," she said with a laugh. "You'd think the two of you were leaving for a year, instead of four days. She's been to Europe a dozen times and never had this much trouble."

"She's a little nervous, I think." Adrienne smiled, tossed her briefcase on the table in the hall, and went upstairs to the master bedroom she and Tanner shared.

"Honey?" As she entered the room, she stopped abruptly and stared. "Tanner?"

Closet doors stood open with half a dozen garments hanging askew from their hangers. The entire surface of the large bed, as well as several chairs, was piled with layers of clothing. Tanner, looking frazzled, stood in the midst of the chaos, an open suitcase on the floor beside her.

"It's hopeless," she cried in despair. "Maybe we should cancel."

"I don't think that we can do that. It's your mother's wedding."

"I hate these black-tie functions," Tanner grumbled, stalking about with her hands in the pockets of threadbare jeans. "Insufferably pompous people trying to impress each other."

"It's not going to be like that." Adrienne caught Tanner in her arms and rubbed her back until she felt some of the tension relax in the tightly coiled muscles. "Small and intimate. It will be beautiful."

"I still can't figure out what to take."

"Well, not all of this." Adrienne kissed her, barely hiding a grin. "So, what's really bothering you about this weekend? You know damn well you'll look great in whatever you decide to wear." She regarded Tanner, fit and more handsome than ever, and remarked musingly, "In fact, I'll probably have to go armed just to protect my interests."

"Hey!"

Adrienne ignored the outraged expression in her lover's eyes. "You've been out of circulation for so long, I—"

Tanner tackled her and threw her onto the bed with no regard for the clothing under them, smothering her words with a kiss. "Take that back."

"What?" Adrienne inquired innocently. "And you're wrinkling my uniform."

"Take back that insult to my honor," Tanner insisted, unbuttoning Adrienne's shirt. She slipped her hand inside and caressed Adrienne's breast, until Adrienne's eyes grew liquid.

"What?" Adrienne whispered, her brain a bit fuzzy.

"Say you know you're the only one."

"I know," she murmured, her voice husky as she drew Tanner down for another kiss.

"Better." Tanner relished another minute of exploring Adrienne's mouth. Then resting her head on her lover's shoulder, she sighed. "What are you going to wear?"

"That's easy, I'll wear my dress whites."

Tanner kissed Adrienne's neck and teased, "Oh, good. I've always liked you in uniform."

"You'd better." Adrienne was aware of Tanner's nearly successful ploy to distract her. "What are you worried about?"

"It just seems so...final." Tanner sighed.

"The wedding?"

"Yeah."

"Tanner," Adrienne said softly, adoring the tenderness so few ever saw in her lover, "nothing is going to change. At least not for the worse...and Constance will never change. You're the light of her life.

And I guarantee she'll be here for the opening party on Memorial Day weekend—and all summer, too."

"Dumb of me to worry, huh?"

"Not dumb at all." Adrienne kissed her. "And don't worry about this weekend. I intend to keep you very busy."

"Yeah?" Tanner's tone had lightened considerably. "Promise?"

"You know I do," Adrienne answered softly, thinking of how precious a single day could be. She looked forward now to the promise of each tomorrow with Tanner, knowing that every one would bring joy.

The End

About the Author

Radclyffe is a member of the Golden Crown Literary Society, Pink Ink, the Romance Writers of America, and a two-time recipient of the Alice B. award for lesbian fiction. She has written numerous best-selling lesbian romances (*Safe Harbor* and its sequel *Beyond the Breakwater, Innocent Hearts, Love's Melody Lost, Love's Tender Warriors, Tomorrow's Promise, Passion's Bright Fury, Love's Masquerade, shadowland,* and *Fated Love*), two romance/intrigue series: the Honor series *(Above All, Honor, Honor Bound, Love & Honor,* and *Honor Guards*) and the Justice series (*Shield of Justice,* the prequel *A Matter of Trust, In Pursuit of Justice,* and *Justice in the Shadows)*, as well as an erotica collection: *Change of Pace – Erotic Interludes*.

She lives with her partner, Lee, in Philadelphia, PA where she both writes and practices surgery full-time. She is also the president of Bold Strokes Books, a lesbian publishing company.

Her upcoming works include: *Justice Served* (June 2005); *Stolen Moments: Erotic Interludes 2*, ed. with Stacia Seaman (September 2005), and *Honor Reclaimed* (December 2005)

Look for information about these works at www.radfic.com and www.boldstrokesbooks.com.

Other Books Available From Bold Strokes Books

Course of Action by Gun Brooke. Actress Carolyn Black desperately wants the starring role in an upcoming film produced by Annelie Peterson, a wealthy publisher with a mysterious past. How far is Carolyn prepared to go for the dream part of a lifetime? And just how far will Annelie bend her principles in the name of desire? (1-933110-22-8)

Rangers at Roadsend by Jane Fletcher. After nine years in the Rangers, dealing with thugs and wild predators, Sergeant Chip Coppelli has learned to spot trouble coming, and that is exactly what she sees in her new recruit, Katryn Nagata. But even so, Chip was not expecting murder. The Celaeno series. (1-933110-28-7)

Justice Served by Radclyffe. The hunt for an informant in the ranks draws Lieutenant Rebecca Frye, her lover Dr. Catherine Rawlings, and Officer Dellon Mitchell into a deadly game of hide-and-seek with an underworld kingpin who traffics in human souls. (1-933110-15-5)

Distant Shores, Silent Thunder by Radclyffe. Ex-lovers, would-be lovers, and old rivals find their paths unwillingly entwined when Doctors KT O'Bannon and Tory King—and the women who love them—are forced to examine the boundaries of love, friendship, and the ties that transcend time. (1-933110-08-2)

Hunter's Pursuit by Kim Baldwin. A raging blizzard, a remote mountain hideaway, and more than one killer-for-hire set a scene for disaster—or desire—when reluctant assassin Katarzyna Demetrious rescues a stranger and unwittingly exposes her heart. (1-933110-09-0)

The Walls of Westernfort by Jane Fletcher. All Temple Guard Natasha Ionadis wants is to serve the Goddess, and she volunteers eagerly for a dangerous mission to infiltrate a band of rebels. But once away from the temple, the issues are no longer so simple, especially in light of her attraction to one of the rebels. Is it too late to work out what she really wants from life? (1-933110-24-4)

Change Of Pace: *Erotic Interludes* by Radclyffe. Twenty-five hot-wired encounters guaranteed to spark more than just your imagination. Erotica as you've always dreamed of it. (1-933110-07-4)

Fated Love by Radclyffe. Amidst the chaos and drama of a busy emergency room, two women must contend not only with the fragile nature of life, but also with the mysteries of the heart and the irresistible forces of fate. (1-933110-05-8)

Justice in the Shadows by Radclyffe. In a shadow world of secrets, lies, and hidden agendas, Detective Sergeant Rebecca Frye and her lover, Dr. Catherine Rawlings, join forces once again in the elusive search for justice. (1-933110-03-1)

shadowland by Radclyffe. In a world on the far edge of desire, two women are drawn together by power, passion, and dark pleasures. An erotic romance. (1-933110-11-2)

Love's Masquerade by Radclyffe. Plunged into the often indistinguishable realms of fiction, fantasy, and hidden desires, Auden Frost discovers a shifting landscape that will force her to question everything she has believed to be true about herself and the nature of love. (1-933110-14-7)

Beyond the Breakwater by Radclyffe. One Provincetown summer three women learn the true meaning of love, friendship, and family. Second in the Provincetown Tales. (1-933110-06-6)

Tomorrow's Promise by Radclyffe. One timeless summer, two very different women discover the power of passion to heal and the promise of hope that only love can bestow. (1-933110-12-0)

Love's Tender Warriors by Radclyffe. Two women who have accepted loneliness as a way of life learn that love is worth fighting for and a battle they cannot afford to lose. (1-933110-02-3)

Love's Melody Lost by Radclyffe. A secretive artist with a haunted past and a young woman escaping a life that proved to be a lie find their destinies entwined. (1-933110-00-7)

Safe Harbor by Radclyffe. A mysterious newcomer, a reclusive doctor, and a troubled gay teenager learn about love, friendship, and trust during one tumultuous summer in Provincetown. First in the Provincetown Tales. (1-933110-13-9)

Above All, Honor by Radclyffe. The first in the Honor series introduces single-minded Secret Service Agent Cameron Roberts and the woman she is sworn to protect—Blair Powell, the daughter of the president of the United States. First in the Honor series. (1-933110-04-X)

Love & Honor by Radclyffe. The president's daughter and her security chief are faced with difficult choices as they battle a tangled web of Washington intrigue for...love and honor. Third in the Honor series. (1-933110-10-4)

Honor Guards by Radclyffe. In a journey that begins on the streets of Paris's Left Bank and culminates in a wild flight for their lives, the president's daughter and those who are sworn to protect her wage a desperate struggle for survival. Fourth in the Honor series. (1-933110-01-5)

BOLD
STROKES
BOOKS